The Abduction

by

Ester López

www.esterlopez.com
www.writingontheedgeofreality.esterlopez.com
www.authorblogspot.esterlopez.com

The Abduction

by

Ester López

Published by
Writing & Photographic Services, LLC

This book is lovingly dedicated to my mother who always
encouraged me
and called me her dreamer.

For my son, Brian, who was the inspiration for Adam.
And for my son, Jason, who encouraged me to follow my
dream.

CHAPTER ONE

Adrenalin pumped through his veins. His fisted hands were ready to fight. He stared into eyes the same pale blue as his and faced a man identical to himself, his brows narrowed in anger. He wrestled him to the ground. The other man's strength was a match for his own. When he shoved him down, the man reached for a strange-looking gun and took aim. He awoke the moment the man pulled the trigger.

Adam Davis bolted upright in his bed. His heart pounded from labored breathing. His body, moist with sweat, was still pumped and ready to fight but he was alone. He glanced around his dark cabin.

The sheet and thin bedspread fell away exposing his bare arms and chest. Rubbing the sleep from his eyes didn't eliminate the lingering dream. It was more like a premonition, like the one he'd had years ago that foretold the death of his parents.

Thunder growled outside. His pulse raced as other images came to mind. The first was a light bright as the sun. The second was a beautiful, dark-skinned young woman with high cheekbones and dressed in a white glowing jumpsuit. She spoke to him, but he didn't understand the words.

Lightning flashed and a rumbling boom shook the tiny log cabin nestled in the foothills of the Smoky Mountains.

Thunderstorms were rare here but on a stormy night like this, his parents had died sixteen long years ago, when he was ten. The memory still tugged at his heart. Storms made him restless.

Another flash drew his attention to the picture window centered in the room which overlooked the pond.

Crack! The dwelling shook again. Two lights shone over the water, then moved toward the wooded area surrounding his home.

A plane? He threw off his bedding and approached the glass.

The soft glowing orbs sat low in the sky. Aircraft didn't fly below tree level did they? He ran a hand through his hair as he watched the flight path.

Suddenly, lightning struck one of the objects, brightening the entire sky. The explosion startled him. The cabin shook so hard the bed moved a few inches across the wood floor and the glass panes rattled.

"Oh my God!" Remembering the vision, he watched in horror as the fireball fell from the sky.

He yanked his clothes off the chair and pulled on his jeans. Hopefully someone would survive the crash. He slipped a sweatshirt on then struggled with his wading boots.

His raincoat hung by the door. Grabbing the yellow garment from the hook, he knocked his fishing poles on the floor.

"Damn!" Pulling the slicker on, he fastened the top two snaps. He considered the coiled rope on the chair for stabilizing broken bones then slipped it across his chest. Wood for splints was plentiful outside.

He hesitated at the door and lifted the bow and quiver of arrows off another peg. The black bear he had seen the other day might return for the berries beside the pond. His old Boy Scout motto, "be prepared" crossed his mind so he grabbed a flashlight.

The covered porch protected him from the rain but he left the warmth of his dry cabin to search for survivors.

The approaching daylight accompanied a heavy, cold rain, usual for August in the mountains. His boots stuck in the east Tennessee clay-like mud as he rushed through the woods. Each step got heavier as his waders gathered more muck. Icy droplets stung his face like sharp pellets. Breathing the moldy air, he quickly followed the worn path around the reedy pond. A glimmer of light shone in the distance.

God, he hoped no one had died. Memories of his parents' death came to mind--'Burned beyond recognition'--a shiver ran down his spine. He quickened his pace, an uneasiness pulling at his gut. He hoped he wasn't too late. If someone had been there to help his parents, maybe they would be alive today.

Early daylight coupled with lightning, enabled him to find his way through the thickly wooded area. The secluded location of his home allowed him his privacy. He often thought of it as a blessing, since the place had once belonged to his grandparents. Injuries, though, would be a curse. Cell phones didn't work here in the mountains and the downpour would have washed most of the gravel away again. There was no way to get emergency help out here.

He arrived at the wreckage. The rain had almost put out the fire. The burned-out, smoldering shell that remained vaguely resembled a mangled football. Did anyone survive? Anxiety flowed over him as eerie shadows played around the object in the predawn light.

His gut told him to get out of there. He glanced up. No parachute. Maybe the pilot had bailed before the aircraft hit the ground. He blinked, wiping the drizzle from his face.

There were no signs of life. He walked toward the small plane. Another flash of lightning lit up the mangled mass.

Silently, he counted...one thousand one, one thousand two, one thousand three, one thou--

Boom! The storm moved farther away and the rain let up.

"Hey, is anybody here?" he shouted above the rumbling. No response. Closing the distance, he tried again. "Can you hear me?" Apprehension crept up the back of his neck, like someone watched him.

He pulled the bow off his shoulder, nocked an arrow to the bowstring and swung around to check the woods behind him. His bow, fully drawn was ready to release but aimed at nothing.

Lowering his draw, he blinked the rain from his eyes. He couldn't shake the feeling someone was out there. Facing the small plane, he walked toward it as another bolt lit up the area, brighter than before.

He gasped and his heart thudded. The flattened football-shaped object had no wings or tail. It was unlike anything he had ever seen. His first thought was to run like hell! But somebody might be alive in there. He shoved his arrow back in the quiver, and glanced over the area. He slung his bow on his shoulder and cracked his knuckles as he circled the heap of metal. The search for a way to get into the craft was futile.

He needed help. Adam darted down the path, and back to the cabin.

A stand of trees separated an overgrown field from a pond. Genesis sat at the control panel of her ship, **The Guardian.** She'd landed here after she'd watched lightning strike Dram's cruiser. His craft had burst into flames. She held her head in her hands and trembled.

"That was close. I could've been killed." The sight unnerved her. She forced herself out of her seat and switched off the controls. She had to find Dram and bring him back to headquarters, alive if possible.

She pulled the scanner from its holder. Her hands shook as she slipped the strap across her chest. Slow, deep breaths helped calm her.

This was the worst storm she had ever seen where bolts of electricity shot out of the sky. That rarely happened in the mountains on her planet, **Atria.** This field surrounded by woods reminded her of her home, a place she had not seen in ten *anos,* and she missed it.

She strapped a holster to her thigh and slipped the laser weapon inside. She knew what kind of animals lurked in the woods of **Atria,** but not here.

Beasts, larger and fiercer than those the men of her tribe hunted, showed in the database. The ancient ones had reported their findings after visiting this place thousands of years ago.

She clipped Interplanetary Space Patrol issued hand restraints on the holster and opened **The Guardian's** hatch, stepping onto the ramp. A heavy rain fell. Thick *yetik* protected the scanner box from the elements, but not her. Within minutes, her *unicrin* was drenched.

Thank goodness her ship's earlier analysis of the atmosphere had showed the oxygen quality and content would sustain her, although the air held more contaminates than **Atria's** atmosphere. The difference was palpable.

She tapped the screen of the scanner's database and compared ancient reports with current information and displayed significant changes since the first visit. Blinking rain from her eyes, she aimed the scanner toward the crash site.

The heavier gravity slowed her movement, and the surrounding moisture smelled musty, reminding her of **Persus**.

She looked forward to the moment she would face Dram. He deserved to die for his crimes. But if he was killed in the accident, the location of her parents and the women of her village died with him. Under strict orders from the Interplanetary Space Patrol, she must bring Dram back alive to face his charges.

Failure of her mission meant the end of her tribe. Only men remained at White Mountain, unless they joined another tribe, or took mates from other villages to procreate. If Dram and his men hadn't captured the women and children while the men of her village had been hunting, she would be on **Atria** with her mate, raising a family of her own.

She touched the jeweled translator across her forehead and sighed. It was all she had left of her mother, Herda, besides her medallion. The heartbreaking memories brought a lump to her throat and her eyes watered. She should have run faster.

Herda had communicated with her telepathically until the distance between them had made it impossible.

She wiped the rain and sadness from her face, and rested her hand on the weapon. She wanted to kill Dram for what he had done.

Sharp-thorn vines grew throughout the woods with clusters of dark berries. Her hunger increased at the thought of eating the fruit. Her memory of the last real food she had eaten escaped her. The plants here seemed like those on **Atria.** She plucked one and inhaled the aroma. A purple stain formed on her fingers. She scanned the berry and read the results: 'Similar in structure to *nelu*, containing essential nutrients to sustain higher life forms.'

She popped several into her mouth. Mmmm. Not bad, and much sweeter than those from home.

Something crackled to her right, startling her. Her pulse quickened. The scanner indicated a large object running in her direction. Was it a beast or Dram?

Crouched behind a wide bush, her wet *unicrin* stuck to her skin, Genesis felt chilled as she peered above the foliage. A wooden dwelling stood in the distance to the left, beyond the pond. She let the scanner fall to her side. Grasping the weapon, she slowed her breathing as she eased the laser from the holster. Then she nudged the lever to stun with her forefinger. The rustling grew closer and her heart beat harder.

Adam ran through the woods. His pulse raced and his body filled with nervous energy. He had to get help. He could take the Jeep to the highway and make the call. Hopefully, the pilot was still alive.

Stories of aliens formed in his mind. He had read UFO sightings happened in fields in other states or along the coast of Florida, but not here in the Smokies. Knoxville had the closest military base.

Depictions in the newspapers had shown them resembling small, child-like creatures with large eyes. One story said they sucked the blood from cows in a field. UFOs fascinated him, but he'd never dreamed he would actually encounter one, let alone have it crash in his backyard.

The briars and vines scraped at his slicker and rubber boots, but tore through his jeans at the knees, causing sharp pain. He couldn't stop. Someone's life may depend on him.

Breathless, he considered calling the Sheriff's Department for help. But would they believe his story? Without them seeing the spaceship, he'd be put in a straitjacket. A report of a plane crash made more sense. Yeah, that's what he'd do. Then he'd call his boss, Jeremy. He could always count on Jeremy to come.

The sound of a branch breaking halted him in his tracks. His racing heart thudded twice before beating normally. He pulled the bow off his shoulder and fixed an arrow to the string. This was where he had seen the bear.

He glanced around and slowly stepped from the woods and onto the path by the pond. The rain had stopped now. The thick cloud cover obscured dawn's light. A heavy mist saturated the air, while fog rose over the water. In the soft mud, footprints, much smaller than his size eleven, headed toward his home. They came from the old cornfield he and his father had planted years ago. He had no neighbors, so no one else should be here. He turned toward the cabin. Maybe someone--

Another twig snapped behind him and he swung around, his bow fully drawn. He froze, aiming at the woman from his dream.

Did she come from the crash site? She didn't look like an alien, so who was she?

Her long, blue-black hair draped forward over one shoulder in a braid that came down to her waist. Her dark, tanned face stood out against the white jumpsuit she wore. White so bright it glowed. Her body gave the suit curves in all the right places, but her flawless skin accentuated furrowed brows and an expression that could kill.

On her forehead, a jeweled band made of a coppery-silver metal shimmered, and the jewels sparkled different colors. Straps across her shoulder attached to a box at her hip. She had a gun in one hand, pointed at his chest. His pulse quickened at the thought of being shot.

"Tannae se ut!" she shouted.

"What?" Adam cocked his head, his draw on the bow straining to release.

She tapped the band across her forehead with two fingers.

"Tannae se ut!" "Hold there, Dram!" she said.

Dram? "Hey, wait a minute," he lowered his bow slightly. "I'm Adam."

She shot a red beam of light from the weapon and hit the dead branch he stood on. The wood caught fire. He jumped and released his arrow between her feet.

"What the hell?" She meant to hurt him. Confusion and anxiety grabbed him as he nocked another arrow to the bowstring. She's got the wrong guy.

"Next one won't miss," she said, her eyebrows narrowed.

"Neither will I." His mouth went dry and he swallowed hard before responding again. "I'm not Dram. There's been an accident." He glanced in the direction of the crash. "I've got to get help."

"Drop the weapon," she ordered.

"Drop yours first!" With bears and aliens in the woods, he'd keep his bow and arrows.

She stepped closer and raised her pistol toward his face. He aimed his arrow for her heart, his own heart racing at the thought of killing someone. The branch she hit with the laser beam still burned and he didn't want the same thing happening to him.

"I said, drop the weapon." Her voice grew deeper and louder.

"Hell, no! Who are you and what are you doing on my property?" His anger gave rise to courage as he held his draw.

"So this is your base of operations?" She glanced around.

"Who are you and why are you here?"

She lowered her weapon toward his chest and pulled the trigger.

He released his draw as a biting electrical shock flowed through him, paralyzing his extremities.

The woman dove away from the errant arrow as he fell to his knees, then onto his face. "Ugh." He had heard about tasers but had never seen one. The cold, wet ground smelled moldy. He spat out dead, bitter leaves. She didn't appear to be a cop.

"Why...did you shoot me?" he moaned. He couldn't see her, but she tugged at his arms. He managed to turn his face a little.

"Are you there?" he called out. What's she doing?

"Get up," she ordered.

"Yeah, that's easy for you to say. How about giving me the taser and I'll use it on you." His arms and legs refused to obey him.

She pulled at his waist, drawing him back, as his face dragged across the wet, rocky ground. A tingling sensation began at his deltoids and moved down. She squeezed his shoulders, pulling him back, until all his weight rested on his knees. She kicked his boots.

"Get up!"

He brought one leg forward and pushed himself up, then the other leg. He wobbled on his feet. Her grip tightened on his arms. Queasiness hit him in the gut. Behind him, his hands still tingled. Helplessness didn't suit him.

"What did you do to me?" He tried moving his upper body, and found his wrists were bound. Panic seized him.

"Go!" She pushed him forward.

"I'm not going anywhere until I get answers." He turned to face her, anger welling up. No one ordered him around, least of all someone he didn't know.

"You get questions answered when we arrive at headquarters."

She pushed him again.

"Are you an undercover cop or something?" He stumbled forward. Maybe he'd take her down in a wrestling hold he'd learned back in high school. That is, if his limbs returned to normal.

His rope coil hung across her chest. On one shoulder, she had his bow and quiver of arrows. She carried the taser she'd used on him. He clenched his jaw.

She pushed him in the direction of the cornfield.

"Go!" She gave him another shove. The tingling in his legs and arms faded.

"Wait just a minute! I'm not leaving unless you tell me what's going on."

She grabbed his wrists from behind and yanked up sharply.

He doubled over in pain. "Ouch! Damn that hurts."

She stuck the cold metal of the gun against his forehead as he straightened. His breath caught in his throat as he stared at the weapon. His heart beat so loudly, he heard the pulsing in his ears.

"I would love to finish you off now, but the I.S.P. wants to speak to you personally."

I.S.P.? He swallowed hard, his throat and mouth parched from the effort. He'd never heard of that agency. He took his gaze off the barrel momentarily and glanced into her dark, brown eyes framed in long lashes. Her brows furrowed in anger and her lips frowned.

"Look, I don't know what you're talking about, Scout's honor but I need to get help. There's been an accident and we're wasting time." He turned away, but she caught his restraints, twisted his wrists and immobilized him.

"Ouch. This has gone on long enough. Show me your I.D."

"What are you talking about? Go!" She waved her weapon at him. He refused to move.

"Not until you tell me what's going on. And who are you, anyway?"

"You *will* go." She shoved him so hard he lost his balance, stumbling backward. He tripped over a dead tree in the path, falling on his backside.

"Oooof!" He glared up at her. He turned on his side to get up then froze when he saw it. Another space ship, only this one was whole. He recalled what he had seen earlier. There were two lights in the sky. Two space ships!

Genesis watched as Dram tried to get up from the wet ground.

Her patience with him had ended. Now what? He stared at something through the underbrush. Exasperated, she bent down to locate the object of his attention. **The Guardian**? Before she could straighten, he wrapped his legs around her ankles and yanked her to the ground. She hit the dirt hard and the laser flew from her hand.

"Ugh!" She groped for the weapon. He threw himself on top of her, his body pressed against her breasts. She should kill him for his transgression.

"Look! There's the other spaceship. They're probably searching for the one that crashed. We've got to get help before the aliens show up. So quit this game you're playing and untie me."

Confusion engulfed her. He talked nonsense. His face, close to hers, breathed warmth against her cool skin. Blue eyes, wide with fear, captivated her and the heat from his body warmed her. Her pulse quickened, as a tingling rippled through her at light speed when their gazes met. They were motionless for an instant. His lips, inches from hers.

Her fingers found the laser. Good! She pulled it up to the side of his face. Anger infused her as she itched to fire the weapon. "Get off me now, or you will die right here." She tensed her jaw. Her carelessness had almost cost her. This man who had abducted both her parents and all the women from her village had abducted others as well. He deserved to die.

His legs straddled her as he used strong back muscles to pull himself up. He rolled off her and to the side where he rocked forward onto his hands, jamming his heels into the ground. He jumped to his feet in one motion. His gaze fixed on her as she scrambled to stand. She kept the weapon pointed at his head while he tensed his jaw.

How did he do that? "No more tricks!" She shouted as she waved the laser at him. Cautiously, she kept watch on him and gathered his things then pressed the hatch release button on the scanner.

Dram's gaze darted toward **The Guardian** and back to her. His eyes widened.

"Oh, my God, *you're* the...alien?" He stumbled backward.

She grabbed his shoulder to keep him upright. She couldn't let him escape now.

"Go." She turned him around to face **The Guardian** then pushed him forward. He acted strange. Maybe he'd suffered brain damage after the crash.

She shoved the laser in his back as he moved toward the ship. He walked differently now and seemed dazed going up the ramp. She held his arm, guiding him inside.

The I.S.P. reported him as cocky and arrogant with no regard for authority. His injury must have changed his behavior. Ten long anos of searching for him was finally over.

She studied his yellow tunic, made of strange material she had never seen. It repelled water. She glanced at her own unicrin, the wet fabric stuck to her skin. Her body was chilled from the rain seeping through to her extremities.

Dram stopped when he reached the cage.

She pulled the *yav* from her scanner, zapping the lock mechanism and slid the heavy malloid door sideways. She shoved Dram inside.

Suddenly, a biting sting paralyzed her. Dizziness overtook her and she fell.

Numb with fear, Adam heard a body hit the floor. He swung around to find the woman at his feet. A man, wearing a light blue suit, like the woman's, hovered over her, taking the black box off her shoulder. He had her weapon in one hand, and another one in a thigh holster as he straightened and turned to face him.

His mouth dropped open in shock and his pulse quickened as the man facing him appeared a mirror image. From the white-blond hair, pale blue eyes and medium tan, to the same build and six foot frame. The stranger stared back as he squinted to examine his face more closely. The older man had the beginnings of crows' feet where he did not. Did he smile or was that a smirk?

"You must be Dram."

"How did you know?"

"She mistook me for you." He glanced down at her still body. Did he hurt her? "Is she dead?" The thought bothered him more than he expected.

"No, but she will be when I get through with her."

Dram grabbed her arm and dragged her into the cell then turned to leave. He stepped over her, following Dram out, but Dram shoved him back.

"Sorry, boy." He slammed the door shut.

"Hey, wait! I don't belong here. The whole thing is a big mistake."

"Actually, everything is working out perfectly." Dram raised one blond eyebrow and smirked again. He hesitated before picking up his possessions then stowed them in some kind of compartment.

He watched as anger boiled inside. "Be careful with my stuff." His father had taught him how to hunt and his bow and arrows were all he had left of his dad.

Dram ignored him and headed toward a door. He turned back and pressed a button on the black box. "You won't need those anymore." The ramp to the ship closed as Dram entered the other room. Dazed, he watched as the opening hissed shut behind Dram.

He glanced around the interior of the vessel as his gut tightened in fear. "God, help me."

Shiny metal, like new stainless steel, covered everything including the floor, the ceiling, and the walls. Inside, the place seemed round. Outside, it had appeared football shaped. Three doors, evenly spaced apart, stood across from the main entrance. The one Dram walked through was on the far right of the cell. On the far left was a pedestal table, encircled by two benches. Compartments of various sizes lined the walls on either side of his prison.

Between the left lockers and his cage was a large circle flush with the floor. It took up space with a man-hole cover of sorts. No hinges or handle adorned it. Above that spot, in the ceiling, another similar shape existed.

He leaned against the bars and closed his eyes. He should have stayed in bed this morning. Two of his visions had come true. The first time he'd had premonitions, his life had changed drastically, making him an orphan. And now this had happened.

He shook his head. Loneliness he could deal with. Only God knew what would happen now. He felt nauseous and wanted to puke.

Lord, don't let me end up a science experiment for aliens.

His twenty-six-year life flashed before his eyes. Memories of his family, days at the orphanage, right up to his current construction job, working for his friend, Jeremy. He liked his job, too.

Suddenly, a quiet hum started, causing a light vibration under his feet. *We're moving.* His life had just changed. He lowered his head.

He noticed the young woman sprawled out across the metal floor. He let his tired, hungry body slide slowly to the ground. He understood how she had mistaken him for Dram. To share the face of a total stranger seemed uncanny, especially an alien. How ironic, though, that the man she thought she'd captured had turned around and abducted her. Now they both suffered the same fate.

Her dirty, drenched white suit clung to her unconscious body, showing off luscious curves and bare skin underneath.

"Hmmm." *How interesting.* He leaned closer to get a better view. *Why hadn't he noticed before?*

His flesh was chilled because he wore jeans soaked at the knees and a sweatshirt wet around the neck. He turned sideways, pried off his muddy boots, and wriggled his toes. Then, sitting cross-legged, he leaned against the bars and realized he had no other shoes when the air cooled his feet.

Thoughts of things he'd left behind on Earth like his fishing poles, cabin, and Jeep, crossed his mind. He banged his head against the bars. Would he ever return home again? He thought he had problems with a clingy girlfriend and a stray cat. When Jeremy comes over later this morning to go fishing, he won't be there. Would Jeremy search for him?

In the Navigation room, Dram straightened in his chair. Thank goodness the storm had dissipated. Flying in bad weather had been difficult. He lifted a lever then tapped 'location' on the keypad of the Nav-U-Com.

The monitor flashed astronomical charts across the screen until stopping on one with ten planets. He punched in 'system?' The display showed: 'SSO, or star system one. Two questionable, might be moons.'

"Great," he mumbled, as he typed in 'location within system?' Twenty-seven anos had passed since his last visit. He smiled and his heart lightened at the memories while the monitor displayed: 'third planet from un-named star.'

"Now you're talking," he said. He identified 'Earth' for the database. His fingers flew across the keys, spelling 'escape trajectory?' The display showed Earth and changing graphics of a window outside the planet. It aimed at the star with coordinates listed above the drawings.

He typed 'enhancement' to get a closer view.

Hmmm, what had Emma called it? He entered 'sun' for the database then hit the keys and spelled 'Plexus?' His mind briefly reflected on the only woman he had ever loved.

The coordinates appeared along with the wormholes and trajectory through hyperspace from the sun.

He punched in 'window' and the graphics displayed once more, aiming at the sun. He set the destination for its gravity well, entering the parameters, and then pulled back on the controls. The ship lifted off the ground 300 *centikiks*. He pointed the ovoidal shape toward the giant star.

Relieved, he settled in his seat, his clothes sodden from his recent ordeal. He would have to find something to change into once he left the Earth's gravity. He glanced around the Nav-room. State of the art technology, compliments of the Interplanetary Space Patrol. *How nice.* Their seal was stamped on the center of the console. No doubts as to ownership. *How did the woman get a ship like this?* Unless she worked for them. She seemed a little young to recruit into service.

He clasped his hands behind his head and remembered sadly the times he and his partner, Timna, had close calls with the I.S.P. But Timna no longer had to worry about them. One minute he'd controlled the ship, the next, Timna was dead. Luckily, he'd survived.

He gazed out the view port at the sun. Until he got within this system, he hadn't realized someone pursued him. Emma called this the solar system.

He and Timna had tried to shake off their pursuer, but nothing had worked. *Why would a lone, young woman chase them, anyway?*

How ironic that she'd found the very person he had come to find, thinking the man from Earth was him. *Perfect.* She seemed convinced of the boy's identity. Perhaps others could be, too. The boy resembled him more than he had anticipated. Now hopeful, he had to create a flawless plan.

Already behind schedule, he had to return to his base on **Meta** to get the last shipment out to Z. If Z didn't approve the merchandise, his business was *kunnarled*. Hmmm. An idea formed in his brain. He just might succeed with the boy's help.

Back in the cell, Adam yanked and wriggled his wrists in frustration. Whatever the woman had used to bind them, held fast. He couldn't reach his Swiss Army knife in his jeans pocket. If she woke, maybe she'd help him.

He thought of Dram again and how disturbing it was to share features with a man not related. He was an only child, something he and his parents had in common. No chance Dram could be related. He shook his head. He had to get those thoughts out of his mind. Both of them were aliens, yet they appeared human. When he was on top of her, though, she'd had all the right equipment.

Did they have red blood? Maybe a star out there had a twin to everyone on Earth? *Was it possible two planets shared the same history or God?*

He was taught that God had created the universe and everything in it. Perhaps God didn't stop with Earth. What if He made men on other planets as well? It would be a waste to set people in just one place when He initially had so many stars and galaxies.

God meant for him to meet this woman. Otherwise, why have that premonition?

Stories of aliens looking less than human must be true, too. Somebody had witnessed them, hadn't they?

Confused, he leaned his head against the bars of the cell. He had too much to think about now.

He heard the woman stir. Her lids fluttered open, and her lips moved.

"Malek?" Her eyes widened at the sight of him.

"What?" He leaned closer to hear her.

She lunged for his throat.

"Whoa!" He fell back as her hands squeezed tight around his neck, his airway closing off. He twisted and turned, trying to shake her loose, but she held firm. Her weight, pressing against him, knocked him off balance and he rolled to his side. He flipped to his back. He didn't want to die. Not now. Not this way. He had to survive.

Something struck him in the face while she pressed harder on his throat. A couple of medallions dangled in front of him. Both identical and shaped like trees encircled in metal. They hung around her neck with long leather straps.

He remembered a wrestling maneuver and drew his knees tight to his chest. He wedged his feet between him and her soft body, beneath her breasts. Then he forced his legs out straight, shooting her across the small cell. She slammed into the bars opposite him.

She sat there, dazed. Her eyes were wide in surprise. Two large footprints were imprinted on her outfit, just under each breast.

He rolled onto his side, coughing and gagging. He coughed so hard, he heaved, almost puking. He managed to roll into a kneeling position, his head against the floor.

"I am not Dram!" His voice was hoarse.

He pulled himself up and sat back on his heels, wiping his mouth on the shoulder of his rain slicker.

"Dram is flying this space ship." The awful taste would not go away. "Dram..." He coughed again, anger infused him. "Dram put you in here!"

"You tricked me," she said, glaring at him.

"Yeah, well if I was Dram, how did I knock you out? My hands are tied behind my back." He twisted his body around to show her his bound wrists, aching from the restraints.

"And," he continued. "I certainly wouldn't be in this cage with you!" he snapped. "I had a life on Earth before you came along. You've changed everything!"

Her eyes narrowed as she glared at him. She pulled her knees up to her chest and lowered her head.

"Your fate could be worse, Earth man," she replied, tensing her jaw. Her brows deeply furrowed.

"Oh, yeah? What could be worse than being abducted from my home?" He tightened his fists, irritating the raw areas under the restraints.

"I could have *killed* you," she whispered harshly.

CHAPTER TWO

Stunned and overwhelmed with emotions, Genesis sat where she had landed, against the cage bars. She hugged her knees and rested her head on her forearms.

What had she done and how did everything go so wrong? The bolt of electricity had hit Dram's ship. *So, who is he and why does he resemble Dram?*

The Guardian's vibration meant someone flew her. The Earth man's story now made sense. It explained his strange behavior. *How would she escape?*

Her heart fell, like a shooting star. She was trapped. The fate of the others had rested in her hands. With one careless mistake, she'd failed her parents and her mission as well.

She took a deep, jagged breath, as her eyes watered. No. She blinked back the tears and glanced over her arm. She had to be strong. The man leaning against the bars watched her. She would fight Dram for as long as necessary.

The door to the Nav-room hissed open.

"Have you two killed each other yet?" Dram walked into the room.

She stood. Shock washed over her. She looked first at Dram and back to the man she mistook for him. Her pulse quickened.

"Clones?" She cocked her head. The Council of Nations had outlawed cloning on all the planets. She studied both men again.

"I told you who I am. I'm no clone, you got that?" The man next to her raised his voice. His face was close to hers, his eyebrows narrowed. She breathed in his scent. His nearness sent a familiar warm shiver throughout her body. *What power did he possess over her?* She turned toward Dram, grasping the bars with both hands. Anger infused her.

"Where's Malek?" She shoved her arm through the cage and grabbed at Dram's throat. She wanted to tear his heart out, the way he'd done hers when he'd taken her mother so long ago.

Dram jumped out of her reach. "Let's say he's living a new life somewhere in the **Vaedra** System. Why do you ask?"

Her heart dropped again. **Vaedra** was such a large area to search. "I am Genesis, daughter of Malek," she struck her chest in salute to her father. "He is Chief of the White Mountain tribe, on **Atria**."

"Do you realize how much trouble you've caused?" Dram pointed a finger at her as he paced back and forth. "I ought to let you rot in there."

She glared at him, her anger building. "You created more problems for others than I *ever* did," she clenched her fists. She ignored the guilt for her recent blunder.

"Hey, since you two are working things out, can I go back to Earth now?"

"Look," Dram pointed a finger at the man. "You're not going anywhere. I've got plans for both of you." He glared at the Earth man and her. He spun around and walked toward Malek's sleeping compartment.

"Well, *he* was in a good mood," the man beside her said, leaning against the bars. He rolled his eyes.

She grabbed the cage and banged her forehead on the cold *malloid*. She wanted her family. She choked back the tears and thought of her tribe. She had let everyone down.

Dram came out of the compartment, wearing her father's flight suit.

"That belongs to Malek!" she shouted at him.

Dram shrugged his shoulders. "Yeah, well, he's not here now, is he?" He walked to the Nav-room. The door hissed closed behind him. The Interplanetary Space Patrol was right about him.

She clenched her fists and tensed her jaw. Why didn't she kill him when she had the chance? Her heart fluttered as she realized her mistake. Had she shot the one she mistook for Dram, an innocent man's blood would be on her hands. She stole a glance at the Earth man.

"At least tell me what's going on," he said, catching her gaze.

Disheartened, she turned her back on him and crossed her arms. To face him now would mean admitting she was wrong and she wasn't ready to acknowledge her mistake. She had sealed his fate with her actions.

She shivered and her wet unicrin clung to her skin. She rubbed her arms for warmth, the gesture useless. She leaned her shoulder against the cold bars.

Now she needed an escape plan.

Adam glared at the woman's back. He didn't like being ignored when he spoke to someone. He wanted answers! His arms were useless behind him. He thought of another tactic and bent down to slip his bound wrists over his butt.

This had to work. He had tried everything else. Carefully, he stepped through the loop his hands made, one foot at a time, until the plastic restraints were in front of him.

He moved close behind her. The wet, almost transparent material of her suit adhered to the curves of her body. *Oh, and she had some nice curves, too,* but he had to be careful. She had already proven herself to be dangerous.

He slipped his arms over her, pulling her to him. He bent down, picked her up and pinned her against his chest.

If he kept her hands still, his neck would be safe, but she fought him. Although her hands were at her sides, her legs kicked furiously. He spread his legs to keep from being injured. Her head thrashed side to side and he forced her to stop by nuzzling her neck with his nose. She stilled at his gesture.

"Now that I have your attention, would you release me?" he whispered hoarsely in her ear. The proximity of their bodies reminded him he hadn't held a woman this close in awhile. The clingy girlfriend he tried to forget would have been worse if he had given in to her.

He inhaled deeply to calm his pounding heart, but her exotic fragrance intoxicated him. She cringed as he exhaled down her neck. He wanted answers and he wanted his freedom.

"Why should I release you?" She tensed in his arms, but she quit kicking and thrashing.

"Because we're both stuck in a situation we don't like and instead of fighting, maybe we can help each other."

She nodded and he lowered her to the floor. She slowly turned to face him. He released his hold and carefully raised his arms over her. The top of her head came below his chin.

He held his bound wrists before her.

"Please release me?"

She worked on the restraining device, pulling and wriggling the fastener. He watched her determination.

"I cannot unfasten you." She finally looked up through long, dark lashes. "The yetik won't yield. I need a laser to cut the restraint."

"I have a Swiss Army knife."

She looked puzzled.

"You know, a pocket knife?"

She shook her head. "What is pocket?"

He chuckled and glanced at his right side. "On my hip is an opening in my jeans. Inside is a knife. Reach in and get it." He would have to trust her now or stay this way until Dram decided to release him. And who knew how long that would be? *But could he trust her*? Would she try to kill him...again?

"I can understand how you mistook me for Dram, but I assure you, I am nothing like him."

She locked gazes with him as her hand snaked through the slicker, sliding down his torso toward her goal. His flesh jumped at her icy touch. She froze at his reaction, her eyes widened.

He shrugged. "Your hand is cold."

She resumed her pursuit until her hand reached the Swiss Army knife. She pulled the object free and he let out a breath.

Genesis stared at the prize.

"Let me show you."

She gave it to him and watched as he opened the blades.

"Here," he handed the knife back.

She worked the blade against the thick plastic band with frosty fingers. He breathed in her sweet, woodsy scent of flowers. *Genesis smelled good. Did she wear perfume? Were such products used on her planet?* He imagined loosening her braid and running his fingers through her blue-black mane. He had never seen hair that long on anyone. He shook away the thoughts, remembering she was an alien. But the parts he saw and touched sure felt human, though.

Finally, she cut through the band and handed him the knife.

He pocketed his tool after closing it.

"Thank you." Relieved, he rubbed his wrists and turned away. She caught his hands and yanked him back. His pulse quickened as he pulled away. What was she doing?

"You're bleeding." She glanced at his hands.

"Yeah, well, it hurts."

She gently reached for his wrists and turned them over, studying the raw areas. Her attention and the coolness of her touch made him uncomfortable.

"I will heal you," she said, gazing into his eyes.

"What did you say?" Did he hear right?

"Take this off." She released him and reached for the snap on his slicker.

He caught her hands in his. Her choke hold was still a fresh memory and so was her feistiness. Her strong, cool fingers were soft to touch.

"Why?" He was still suspicious of her motives. Her dark brown eyes met his gaze.

"I need to attend to your injuries," she whispered.

He cocked his head. "Why do you care now? You almost killed me." He tightened his grip on her wrists as he remembered her fierce strength. She lowered her gaze to her captured hands resting against his chest.

"I am sorry. I thought you were Dram. I didn't know." She gazed at him, her eyes glistening.

He released one of her hands and lifted her chin with his finger. One blink triggered the tears trickling down her face. His heart softened at her pain.

"I forgive you, okay?"

She blinked again, a single droplet clung to her lashes. He noticed her trembling hands and realized her chilled body shook uncontrollably.

"Good gosh, you're freezing." He pulled away and unsnapped his slicker. Shrugging the garment off, he wrapped her shoulders with the raincoat and held her body close.

"You'll be warmer once you get those wet clothes off."

She stared up at him, her eyes wide. He'd forgotten her predicament. She had nothing else to wear and they were both stuck in this cell.

"I mean take your top off and keep the slicker on instead. It's not real warm but it *is* dry." He faced away and gave her privacy while he cracked his knuckles, one at a time. He hoped the coat would warm her.

"You can turn around now," she said, finally.

"Are you sure?"

"Yes," she chuckled. He loved her laugh. She smiled. Her arms disappeared in the over-long slicker.

"Thank you." She lowered her gaze.

He reached out and rolled up the sleeves of the raincoat. An unfamiliar tenderness swept over him, like he wanted to care for her. *Where did that come from?* The only person he looked after was himself. He finished and she grabbed his hands.

"Any other injuries?"

A warm sensation rushed through him at her touch.

"Uh, yeah, my knees hurt."

She raised an eyebrow.

"From the briars, when I ran through the woods." He wouldn't admit he had been a little scared.

She cocked her head.

"After I found the spaceship, I ran for help. Apparently, Dram didn't need any."

She nodded. "Sit." She pulled him to the floor and tore open his jeans where the briars began the job at the knees.

"Careful, I have no other clothes." The soft touch of her fingers brushing his flesh sent a fire through his loins. Afterward, he forgot about the deep cuts and abrasions in his skin.

"Hmmm." She checked his wounds.

"Well, it hurt at the time. Mostly it itches now." He sat with his legs crossed. The position was uncomfortable.

Genesis knelt before him, holding his wrists with his palms facing up. She closed her eyes and mumbled something in another language. He watched her. *God, she was beautiful, even if she was an alien.* He had a hard time letting go of the thought.

Genesis outwardly appeared like any other Earth woman. Inwardly was another story. Shock had ripped through him when he'd realized the truth. His legs had been like Jell-O when he'd walked up the ramp. He had never been so scared in all his life.

He glanced at his wrists while she held them. The raw places had disappeared.

"That's amazing. How did you do it?" He caught her gaze.

"It's a gift." She let go of his hands. She touched his knees and mumbled again. He thought the last touch sent fire to his groin. Her stroke nearly knocked him over the edge. He shook his head to clear the trance rippling through him. The pain was gone but the throbbing between his legs was more intense.

"I can't believe you did this." He stared at the places he had been injured. She leaned forward and touched her fingers to his lips.

"You must have faith for your healing to manifest."

Her gentle tap undid him. He closed his lids momentarily and groaned. Opening his mouth, he sucked the pad of her finger still pressed on his flesh and planted a kiss.

Genesis' eyes opened wide as she slowly pulled her hand back and moved toward the bars. Sitting against the cell, she drew her knees to her chest and wrapped her arms around her legs. He sat beside her, and tamped down his lust.

"Thank you," he said.

She lowered her head. "After what I did to you?" She shrugged and rested her chin on her knees. He watched her a few minutes, hoping she would open up.

"How is it you speak English?"

"English? I speak **Vaedran** and **Micca Nulee**. You use ancient **Vaedran**." She tapped the gemstone band across her forehead. "My translator helps me interpret your words as well as say them." She took the jeweled band off, handing it to him.

He studied the intricate details. The underside was enclosed. Two openings at either end served as microphones. He put it on his forehead.

"Set se naquay?"

"Do you understand me?" He repeated the words he heard from the small speakers.

Genesis smiled.

He handed the band back. "Was that **Micca Nulee?**"

"Yes," she answered before wearing the translator.

"How is it I speak ancient **Vaedran** when I haven't been to your home?"

"Thousands of years ago, our people explored different systems looking for habitable places to live. The mixed races settled on Earth. The pure chose the **Vaedra** System. Each group colonized a whole planet."

"What do you mean by mixed?" He scratched his head.

"The Council of Nations passed an edict before the Exodus. Anyone taking a mate from a different race would be exiled. Some chose Earth, others, the isle of **Pathos** on **Vestra Major**."

"That's a stupid rule if you ask me. On Earth, you can marry whomever you want."

"And Earthens accept the mixed races?"

"Well, sometimes people don't understand. You can't decide who you fall in love with. It just happens."

Genesis sat, leaning against the bars, her arms crossed under her breasts.

"Why do you hate Dram so much?" he asked, breaking the silence. She glanced at him.

"Dram abducted my mother, Herda, and all our village women when I was fourteen. I escaped to get help. I returned with the men but everyone was gone, including the old ones and the babies."

"Why?"

"Do not worry yourself, Earth man."

"Adam. The name's Adam, if you don't mind and it is my concern since you dragged me into this."

She pouted and glared at him. "Malek and I searched for Dram throughout the **Vaedra** System for ten long anos. He ambushed my father a week ago. I was instructed to bring Dram before the I.S.P."

"The I.S.P.?" Genesis' lips distracted him. He wanted to kiss the frown off her face. He moved closer.

She glanced at him. "I work for the Interplanetary Space Patrol as a bounty hunter. My sole job is to bring Dram to justice. He must answer the charges against him."

No wonder she hated Dram. He certainly understood. He despised the hit and run driver who had killed his parents. The man was never found after he took Adam's precious family, something he couldn't get back.

Why did he share a criminal's face? He ran his hand through his hair. "Do you know if your parents are alive?"

She nodded. "I communicated telepathically with Herda until she was taken off planet. Malek does not possess that gift. Herda's destination was kept from her when she was captured, so we don't know her location."

He lifted her chin. Her sad, brown gaze locked on his and melted his heart.

"If I promise to help you, will you take me back to Earth?" He ran the pad of his thumb across her soft, moist lips. Her lids closed momentarily. He gently pulled his hand away before his desire for her grew stronger.

"Why?"

"Because I know how it feels to lose a parent. Mine both died in a car accident when I was ten. If I had the chance to get them back, I would."

"You help me capture Dram and I will return you to Earth."

He offered his hand. "Deal." She shook it.

"I give you my word." She hit her chest with her fist.

He sat back against the bars. Genesis' presence warmed him. He was comforted knowing both of them shared something, even though the event was the tragic loss of their parents.

The door hissed open and Dram came to the cell.

"And what's this?" he asked.

Adam helped Genesis stand to face Dram.

Dram studied them.

"I asked a question," he raised his voice.

"Why is she wearing your tunic?" Dram glared at him while he pointed to Genesis.

"She was cold so I gave her my slicker. It's a raincoat." *What's his problem?* He glanced at Genesis. She rubbed her arms for warmth.

"Well, that's too bad. I'm not concerned with her comfort." Dram walked to the cell door and aimed a small object at the lock mechanism. "I need your assistance."

"Oh? Why should I help you?" He crossed his arms over his chest. Dram had some nerve. Dram was the last person he wanted to assist.

"Because I have a weapon and you don't, that's why." Dram slid the door open and pulled his laser, pointing at him. "And you don't have a choice. Now, move it." Dram waved the strange-looking gun at him.

Déjà vu washed over him. In the premonition, though, Dram had used a rifle. He swallowed as he stepped from the cell. He didn't want to anger Dram any more than he had. He liked cooperating even less.

Somehow he would figure a way to escape. He would wait for the right opportunity to present itself.

The lesson his father taught him about hunting deer applied to this situation. 'Be patient for the animal to feel comfortable and drop their guard. When they do, shoot to kill.'

"What about Genesis?" He glanced at her. Worry etched her features. She grabbed the bars with both hands. Dram slammed the cell door shut.

"The woman stays right there." Dram pushed him toward the room he had vacated. Then the door hissed closed behind them.

Genesis turned and sat on the floor. She drew her legs up and hugged her knees for warmth. She must trust Adam to devise an escape plan. Otherwise, she would do it herself. She didn't know if he knew how to fly. **The Guardian** was voice activated but only Malek's voice and hers could guide the ship. Dram had to operate the craft manually. Without voice control, Dram needed Adam's assistance if he was going back to the **Vaedra** System. He would have to sleep sometime.

If she and Adam worked together, they could overpower Dram and take back the ship. Somehow Adam had to get the yav to unlock the cage. Dram had worn the scanner when he came out and she kept the yav there. She had a problem.

Cold and weary, she closed her eyes and reviewed the last few moments in her mind. The power the Earth man had over her was unlike anything she had ever experienced. His whispers in her ear sent warm shivers rushing through her body. She forgot her discomfort when he did that. His glance at her with his wrists bound, begging her to release him, had made her feel powerful, yet her knees had weakened when he held her in his arms. What had he done to her?

She sighed as she loosened her long, thick braid. She ran her fingers through the damp mass to let her hair dry naturally.

Herda, hear me. Tell me about men. This Earthen forgave me after I tried to kill him. He promised to help me. In return I must take him back to Earth. Should I trust him?

Herda's thoughts didn't come. In the past, Herda's words had always comforted her. She rubbed her arms for warmth. The raincoat Adam let her wear helped in warding off the cold. It still contained his body heat.

Why did he resemble Dram? She'd spent the last ten anos hating Dram's face. As long as Adam remained with Dram, he was in danger. Dram deceived people. The I.S.P. had warned her of Dram's cunning ways. She had experienced his treachery first hand when he took her mother. No one had ever crossed Dram except one man and he hadn't lived to tell about it.

CHAPTER THREE

Adam's mouth dropped open when he stepped in the room where Dram had taken him.

"Good gosh, look at the view!" He stood there, awestruck, and gazed out a large windshield to the vastness of space. None of the images he had seen on the internet had prepared him for this reality. "Wow!" He cracked his knuckles. The panorama was incredible.

"How could anybody ever doubt the existence of God?" He shook his head slowly, amazed.

"Who?" Dram asked, sitting in a seat facing a large dashboard-type area. The rounded surface of the dashboard panel contained different colored levers where the speedometer and radio would be in a car. Below, a long shelf-like tray existed. Dram pulled it to waist level.

Two separate elongated keyboards sat on the shelves in front of each seat. Dram pressed a button on his keyboard and two monitors rose from the dashboard.

His attention moved to Dram. "You know, God, the Creator of Heaven and Earth. You *have* heard of him, haven't you?"

Dram nodded. "Yes. God."

He couldn't imagine a planet where inhabitants didn't know God.

"There are some who believe in God and those who do not," Dram said, glancing his way.

"And you?" he asked.

"I used to, when I was your age."

"What happened?"

"Sit," Dram pointed to the only empty chair in the room.

He sat beside him.

"Do you have a name?"

"Adam Davis." Dram ignored his question.

"This is the Nav-room," he said, waving his hand in the air. "The view port," Dram pointed to the glass window he had been looking through. "And," he tapped the sophisticated computerized panel and tray, "the Nav-U-Com, or Navigational Unit Computer, state of the art technology, Adam Davis."

"Okay?" Puzzled, he took in the information. Why tell him this? "You can call me Adam."

Dram glanced at him. "Wasn't Adam the first man on Earth?"

"Yes. How did you know?"

"I acquired a lot of knowledge about your Earth."

He studied Dram's face. "What exactly do you mean?"

"Would you like to learn how to fly?"

"You're kidding, right?" Had he heard correctly? Dram smoothly avoided his new question.

"This ship is normally voice-activated, but we're going to fly manually. Therefore, I need your assistance with a few things."

Hmmm, could be a bad thing, but right now, it sounded pretty cool. He tamped down his excitement. Jeremy would never believe this, if he ever got back to tell him. He crossed his arms over his chest. Stay calm, this could be a trick.

"It's a three-day trip to **Meta**," Dram stared out the view port.

"**Meta**?"

"Our destination." Dram glanced at him. "Now do you understand my problem?"

Yes, Dram needed his help. He sure as hell wanted to do otherwise, especially since Dram kept him imprisoned. He was here against his will. Then again, the opportunity to escape might be presented. Either way, he would stay alert around Dram.

"Yes, I think I do. You need me to take turns flying so we can each get some sleep."

"You catch on pretty quickly. Now, a lot of things can go wrong on a flight. For instance, unexpected debris in space or asteroids can collide with the craft." Dram waved his arm toward the view port.

"Really?" The thought of floating junk had never occurred to him.

"Yes, on long trips, if we ran on voice command, unpredictable things can show up. Only people can make course corrections to avoid these collisions, so we need someone here all the time." Dram glanced at him, his eyebrows raised.

He swallowed hard. Anxiety welled up as he realized he actually had to fly this ship. Alone. He hadn't anticipated much trouble, but Dram's explanation made sense. Earth had put a lot of stuff into orbit over the years from its satellites and shuttles.

"I don't know if I'm ready for that responsibility." He shook his head.

"Adam, I can show you the basics. The sensors on the ship will pick up anything unusual and give you enough warning time to wake me. It practically flies itself. Besides, if that woman out there can fly, so can you." Dram glared at him as he aimed his thumb over his shoulder toward the other room.

Genesis flew alone. How did *she* manage to get any sleep?

"Power comes from a fusion engine," Dram continued, "with a warp drive and worm hole generator."

He raised an eyebrow. Vague scientific references from his physics class, years ago, came to mind.

Dram showed him levers and switches and briefly explained their functions. He hoped he would remember this stuff when he needed it. Then Dram went on to explain the larger lever between the seats.

"For lift and down."

"And what about this gadget?" He pointed to a half steering wheel, rising from the floor. The column holding the object stood keyboard height in front of him.

"Yawing right or left, depending on the pitch. You'll need a lot of practice, Adam. Are you up for it?" Dram raised an eyebrow.

"Sure." He contained his excitement.

Dram pushed back the keyboard tray and pulled the wheel up in front of him, bringing it to waist level. He flipped a lever.

"Inertia Canceler," he said. He lifted the wheel toward the right. The ship tilted and turned abruptly in that direction. Then he reversed everything.

"When we get to **Meta**, you'll have more time to practice. The main thing I need you for now is to stay awake while I sleep. I'll leave the controls on computer command. If anything happens, an alarm will sound. All you have to do is wake me. I'm a *very* light sleeper."

He took in the information Dram had given him. All the video games he had played since high school gave him fast reflexes. It helped him get over the loneliness.

Knowing Dram slept lightly might mean problems in finding the key to the cell, and the means to escape. Dram must keep the key in the black box he had strapped across his chest, the same box Genesis had carried when she locked him up. The empty holster on Dram's right thigh meant he didn't trust him. That was okay. They were on equal ground as far as he was concerned.

"We'll have to make mid-course corrections soon, so use the Nav-U-Com," Dram said, bringing his thoughts back to the reality of flying.

"First, you'll need to triangulate our position. Type any questions or commands here." Dram motioned toward the keyboard-type instrument.

The alphabet, located differently from the keyboards on Earth, had other strange symbols as well. It took him a few minutes to adjust to the shift in letters.

"Gotcha," he said as he typed in the words: 'what is ship's position?' The monitor flashed: 'analyzing radio waves.' Then a graphic appeared with location coordinates at the top.

"What are these?" He pointed to the waves in the graphics.

"Time tunnels."

A dot flashed. "Is this significant?" He pointed to the speck.

"That's our location. We hit hyper speed here," Dram said. He connected the dots with a stylus. "We'll sail through these short cuts," he pointed to two waves beyond the dots. "Then, we'll triangulate our position again, when we get there," he pointed to another flashing spot at the far edge of the screen. Dram flipped on the Inertia Canceler and moved the warp drive lever on the control panel. "Strap in, Adam, we're going to hyper speed."

A great weight pushed against his chest. The pressure was tremendous. His body sank farther in the seat. Breathing deeply became difficult, so he took shallow breaths. He felt paralyzed. He couldn't move his head right or left. The sensation lasted a few minutes then stopped.

"Strange, wasn't it?" Dram asked, switching off the Inertia Canceler.

"Yeah, like the fastest roller coaster ever." He couldn't help the smile that escaped his lips.

"Roller coaster?"

"It's an amusement ride. How much longer to the next point?"

"We've got three parsecs to go. Even with a time warp generator, it'll take some time to travel the distance. Why don't you find something for us to eat?"

"That's the best idea I've heard so far." He stood to leave. His hunger roared in his stomach. The thought of food reminded him he hadn't eaten since last night. He glanced out the view port into total darkness, except for the glittering of millions of stars. How did they tell time here?

"Don't get your hopes up, Adam. Space food isn't that good."

The door hissed open at his approach. After he passed through the entryway, it closed much faster than any automatic entrance on Earth. Earth should have the technology these people had.

The thought of flying this space ship excited him, yet the task daunted him as well. What if he made a mistake or got them off course? Navigating had seemed simple enough until Dram had used the warp drive. He hadn't explained when to use those levers at all.

He glanced at the cell. Genesis sat on the floor, her head on her knees. He walked toward her.

"Are you getting hungry?" he asked softly. He squatted to her level. His concern for her comfort was becoming a habit. In the past, he had only cared about himself.

She lifted her head and gazed up at him with tired, brown eyes. She nodded. Her long, shiny hair fell over her shoulders and touched the floor. She looked drained.

"Where do you keep your meals?"

She pointed to the lockers on the far left, near the table. "All the food is in small compartments in the galley and each is labeled."

Strange dials and windows, like appliances of some sort, were on the bottom. He hadn't seen those before.

"You know, Gen, Dram doesn't seem as bad as I thought."

She frowned at him. "My name is Genesis and he wants you to believe that."

"Are you cold?" He reached between the bars to touch her still damp tresses. In the dim light over the cell, her hair appeared soft and touchable. He had only seen blue-black hair in pictures before. He let his fingers run through the silky strands like a comb. He studied her face as she closed her eyes briefly while he played with it. She seemed to enjoy his touch as her features softened.

"Yes."

He could easily warm her in his arms, but they wouldn't fit through the bars.

"Do you have any extra clothes to change into?" he asked.

"Over there," she pointed to another doorway, "In my sleeping compartment."

He stood and walked to the door and it hissed open. He glanced at the Nav-door to make sure Dram hadn't heard him. He stepped inside Genesis' room. Shiny, silver metal was everywhere, including the wall cabinets, shelving, and the bed frames. Storage units attached to one end of the bunks. At least there were mattresses.

Searching through the drawers, he located a small flight suit. He found it odd that there were no other clothes, not even panties or bras, just a pair of socks. Did women wear lingerie on **Atria**? "Hmmm." He would enjoy the view while he had the opportunity.

He shook the thought from his mind and walked back to the cell.

"Here, Gen, put this on. It'll help warm you."

"My name is Genesis!" She grabbed the suit from his hands.

"I said that."

"No. You called me Gen."

"Gen is a nickname. Don't you use nicknames on your planet?"

"No." She pouted as she sat to remove her boots. The thought of undressing her put a smile on his face. He shook his head.

Food. He needed to find some and get his mind off her body. He pictured himself *on* her body instead. He should have kissed her when he had the chance. He grew hard at the thought of tasting those lips.

He walked to the galley area and looked through the small compartments and located the food. They were labeled protein, vegetable, fruit, and carbohydrate matter.

"Hmmm." Their bodies required the same nourishment as humans on Earth. Another locker identified H2O. Good. He was thirsty.

He pulled his sweatshirt out at the bottom, making a well in the center. Then he filled it with items from each food group for all three of them. Unfortunately, everything looked like tubes of toothpaste, except the water bottles and sipper seals. He figured he'd suck the stuff out. Hopefully, the paste tasted better than it appeared.

He returned to the cell and caught sight of Genesis. She bent at the waist. The raincoat rode up her thighs. Her bare, muscular hamstrings were exposed to his view. Wow. She lifted the dry flight suit up her shapely calves, her back toward him. She straightened and he moved forward until the slicker fell to the floor. He froze in his tracks. His pulse quickened. Her muscles flexed as she pulled the top over her shoulders. Her dark skin showed no tan lines. Her long hair lay in front on her right side. When she slipped her left arm into the sleeve, he was blessed with a glimpse of a well-rounded breast. She finished covering herself.

He glanced up and took a deep breath. "Thank you, God," he whispered and let out his breath. He headed to the cell. This would be one long trip.

"Here, Genesis. I brought you some food." Their gazes locked momentarily as she reached into his sweatshirt.

"Thank you," she said and pulled out several tubes and a bottle of water. She lowered her head then gazed up at him through her long, black lashes. Her eyes seemed so large, so beautiful.

"Do you know where we are going?" she asked.

"He mentioned a place called **Meta**." He couldn't keep his mind off her mouth.

"**Meta?**"

"Yes. He said it was three parsecs from here. We make course corrections when we get to the next point."

"He is returning us to the **Vaedra** System. **Meta** is a moon of **Plexus.**"

"Is that good?"

She sipped her water, and he wondered how she would taste as he licked his lips.

"Yes. **Vaedra** is where I come from. We must search for Malek there."

"Good. Hang on, Gen." He turned away. He had to leave before he did something stupid.

"Genesis, my name is Genesis," she whispered loudly. The door hissed open.

"What took you so long?" Dram snapped.

He glared at Dram, feeling defensive.

"I had to *find* the stuff first. I don't know where anything is on this ship, remember?" He'd give Dram attitude right back.

Dram scowled at him. He took several tubes of food and some water from his outstretched shirt. "Don't waste your time on that woman, she's nothing but trouble."

How did Dram know he had been with her? He straightened in his seat as he opened the first tube.

"She's bad news." Dram took a swig of his water.

He squeezed the paste into his mouth. He didn't care for Dram's opinions, anyway. He choked down the dry, thick stuff. It reminded him of bland baby food.

They had more technology than Earth and this was their idea of nutrition? He wondered if NASA had anything better.

He cocked his head toward Dram. "What has Genesis done to you?" He hoped to get Dram's version. He'd only gotten half the story from Genesis and she didn't give up many details.

"She interfered in my business and delayed a big shipment. She's cost me a lot of time and *kashis* on this deal, including the life of my partner.

If things don't go well when we get back, I'll take it out of her hide." Dram's blue eyes flashed with anger.

"Kashis?"

"You call it money, I think."

His curiosity piqued. "How did she cost the life of your partner?"

"She chased us into that storm! Otherwise, Timna would still be alive today."

"You can't blame her for killing him when lightning hit the ship. It's not her fault."

"Damn sure is!"

What the hell? "All she wanted was her father. Couldn't you tell her his location?"

Dram glared at him. "I don't *know* where he is. The last time I encountered him, he was leaving Tarsius on another ship."

"How did you meet her father?" He sipped his water.

"He followed me and interfered in my business, just like *she* did. So I ambushed him and sent him off with an acquaintance."

"Why?" Curiosity got the best of him.

"To get rid of him. He cost me hundreds of dinnaras, uh, dollars in delays of my shipments."

"What business *are* you in?" he asked.

"I have a trading company. I trade services for goods or kashis, whichever benefits me most at the time."

He finished his tubes of food and he sat back in his seat. He thought about what Dram had said or *didn't* say.

Genesis had chased Dram and interfered in his trading company. Dram had neglected to mention he was a wanted man. No doubt his business was illegal as hell. He laced his fingers behind his head.

Genesis and her father had searched for Dram ten years because Dram had abducted all the females from their village. What did Dram do with all those people? He closed his eyes. He believed Genesis' story but Dram's was believable as well, from a criminal's point of view. Of course she would be bad news for Dram.

What was he thinking when he'd offered to help Genesis find her father? No woman had ever affected him so much. His only choice now was to do as he was told. Dram had weapons and he had a pocket knife. When the time was right to escape, he would know.

He crossed his arms over his chest and glanced at Dram as Dram stared out the view port. Dram's jaw was tensed and his bottom lip protruded a little. His eyebrows scrunched together. Dram was either deep in thought or mad at someone.

He cracked his knuckles, one at a time. He wanted to hate Dram but there was something familiar about him--

"Why don't you get some sleep, Adam? You'll need to take over later while I rest." Dram ran a hand through his thick, blond hair.

He wasn't tired, just keyed up. He had too much to think about and not enough answers.

"Do you suppose I can fly this ship by myself?" He had lots of doubts. He drove any kind of wheeled vehicle or boat but a spaceship--

"Sure. I'll call you in to assist me when I make course corrections. After that, you can handle it."

He left the Nav-room. Genesis slept. He walked to the cell and squatted. He gazed at her face and gently brushed away a long strand of hair. His heart warmed at seeing her. Genesis had experienced more things in her short life than he would in a lifetime. She lay on her side, in a fetal position. Her hands crossed her chest. Her face was drawn as she shivered. He remembered the anger and hate in her eyes when she'd lunged at his throat earlier.

Thinking she was cold, he went to her sleeping compartment and took a blanket off the bottom bed. He pulled it through the bars and draped the soft material over her body. He felt better knowing she would be warm.

He returned to her quarters and climbed up the top bunk. He locked his fingers behind his head and rested on her pillow. Thoughts of the day's events ran through his mind. A lot had happened. Maybe he'd wake up and find this all had been a dream. Two things he knew for sure. One, Dram made him feel uneasy. Two, he realized his secluded, lonely life was no longer attractive.

He glanced at the ceiling and found something stuck in a seam. Curious, he pulled out a piece of paper. He opened a poster. His face stared back at him. His heart rate shot up a notch. It was Dram when he was younger. The image moved. *A hologram?* Above the picture were the words: 'Dead or Alive.'

His stomach churned. Below it--Dram, from the planet **Chroma**, is wanted for--' the remaining piece was missing.
Nausea set in as he thought about all the people who would see the poster. Would someone mistake him for Dram and shoot first, or try to arrest him? As long as he remained *with* Dram, they had to believe his story because only one of them could be Dram.

He sat up in bed. The poster *did* say, dead or alive. He rubbed his neck as he remembered how close he'd come to death at Gen's hands.

Tired and exhausted, Dram sat at the controls in the Nav-room and ran a hand through his hair. Hopefully Adam believed him. He actually held his interest for awhile. Sure, he'd show him some things about flying but not too much. Not yet.

He must keep Adam separated from the woman. He certainly didn't trust her at all, especially when she had been tracking him for so long. If she *did* work for the I.S.P. then she might enlist the boy's help to escape.

First, he had to convince the boy of his importance. Since Timna's death, he needed another copilot. Adam was his ticket out of this mess.

Once they made it to the **Vaedra** System, he could communicate with Ramen and have him set things up. He had to convince Z the delay would be worthwhile.

CHAPTER FOUR

Genesis woke, wiping sleep from her eyes. She depended on the Earth man to escape Dram. There was no other way. He'd offered to help her. He didn't have to do that, especially after what she'd done to him. She owed him and she would keep her word as the daughter of the Chief of her tribe. She still had a chance to accomplish her mission.

Her thoughts drifted to the Earth man again. Something about him gave her sensations she had never experienced before. Worries seemed to disappear from her mind at his nearness. A warm surge flowed through her body, along with the sudden pounding in her heart. She wished Herda was here to explain these things. Had her mother not been abducted, she would be home on **Atria**. Jolu had promised to take her as his mate on her eighteenth ano, but that was six anos ago. Did he still wait?

Malek never spoke of his love for Herda but Genesis knew he cared for her. The way he had talked about her and had gazed in her eyes showed his affections. Genesis wanted someone to caress her cheek and look at her like she was the only one in his life.

Adam lay on the top bunk in Gen's room. He tossed and turned as sleep eluded him. The day's events played over in his mind. If he had reacted differently maybe he wouldn't be here. Then, again, he could be dead. His thoughts kept coming back to Genesis. No other woman had affected him the way she did. Every time he came near her, his pulse raced and his body reacted in a way he had no control over. Her penetrating brown eyes drew him in. Her soft, sensual lips begged to be kissed. He hardened at the thought of her and sat up.

"Great! Now I won't get any sleep at all." He tossed the blanket off and jumped from the top bunk to the floor. Maybe she was awake and willing to talk. Yeah, right. That was the last thing he wanted to do with her. He needed to speak to someone, though.

The sleeping compartment door hissed open. He glanced toward the Nav-room. Good, it was closed. Straight ahead, in the cell, however, Genesis sat propped up against the bars, her arms folded over her knees. She watched him.

"I couldn't sleep, how about you?" He walked toward her in his bare feet. The cold metal floor was uncomfortable. He squatted to her level when he reached the cell.

She moved closer and kneeled in front of him. He lowered his knees. His body touched the bars, the only thing that separated them. Her warm breath brushed his face.

"I want my ship back." She tugged the blanket around her shoulders. Genesis bit her lower lip. He wanted to kiss her and found concentration difficult. He moved his arm through the bars and slipped his hand to the nape of Genesis' neck, drawing her near him. Her mouth opened slightly and her eyes widened as he met her soft, moist lips. The tender, sweet kiss grew passionate when he explored her with his tongue. The tension in her shoulders disappeared as she sagged toward him. Her arms reached around his back.

He wrapped his other arm below her waist and pulled her closer to the bars and him. He wanted her body against his but the cold metal prevented that. He let his hand slide down her hips and squeezed gently. She whimpered in his mouth as her tongue met his. He deepened the kiss as much as the bars would allow. Her arms moved up his spine. One rose to his neck. Her fingers played with his hair. His body burned as she returned every bit of what he gave her. He didn't want this moment to end. Her touch sent him over the edge and he groaned.

Genesis broke away first, gasping for air, her eyes wide as she gazed at him.

"Gen," he gently touched her lips with the pad of his thumb. Her eyelids closed at his touch. He loved seeing her respond to him. He lifted her chin and tasted her again.

Her hands held his face as they kissed passionately, urgently. He gently tugged her bottom lip in his teeth. He wanted more of her. He wanted to trail kisses from her neck down to her breasts and follow with caresses. The bars between them reminded him of that impossibility.

Finally, he pulled away, his breathing labored. The tightness in his groin pained him. Her heavy-lidded eyes told him not to stop.

"Damn!" He yanked against the metal with his hands. "I want to get you out of here, Genesis, believe me."

"Find the yav to this cage and let me out," she said as she grabbed the bars, her fists just below his. Their gazes locked.

"Dram's got the key...uh, yav. How do you expect me to get it?" His breathing slowly returned to normal.

Genesis scrunched her eyebrows together. "Tell him I need to relieve myself. He will have to give you the yav."

He stared at her lips wanting to taste her again.

"Are you listening to me?" she asked, bringing him back from his thoughts.

He gazed into her eyes. "Yeah, I don't think your idea will work, Gen. Dram doesn't trust us. That's why he separated us, remember?"

She reached through the bars and held his face in her hands and caressed his temples with her fingers. He closed his eyes. Her relaxing touch mesmerized him. He didn't want to move. What had she done to him? *Don't stop.*

He had to think but her gentle massage removed all logical thoughts from his mind. He reluctantly tore away.

"Wait! I have an idea." He got up and moved toward the compartments. He tugged several of the inset handles but none released.

"Why won't these open?" He glanced at her.

"Dram locked them. The scanner box controls most functions on **The Guardian** as well as holding the yav to the cage," she said, lowering her eyes.

"I think we should wait for the right moment, Gen, and this doesn't feel right. Not now."

"We need to try something," she pleaded.

"I could pick the lock," he reached into his pocket for the Swiss Army knife. He flipped the blade open and walked to the cell door.

"No!" Genesis got up and ran to meet him.

"No?"

"The mechanism is sensitive. You scratch the chip inside and I may never get out." Her eyes pleaded with him. Already weakened from her kiss, her look convinced him. He closed his tool and put it up.

"Use the knife on Dram," she pointed to his pocket.

"No, Gen, that will only make him mad. I need to get real close to use it and he won't let me." The premonition ran through his mind once more. The two fought somewhere on land. One of them had a strange-looking gun, the size of a rifle.

She clenched her jaw and grabbed the cold metal, squeezing with her hands. She threw her head back and grunted in frustration. He reached through the bars and wrapped his arms around her. He lightly rubbed her shoulders, trying to soothe her. His aching groin reminded him of his disappointment as well.

"I'll think of something, Genesis. Just give me time, okay?"

She nodded against his chest. He kissed the top of her head.

"I really do need to relieve myself," she glanced up through her long lashes.

"I'll talk to Dram." He lifted her chin with his forefinger and kissed her lightly on the lips.

The door to the Nav-room hissed open at his approach. Dram swirled around in his seat, his weapon drawn and pointed at him.

He jumped back, clutching his chest. "Good gosh, you startled me!" His heart pounded.

"Don't ever do that again, boy. You were supposed to be asleep." Dram lowered his gun.

"I couldn't sleep. There's too much to think about." He ran a hand through his hair as he sat in the empty seat next to Dram. The tightness in his jeans started to recede.

"Genesis is awake. She says she needs to relieve herself."

Dram stared at him, his eyes wide.

"I need to go, too," he said, trying to sound casual. Dram continued to study him. Maybe he suspected something. He was uncomfortable. What Dram didn't know was they *had* no plan. At least, not yet.

"Are you going to let her pee her pants?" he asked, finally.

Dram stood and pointed at him. "You stay here and keep an eye on things. I'll take her to the cleansing compartment. When I get back, you can go."

"Sure, just hurry up, okay?" He only hoped Genesis didn't try anything. He crossed his arms over his chest as he gazed out the view port.

He wouldn't have stopped with the kiss if Genesis had been out of the cell. He'd never experienced such a strong connection to any woman before. What pulled him to her like a magnet? He had to get thoughts of her out of his head. A relationship between them couldn't work out. Once they escaped and found Malek, she would return him to Earth. End of story.

Genesis sat in the cage with her back against the bars and her eyes closed, lightly touching her lips. The incredible sensations when the Earth man had touched her still lingered. Did her parents feel this way each time they kissed? Her heart had pounded so loudly in her ears she'd thought Adam would have heard the beating. The tingling rush of warmth had swept through her body and had left her gasping for air. Then he'd kissed her again and the same thing had happened. This time she'd held him, not wanting to break the connection. *Are these sensations normal? I like them.*

While she'd briefly touched his face and caressed his temples, she'd heard his thoughts. He, too, enjoyed her flesh against his. He didn't want to stop, either, but he fought himself to resist.

Had she inherited Herda's mind reading powers? She knew she had her gift of healing, and the ability to communicate telepathically. But to use the skill of mind reading, she must properly learn techniques only her mother could teach her. She had seen Herda use it on the little ones who were sick and too young to speak.

She had heard the Earth man's voice clearly in her head. She had not imagined it. Would she be able to communicate with him telepathically as well?

The sound of the hissing door made her jump. She stood to look at Dram. He shared the same appearance as Adam, but she could see the difference between them. The Earth man's eyes were sincere and kind, while Dram's held nothing but evil.

"So, you need to relieve yourself?" His gaze narrowed at her as if he wanted to inflict pain.

"Yes, I do." She dropped her blanket and fisted her hands on her hips. She would take any chance to escape, whether or not the Earth man helped her.

"Don't even think about trying anything. I'm onto you and the boy." He aimed the yav at the lock mechanism but had her laser weapon pointed at her.

She glared at him as she left the cage. She walked to the cleansing compartment and stepped inside when the door hissed open. Once closed, she removed her flight suit to tend to her needs.

Dram waited outside for Genesis. He leaned his large frame against the wall, folding his arms and crossing his right foot over his left. He needed the stretch. He would take care of himself after he got the woman back in the cage.

He wondered how long the boy had been awake before coming into the Nav-room. He was positive the two planned something, but what? Her laser weapon was still in his hand when he slid the switch to stun with his finger. His full bladder made him uncomfortable. She was in the cleans-com entirely too long.

The door hissed open but she didn't emerge from the compartment. Dram peered inside. A hot, soapy spray hit him in the face.

"What the Vaedran hell?" Dram spat out the sudsy mess and fired the weapon at Genesis. Her body hit the floor. The spraying stopped but the hose snapped and bounced furiously. Water was everywhere. He reached in and turned off the supply. The nozzle hung limply from the ceiling, just over the woman's torso.

He tucked the weapon inside the holster and grabbed her arm. He dragged her across the floor and back to her prison, cursing. She could sleep the rest of the trip. He would zap her periodically to keep her unconscious. At least that way, she couldn't cause any more problems.

He locked her inside the cage and went back to the cleansing compartment to relieve himself.

After cleaning up, he checked the supplies. In Genesis' relentless pursuit, she hadn't thought to restock the ship. However, with her unconscious, he and the boy had enough food to last until they reached Meta.

The boy and Genesis were obviously in this together. He knew she was persistent but what about Adam? He straightened the strap across his shoulder. Adam had to fight him to get the scanner. Hopefully, he was smart enough not to try.

The door hissed open as he approached the Nav-room.

"Why are you soaked?" Adam asked. His eyebrows narrowed.

"Your plan failed." He glared at the boy as he dropped to his seat. He ran a hand through his thick, wet hair.

"What are you talking about?" The boy stared at him.

"You and the woman didn't make any plans, did you?" He raised an eyebrow at Adam.

"Hell, no! She told me she had to relieve herself." The boy stood.

"Where do you think you're going?"

"You said I could pee when you were through, remember?"

"Yes. Well, you needn't worry about the woman anymore. I took care of her."

The boy glared at him. "What did you *do* to her?" He demanded. His hands fisted at his sides.

"Don't concern yourself. She won't be bothering either one of us for awhile."

Adam's jaw tensed as he rushed out of the room. Dram leaned back in his seat and crossed his arms over his chest.

"That's one down and one to go," he mumbled to himself.

Adam stopped short. Genesis' drenched body lay unconscious on the floor of the cell.

"Oh, Gen, what happened to you?" He felt her pulse on her neck. Strong but slow. He breathed a sigh of relief.

"Why, Gen? You should have waited for me. I would have thought of something sooner or later." He reached into the cell and grabbed the edge of the blanket and pulled the fabric over her body. Her being cold and wet on the floor bothered him. She had just dried out from the rain, and now this had happened.

He stood, clenching his fists. Seething with anger, he wanted to punch Dram. The action itself was dangerous. He paced back and forth. He had to help Genesis escape and find her father but an overwhelming need to defend her, seized him. Why was she so stubborn?

He found the cleansing compartment between the two sleeping rooms and relieved himself. The contraption was like a giant port-a-toilet, except everything was shiny metal. The toilet stood in one corner, a sink in the other, but on the floor was a drain. The area was four times the size of a normal one they used on the job site. Above his head, a metallic tube hung from the ceiling with an extra set of knobs by the faucet handles on the sink. The shower-type nozzle retracted at the push of a button he found on the wall beside the toilet. A few drops of water fell loose. Then he noticed the wet floor.

"Hmmm." *That must be how they both got wet.*

"Why, Gen?" he whispered.

A recessed compartment near the sink revealed something similar to toilet paper when he pushed the button above. The substance was much thicker, damp, and softer, like wet wipes he used on the job site for cleaning their hands before eating. Some things were the same everywhere. The one obvious thing about the cleansing unit was the lack of odor. All the port-a-toilets he had ever been in had the overwhelming fragrance of a sewer.

He returned to the Nav-room but paused to check on Genesis again.

"Cool bathroom you got," he plopped onto the seat next to Dram.

"Huh?"

"Er, uh, cleansing compartment?"

Dram glared at him. "What took you so long?"

"I checked on Genesis, do you mind?"

"Yes, I do. I told you she was bad news. Just stay away from her, understand?"

"You don't need to treat her like that. I don't care what she did to your business."

Dram stood and pointed a finger at him. "You're in no position to lecture me, boy. Since you're awake, I think I'll take a nap. Wake me when the alarm goes off." Dram left the room.

"What alarm?" He swung around as the door closed behind Dram. He propped his elbows up on the console with his head in his hands.

"Lord, how am I going to get out of this mess?" he mumbled. At the sound of the door hissing open, he jerked in his seat.

"I forgot to tell you, boy, I'm a light sleeper, so don't try anything stupid." Dram pointed a finger at him.

"I wouldn't think of it." He swallowed.

Dram turned and left, the door closed behind him.

Adam shook his head. Dram was edgy. The longer he knew Dram, the less he liked him.

He stared at the view in front of him. The stars seemed motionless as they traveled at a high rate of speed. Earth needed this capability. NASA could explore their own galaxy and look for planets that held the possibility of life.

He pondered what it was like to be a pioneer in the early days of Earth's history. How did Columbus feel, knowing he explored the unknown? Criticized for believing the Earth was round, he was compelled to prove himself right. Adam admired him for his perseverance.

Scientists held beliefs no one accepted, until their theories were proved. The risk takers made Earth's present day technology possible.

His mind wandered to other planets and the kind of homes they lived in. His crew built log cabins. Did similar materials exist in the Vaedra System and did Meta have trees?

The technological stuff he had seen so far made him wonder what else these people knew. Maybe the diseases that plagued the Earth weren't found in their galaxy.

He sat a long time contemplating the possible differences between Earth and the culture on Meta.

Finally, he grew restless. He needed to stretch but he wanted to check on Genesis. He hesitated at the entrance after the door hissed open. How could he leave and still keep an eye on things in here? He noticed a small button along the right side of the entry. He pressed the knob then stepped through the opening. He walked away from the sensor but it didn't close. Good. He wouldn't take long. He needed to know Genesis was okay.

At the cell, he reached inside to check her pulse. Her body was still and cool. The blanket had not been moved and her heart rate was strong. He let out a breath he hadn't realized he was holding, and gently brushed a long strand of hair off her face.

A strange noise came from the Nav-room. He ran back to the computer. The monitor flashed a **Warning-Two minutes to re-entry!**

CHAPTER FIVE

Adam ran to the first compartment searching for Dram. The door hissed open. Dram bolted from the bottom bunk with a laser weapon in his hand pointed at his chest. The premonition flashed through his mind. In the vision, Dram wore a blue flight suit, not the white one he had on now.

"Dram!" He raised his arms in self defense. "You told me to wake you when the alarm went off." He turned and ran back to the Nav-room. Dram followed. His heart pounded. He would have to remember Dram's lightning reflexes in the future.

Dram sat at the controls. "We need to triangulate our position." He typed some commands onto the keyboard then showed Adam which levers to pull. The monitor flashed the location and trajectory through the wormholes. Many blinking dots appeared on the far side of the screen.

"What are these spots?" He pointed.

"Those are planets. Type in **Plexus**."

He typed the word and the coordinates popped up on the monitor.

"We'll go through the worm holes here," Dram tapped the screen, "and stop there."

"Is that **Plexus**?"

"No, actually, it's **Meta**, a moon of **Plexus**, your new home."

"Home?" He scowled at Dram. The last time someone chose his place to live, he was ten years old and he had just been orphaned. He especially didn't like the idea Dram thought he would stay.

Once they got to **Meta**, Dram promised to teach him more about flying. Afterward, he'd hijack this ship and help Genesis find her father. Then she could return him to Earth. The plan had to work because he didn't have any other ideas at the moment.

Time passed, but how long was anybody's guess. He and Dram

took turns sleeping and keeping watch. Each shift change he checked on Genesis. She always slept. He wondered what Dram had done to her and it bothered him. That much sleep couldn't be normal. Did he give her drugs? She had no food or water. The consequences of going without either for very long were not good.

Dram entered the Nav-room for another shift change.

"What did you do to Genesis, Dram?" His anger was mounting inside.

"Nothing, why?"

"She's been asleep for days and she hasn't had anything to eat or drink in all that time."

"That's the side effects of being stunned with a laser weapon. You sleep for hours."

"It's been days, Dram. She needs water, if nothing else." He crossed his arms over his chest.

"She'll be up shortly. I'll make sure she gets something to eat and drink when we land."

He glared at Dram but wasn't convinced. "She'd better--"

"Or what, Adam?"

"Or I may not cooperate with you anymore." Yeah, like the threat would make Dram shudder.

Dram glanced at him, an eyebrow raised. "We'll see about that." He pointed to the horizon as he yawed right.

The monitor flashed: **Approaching Meta**. This moon appeared smaller than the pictures he had seen of Earth's moon.

The landscape came into view. The mountains reminded him of the rolling hills of the Smokies but unlike the Appalachian chain, these had few trees. A stream wound down through one of the mountains and flowed into a river and lake. Otherwise, there wasn't much vegetation except at the higher elevations. The scrub brush and a few scraggly pines reminded him of Arizona desert photos, except for the gray dirt.

The stars flickered in the dusky sky, more brilliantly and numerous than he had ever seen from Earth.

"Is this place populated?" He asked.

"My employees and I live here," Dram said.

"You mean no one lives here except a few people?"

"Yes, and I plan to keep it that way. It's better for business."

"How?"

"Less hassle."

From the law, no doubt. Dram hid something illegal, but what?

Dram brought the ship into a hover position over a well-lit compound. The vegetation surrounding the area looked vaguely familiar. Huge pines and hemlocks, tulip poplar and mountain laurel grew around the complex. The large building, shaped like a 'T', had a pond on the right side, behind their landing pad. Small holly bushes along with a few boulders, encircled the bank. Except for the fountain in the corner, the area reminded him of a smaller version of his own place back on Earth.

"Nice digs you've got here," he replied but it would never be his home.

"I've spent years preparing this location as well as the business," Dram said, moving a lever. He flipped some switches as they landed then glanced at him.

"Go ahead and check on the woman while I finish up in here."

Surprised to get permission, he forced himself to stand slowly. He took time to stretch, tamping down his emotions. He didn't want to appear anxious.

Genesis awoke at his approach.

"Gen, are you all right?" Relief washed over him when she moved.

She shook her head then lifted her face to glance at him. He squatted beside the cell and reached his arm inside to help support her while she stood.

"How long was I out?"

"A couple of days, I think. We had several shift changes."

She trembled as he held her. Concern washed over him.

"Two? That can't be right. He only shot me once." She gazed at him, dazed.

"Damn him," he clenched his jaw, his anger rising.

"The last thing I remember was he stunned me when I hosed him," she said.

She appeared so vulnerable. A strange new mixture of feelings ran through him seeing her this way. That overwhelming need to take care of her along with the urge to protect and comfort her, drove him. His arms ached to hold her.

"I checked on you several times, Gen, but you slept until now.

Genesis raised her fingers to her forehead, touching the band of jewels, her hand shaking.

"Let me get you some water, Gen. Hold onto the bars for support." He ran to the galley. Dram had been doling out the food and drink. He was surprised to find the compartments empty when he searched, except for one tube of vegetable matter, and two bottles of H2O. He grabbed all three and ran back to the cell.

"Here, swallow this," he lifted her chin with his forefinger. He opened the container and watched as she gulped down the first bottle of liquid without stopping.

She wiped the moisture from her lips with the back of her hand and glanced around the ship.

"Where are we?" She asked.

"We landed on **Meta.** Here, take this," he handed her the vegetable matter.

Her shaking prevented her opening the tube.

"Let me," he gently took the paste and squeezed the contents into her mouth. He watched her swallow. He continued feeding her until she finished then handed her the last bottle of water.

"Dram promised to feed you once we got here," he said.

"Is this his base?" she asked, her eyes wide.

He nodded.

The hatch opened and four men entered the ship, all dressed in the same light blue flight suits like Dram had worn earlier. The men stood over six feet tall and each was as different in appearance as hair, eye color, and body shape would allow. All the men carried weapons, similar to the one used in his premonition.

The men pointed the guns at Genesis, holding them at waist level, one hand supported the barrel and the other touched the trigger.

"Whoa!" He waved his arms, his pulse quickened. "Lower your rifles." The men followed his command.

"Dram?" The one with dreadlocks spoke first, studying his clothes.

Dram exited the Nav-room. "Hello, boys!"

The four men glanced between Dram and him. Puzzled shock on all their faces.

"What the Vaedran hell is going on?" the blond man asked, scratching his head of snarly hair.

"Hey, you've cloned yourself, boss," the one with dreadlocks said, chuckling.

Dram walked to the snarly-haired man and tapped his shoulder as he called his name. Then he moved to the others in succession.

"Bordon, Sim, Ethan, and Rosca, I want you to meet Adam, my son."

He swallowed in surprise and his mouth fell open as he straightened to glare at Dram. He realized he had heard the others echo the word as well.

"That's right, Adam. I'll explain everything later."

He shook his head. Dram avoided explanations to his men by shocking everyone. How could Dram suggest such a thing? Even though they *did* appear alike, Dram was an alien.

"Adam will be one of my pilot trainees," Dram announced, putting his arm around him. He cringed at Dram's touch. Maybe he'd told the truth about teaching him to fly. At least he had witnesses.

The four men exchanged puzzled glances. Genesis glared at him. Her eyebrows narrowed, and her bottom lip poked out. He felt her anger. Why did she act that way, couldn't she tell Dram had lied?

"What happened, boss?" Ethan whispered.

"It's a long story, Ethan. I'll explain later." Dram unlocked the cell door.

"This one is trouble, boys." Dram said as he grabbed Genesis' arm and pulled her from her prison. He pushed her into Sim.

He moved closer. He didn't trust Sim nor did he like what had happened. His adrenalin kicked in.

"Oh, a gift for me?" Sim chuckled, grabbing her arm.

"Hardly," Dram replied. "Put her in section two," he said.

"Where's Timna?" Ethan asked.

"Dead."

"What about *him?*" Bordon pointed to him.

"Ethan, give Adam room ten tonight. He will be my guest at the evening meal."

Genesis resisted Sim's efforts to tie her up, so Rosca assisted. He moved next to Sim, his anger growing.

"A tough one, eh?" Rosca said, pulling her around. Genesis kicked Sim's shin. Sim reached back to slap her but he caught Sim's arm and held on.

"Don't even think about it," he growled, his other fist clenched tight and drawn to take a swing.

"Don't concern yourself with her, boy." Dram said from close behind.

He turned and glared at Dram over his shoulder, tensing his jaw. Sim pulled his arm away. One thing he didn't like was someone mistreating women and most especially, Genesis.

Genesis faced him with hopelessness in her eyes. Somehow he would find a way to escape. He had promised her and he always kept his promises.

"Did Ramen explain about the shipment, boss?" Ethan whispered to Dram.

"Yes, he did. We'll send the merchandise first thing in the morning," Dram patted Ethan's shoulder.

"Sir? I thought you were delivering the shipment to Z yourself," Bordon said.

"We have a change in plans, Bordon. Prepare the team for flight tomorrow."

"Yes, sir." Bordon turned to leave but Dram held him back.

He watched as Sim and Rosca forcefully hauled Genesis down the ramp, her hands confined in plastic restraints behind her.

She pulled but Sim didn't give her any slack.

Why did she have to resist? She knew treatment worsened when she fought. She hadn't learned anything since Dram had stunned her. He wanted to warn her but the consequences might work against both of them.

"Ethan, escort Adam to his room and give him a unicrin to wear," Dram said.

He walked beside Ethan down the ramp and heard Dram whisper something to Bordon.

Ethan led him toward the door nearest the landing pad at the bottom of the 'T'. A large picture window on the left stood beside the entrance and showed a command room inside. An elaborate computer and communications system lined an entire wall.

A tall, thin, dark-haired man sat at the keyboard, talking on a strange-looking headset.

He followed Ethan through the narrow quarters to a double-size door. All of them had sensors to open at approach, like on the ship. Ethan led him into a large dining room. Several long tables and lots of chairs took over the place. *They must feed a crowd here.* He cracked his knuckles, one at a time. The two of them left the room through another double-size door and went down a narrow hallway. A lounge area on the left had a sofa, chair and low table. He noticed an entrance with an 'office' sign.

Ethan continued leading him farther. Doors faced the hall on either side. At the intersection of halls, Ethan paused. He watched Sim and Rosca continue with Genesis farther down on the right.

"This is your room for now," Ethan unlocked the access box with a yav. The last door on the left of the main hallway hissed open.

The three others stopped at a room. Rosca let Gen in.

Genesis glanced back at him, her eyebrows raised, as they shoved her inside. There was nothing he could do until he learned how to fly. He closed his eyes briefly. *Hang on, Gen.* His gut tightened at the thought of not seeing her again. Outnumbered and outgunned, he was helpless. Dram hadn't trusted either of them together on the ship. He wouldn't let his guard down here.

"Okay, Adam." Ethan stepped away from the entrance and gestured for him to go in.

Inside, a king-sized bed took most of the room. The bed, dresser, and a matching mirror framed in gold were set against beige walls. He touched the shiny metal. "What is this material?"

"Tulin," Ethan said as he opened the top drawer. "You'll find a unicrin and boots inside. The cleansing room." He pointed to another doorway. "I'll come back for you when your evening meal is ready." Ethan turned and left.

He pulled the heavy drawer open. Solid gold lined the sides, bottom, and front. How did Dram afford this? Were trees more precious than gold here? Why not use some alloy, or at least something lighter than this metal? He pulled out the only item, a blue flight suit. Everyone wore the outfit. He checked all the other drawers. They were empty, except the one containing the boots. There was no night stand, just an overhead light.

He held the unicrin against his chest. With blue clothes on, he would resemble Dram even more. The thought disturbed him.

The bathroom, located on the left of the bed, appeared similar to the one on the ship, except larger. Two switches operated the lighting in both areas.

After showering and toweling off, he discovered the unicrin had no zippers or buttons. A type of magnetic strip at the shoulders, across the arms, as well as along the inseam of the pant legs, held it together. He suited up. The boots had no socks and went high on the ankles, similar to military shoes on Earth. The tongue of the boot attached on both sides, keeping the leather in place. He liked that idea.

When he caught his reflection in the mirror, he realized he needed a shave. He searched the cleansing compartment but found nothing resembling a razor. A cabinet held a hairbrush and something vaguely reminiscent of a toothbrush with white powder in a container. He had been wiping his gums with his fingers all this time. He took the object from its sterile wrapper and wet it. Then he sprinkled the white stuff onto it. His teeth needed a good brushing but the powder tasted like baking soda. At least his mouth felt clean.

He dug his knife out of his jeans and flipped open the blade.

"This might work." He touched the sharp edge to his cheek but a knock at the door interrupted him. He closed the tool and felt the suit for pockets but couldn't find any.

"Damn." He slid the weapon into his boot. *Better keep this item quiet.*

Bordon stuck his head in the doorway. "Ethan said to escort you to the evening meal."

Farther down the hall, Genesis sat at a table near one end of a dark room. A single hanging illuminator lit the area.

She choked on the food Sim had brought her as she fought tears of despair. Dram seldom showed mercy to anyone. The Earth man would spend the rest of his life on a foreign planet, unless he formulated an escape plan. Even though he forgave her for her mistake, how could she forgive herself? She wanted to see him again. Did he whisper in her mind, *'Hang in there, Gen'*? No one else called her that.

A couple of blonde-haired girls, about eight and thirteen, joined her.

"You'll get used to it," the older one said. She had pale blue eyes like the Earth man and spoke in a whisper. Her skin was white and creamy.

Both girls had the same coloring but the shape of their noses, eyebrows, and mouths appeared different.

"I don't want to be here," she mumbled. She put her eating implement down and rested her head in her hands. She had lost her appetite. The food would not go past the large lump in her throat. She wiped her mouth with the back of her hand.

"There is nothing we can do," the older one answered.

"How many girls are here?" she asked, swallowing her despair. She needed to make her own escape plan.

"We have eight in this room but thirty altogether."

Certainly they could take the handful of men she had seen. Flying a transporter didn't require a large crew. She had to convince them to help her for the plan to work.

"Have you tried to escape?" she asked, sitting up in her seat.

"No. The men carry weapons and make regular rounds. The only hiding place on this moon is the mountains, and there's no way to leave."

"Where are the others?" She asked.

"They're down the hall, in different rooms. The plan is to ship us out tomorrow."

"Do you know the location?" She folded her arms and leaned forward at the table. She pushed her plate away.

"I'm not sure, but I've heard the men talk. We're going to another planet in the Vaedra System."

"Can any of you fly a cargo ship?" she asked.

"Shey can," the older girl said.

"She's our instructor," the younger one added.

"Really?"

"We were outside in our fitness class at the academy when they landed in our field," the older one explained.

"Yes, and the men pointed their weapons at us and made us get in the ship," the little one said. "Shey flew missions with her father on a transporter. She's in another room."

"Good. Tomorrow we will plan our escape." She hoped the Earth man kept his promise but how would they communicate?

She left the table and lay on the cool floor and thought about the kiss he had given her. The memory of his touch sent a flood of heat throughout her body. Was this normal? How did he affect her without being here? She liked the new feelings she got in his presence. She wanted to be near him now and that desire made her ache in strange places. She hoped he was safe.

Then she remembered what Dram had said to his men. 'I want you to meet my son.' As the son of Dram, he appeared like him but his actions spoke differently. After she'd healed Adam, he became nice to her. If he were Dram's son, wouldn't he act the same as Dram in other ways? She'd spent the last ten **anos** hating the man's face. Now, she found it difficult to keep the hate alive, especially after sharing kisses.

Had the Earth man experienced the same sensations as she had? Did his body burn when their lips met? He'd pulled her close and she'd felt his heart pounding as hard as hers. Did he tingle when she touched him? She lay on her back with one hand pressed against her forehead and whispered his name.

"Adam."

Adam and Bordon walked down the hall toward the dining room. "Please tell me it's real food and not the space crap I've been eating for days," he said.

Bordon laughed. "We try to avoid that stuff as much as possible around here."

Bordon stood a few inches taller than his own six-foot frame. He appeared in his late twenties or early thirties. His messy mane was absurd. He wanted to laugh just staring at him. Bordon looked as if he had never seen a comb in his life.

"Who does your hair?" he blurted, without thinking.

"Hey, it's wash and go for me. I haven't got time to fuss."

He stared at Bordon's face. "You have time to shave but not to brush your hair?" He realized all the men had been clean shaven.

"What is *shave?*" Bordon turned his head.

"You're kidding, right?" *Maybe they used a different term.* He tried again. "You know, when you remove the beard from your face, you cut it off with a razor." He gestured toward his stubble.

Bordon's brows furrowed as he shook his head. "Beard?"

"Beard is facial hair."

"We don't have hair on our faces, except eyebrows and lashes. What are *you* talking about?"

"*Adam.*"

He spun around at the sound of Gen's voice. The hall was deserted.

"Did you say something?" he asked Bordon. He knew he'd heard her.

"I said we don't have hair on our faces."

He stared at Bordon a moment, letting Bordon's words soak in and the fact Gen's voice was audible only to him. She had the gift of healing. Did she possess other gifts as well? He sensed her distress but how could he rescue her? Her quarters were close to his. After he ate, he would sneak to her room and release her. Together they'd escape. Alone, he didn't have a chance. To ask for help was not part of his nature.

"Don't tell me you grow hair on your face?" Bordon asked, bringing him back from his thoughts. He nodded as he glanced at Bordon, not explaining further. Hunger pangs roared in his belly when he and Bordon reached the dining room. The smell of real food wafted through the entrance. Bordon glared at him as the double-size door hissed open.

He raised his eyebrows and shrugged, as the two of them stepped inside. "I'm starving," he said.

Dram sat at the head of a long table. He glanced up from his plate. Ten chairs surrounded him. Two seats away sat his food and drink.

"That's all, Bordon. Thank you," Dram said.

"Sure, boss." Bordon bowed and left the room.

"Eat, Adam, we'll talk later."

He wouldn't argue now. He had plenty of questions for Dram, however.

He stabbed at his meal and noticed the resemblance to roast, potatoes, and a green vegetable in the bean family. Delicious, but the food didn't taste like anything he'd eaten before. He tried not to wolf it down. He hoped Genesis ate as well.

Several quiet minutes later, Dram wiped his mouth with his napkin. "I know you have a lot of questions, so go ahead and ask." Dram pushed his plate away and punched a button on the console imbedded in the table top.

"Did you remember to feed Genesis?" he asked, wiping his mouth with his napkin.

A sixteen-year old brunette, wearing a pale blue, sack-like garment came into the room and gathered the dishes. Glancing at him and Dram, she lost control of the plates and dropped them on the table.

"Sorry, sir," she said, looking at Dram. She lowered her gaze as she cleaned the new mess. She quickly gathered the dishes and left.

"Genesis has been taken care of, so drop the subject." Dram sipped his drink.

He thought about the rough treatment she'd had from Dram and his men. If he pressed Dram for more answers, he might get suspicious. Then again, Dram could take his anger out on her. He didn't want that to happen either. Thinking of her in trouble made his pulse quicken.

"How is it you speak English without a translator?" he asked.

"English? Oh, yes. We call it **Vaedran** dialect, Ancient **Vaedran** to those who never left our system. I know many languages and I taught my employees to use Ancient years ago. Not everyone has a translator."

"Why did you lie about me being your son? Did you actually expect the men to believe you?"

"It wasn't a lie, Adam. You *are* my son."

His heart skipped a beat at those words.

"No way in hell!" He stood up. "Joshua Davis was my father. My mother, Emma, and my dad were both killed in a car accident sixteen years ago. No way *you* are my father," he pointed a finger at Dram.

Dram closed his eyes and put his elbows on the table, holding his head in his hands.

"It wasn't an accident," Dram said.

"What?"

"About twenty-seven years ago, I landed in your field. My Nav-unit had malfunctioned and I got off course. I didn't fly state-of-the-art equipment back then. After I discovered the problem, I triangulated my position to the nearest planet--Earth. Emma swam in the pond when I first met her." Dram stared into space.

His knees weakened so he pulled his chair from the table and sat down.

"The prettiest girl I had ever seen and I fell in love with her instantly. We were both eighteen at the time. I told her where I came from, but she didn't care. She helped me find parts to fix the communications device so I could call for help." Dram glanced at him then away again.

"I sent out a distress signal. A salvage crew from **Tarsius** responded. When the ship arrived, I asked her to go with me." Dram leaned back in his chair and folded his arms across his chest.

"And?" He sat on the edge of his seat, awaiting the punch line of a cruel joke. He couldn't believe his mother would fall for someone like Dram. He was an *alien*.

"She refused to go with me. She said she had some premonition about me and wouldn't go."

So his mother was the source of his 'visions.' She had never spoken of them, however. Maybe she saw Dram for who he really was. "No," he found himself saying, "Joshua Davis was my father."

"Adam, why do you think we look so much alike? Did you imagine looking like this Davis man? He had dark hair from what I remember."

"How did you *know* that?" His heart raced and his mind reeled as he realized the possibility his mother and Dram had been *intimate*.

"Emma had blonde hair and blue eyes, too, but you resemble me."

Adam shook his head. He tried blocking the image of them from his mind. No. She wouldn't do that. She couldn't. She loved his dad. Joshua had spent time teaching him how to throw and catch a ball and took him fishing and hunting. The two of them attended Cub Scout meetings and campouts together. He scooted his chair closer to the table. He propped his elbows and held his head in his hands. His dad gave him the bow and arrow for his eighth birthday and taught him how to hunt.

"I know it's hard for you to believe me, Adam, but I'm telling the truth. I thought she loved me but she believed that damn premonition. My life could have been different if she had come with me." Dram glanced at the ceiling and back at him. "Then, again, maybe, I should have stayed on Earth."

"Why didn't you?"

"I didn't belong. I had just started this business with my partner, Timna. I had to return. In exchange for my ship, the salvage crew gave me passage to the **Vaedra** System."

He sat, his head still in his hands, and tried to tame his emotions. Why would she do something like that with an *alien*? Couldn't she tell Dram had used her? Betrayal swept over him.

"The man you thought was your father was Emma's boyfriend at the time. He had a summer job out of town. I was with her for two months and took her for my mate. I knew when she conceived she'd have a son. I think Joshua was the reason she wouldn't leave."

"No!" Adam shook his head and straightened in his seat. He didn't like what he'd heard. The evidence, however, stared him in the face. He couldn't deny the two of them resembled each other. He'd always thought he took after his mother. His stomach knotted.

"She never spoke of you," he managed to say.

"No doubt, it would have been a problem if she had." Dram lowered his head then looked at him.

"Did you recognize any of the trees outside? I got them from her property before I left. She gave me several species to plant when I returned here."

He closed his eyes and leaned back in his chair, taking a deep breath. He exhaled slowly and tried to assimilate all this new information. His stomach lurched at the thought of Dram and his mother together.

He propped his elbows on the table once more, and rested his chin on his laced fingers. The trees and shrubbery he had seen earlier did indeed remind him of Tennessee. The landscaping deliberately appeared like the cabin area at home.

"Maybe this will convince you," Dram said, reaching inside the neck of his flight suit. He pulled out a long chain and slipped it over his head. He handed the object to him. A locket, made of some alloy, dangled from the metal cord. The material resembled pewter. He opened the oval shaped charm and stared at images of two young people. One was his mother when she was eighteen. The other, Emma and Dram.

The black and white photos, taken from a mall booth, showed the two of them smiling. It was uncanny how the image of Dram resembled *him* just a few years ago.

"Do you have premonitions, Adam?"

He wanted nothing of Dram's traits. He didn't mind having any of his mother's. He leaned forward, setting the charm on the table and nodded.

"Good. Trust your premonitions. They're like warnings. You can keep the locket if you want."

Adam swallowed hard. Fatherly advice?

"Thanks." He had loved his dad. He would rather have an image of Joshua and Emma. After his parents had died and he had been sent to the Children's Home, he'd never seen anything they owned again until he'd bought his grandparents' property.

Joshua was the kind of father any kid would want. He closed the locket.

"I'm going to give you flight instructions, Adam. And if things work out, I'll teach you the business."

"Business?" This sounded too permanent to him. He wanted no part of Dram's illegal operation, especially on **Meta.** He had too much to think about now. He didn't want to believe Dram was his father. His mother's affair with an alien was hard enough to swallow.

"I'll go to bed now, if that's okay," he said, standing. His legs felt weak and rubbery. His mind buzzed.

"Sure, Adam. That's a great idea. I think I'll do the same." Dram stood. "You get some sleep. You have a lot to worry about tonight. I'll see you in the morning." Dram pushed a button on the table console and Bordon returned.

"Escort Adam to his room."

"Sure, boss."

He walked toward the door where Bordon stood. He glanced back at Dram once more, his jaw tensed.

"Good night, Adam."

He turned and left with Bordon. Now he trusted Dram even less. Dram hadn't explained his business, yet he'd offered to teach him how to run it.

He and Bordon walked to the room. What did his mother see in Dram anyway? Didn't she know not to trust him? Or maybe he'd fooled her with his charm and fed her lies as well.

Then the thought struck him hard, like a wrestler tossed on his back. *He was part alien*! His red blood and his flesh and bones resembled his mother. Dram appeared as human as everyone else in this place, but he was a poor excuse for one.

Genesis was also an alien but looked and felt human, especially when he had kissed her. She'd tasted better than any woman he had ever touched. Something had happened between them he had never experienced and that warm rushing sensation came back. He thought of her now and wanted to make sure she was all right.

"Can I check on Genesis?" he asked Bordon as they neared his room.

"Who?"

"The woman who was captured with me."

"She's sleeping."

"Well, can I just look in on her?"

"No. The others are all asleep. You can see her in the morning."

Bordon unlocked the access panel and the door hissed open.

Morning seemed so far away right now. He stepped inside the room and heard a click. He stood before the sensor but the door remained shut. He pressed buttons on the inside panel, but nothing happened. Now *he* was a prisoner.

"Great," he mumbled. His *father* trusted him as much as he trusted Dram but then he already knew that. He glanced at the locket in his hand and slipped the chain around his neck. It was all he had of his mother and the bow and quiver of arrows reminded him of his real dad, but they were on the ship.

He sat on the bed and removed his boots. He had been used to sleeping in his underwear and a t-shirt. He couldn't sleep in his clothes or they would be sweaty in the morning. Did the others sleep in the nude? He pulled down the covers then unfastened the top of the flight suit, letting it fall to the floor. He turned off the light and crawled into bed.

How many people lived here? In the morning, he would check this place out. That is, if Dram allowed him any freedom.

He remembered his promise to Genesis. Once he learned to fly, he could get them out. Hadn't Dram thought of that, too? Wouldn't he prevent it? Dram had offered to give him flying lessons in the presence of witnesses. Somehow, this idea didn't seem right. The whole scheme was way too easy.

Dram lay in his bed, his hands intertwined behind his head. For once, telling the truth may have been a good thing.

Hopefully, the boy would develop feelings for him now that he knew they were related.

He had to get rid of the woman, though. He would have to be discreet about it. Adam had grown attached to her already, but she was more valuable as a pawn with Z. Z always had a soft spot for exotic-looking women.

CHAPTER SIX

Adam tossed and turned all night. He fought thoughts of his mother and Dram together. What hurt most was learning the truth about Joshua. His disappointment weighed heavy on his heart. Perhaps Joshua hadn't known? Then, again, if he had and had married Emma anyway, Adam realized how special his relationship with Joshua had been. That was something Dram could never take away from him.

He'd finally drifted off to sleep when a knock woke him.

"Who is it?" he called out.

"Ethan. Morning meal in five minutes."

Ethan escorted him into the dining room where Dram sat at a long table. His men were seated on either side of him. The three others he had met the night before were present as well. Many of the men stopped eating and stared at him. Dram cleared his throat and brought the attention back to him.

"Due to the events of the past few days, I changed the duty roster," he began. "Jonder, you and Berto will begin flight training today with Adam."

"Flight training?" a man asked.

"Do you have a problem, Jonder?"

"Uh, no sir. It was just unexpected."

"Good. Now finish eating," Dram ordered.

The men chatted among themselves. He didn't join them. The stares made him uncomfortable. Some of the men looked rough. Most of the new men seemed Dram's age except one. He appeared in his mid to late twenties. Hopefully, he was someone he could relate to.

He scratched at his stubble. He wanted to see Genesis.

Later, after he left the dining room, he caught Bordon alone.

"Bordon, when can I talk to Genesis?" He touched Bordon's arm.

"Who?" Bordon glanced over his shoulder at him.

"The woman I asked about last night."

"Oh. Well..." he scratched his head, "in a few minutes she'll join the others."

"Others?"

"Yeah. Hey, I've got to go," Bordon trotted down the hall.

Hmmm, Bordon was in a hurry for some reason. Perhaps Dram had given him an assignment. Men exited the dining room behind him. The two men he would train with stood by the sofa, talking. He joined them. Other men filed past, walking down the hall.

"Hey, my name is Adam," he offered his hand to the older man first.

The man studied him then crossed his arms over his chest.

"Jonder," he said, with an evil glare.

The guy oozed bad vibes.

"Berto," the younger one took his outstretched hand and shook it. "We'll be training together."

A commotion arose around the corner before he could answer. Bordon and Ethan lead a procession of girls. They headed through the double-size doors into the dining room, forming two lines following the men. All were blue-eyed blondes dressed in pale yellow, sack-like outfits. The clothes appeared similar to those worn by the girl last night.

Everyone was barefoot and walked with their hands on their heads, silently filing through the doors. He had never seen thirty blondes in one place before, ages ranging from eight to eighteen years. How did Dram find all these girls?

Genesis stood out. Her blue-black hair and dark skin set her apart immediately. Her brown eyes glared at him. She was dressed like the others and she was pissed. The jeweled translator hugged her forehead and her medallions hung around her neck. She was beautiful, though, and reminded him of an angry Indian princess.

He watched her gaze dart from him then to his left. He glanced over his shoulder. Dram stood behind him. He realized with the blue flight suit he wore Genesis couldn't tell them apart. He raised his eyebrows and opened his mouth to call her name, but Dram interrupted him.

"Adam, let's go."

He turned toward Dram. "What's with all the girls and where are they going?"

The tall, thin man from the command room stood behind Dram and watched his reaction.

"They're our guests. The men are escorting them to the morning meal," he said sternly. "We're starting training, so let's go." Dram turned and went inside his office.

Curious, he looked back in time to see Genesis glance his way. She pleaded for his help with her eyes. He raised his chin in acknowledgment. She tugged at his heart. He couldn't do anything for her. Not yet. *Be patient, Gen. I've got a plan.*

He scratched at the stubble on his face. Would guests walk with fingers laced on their heads? They looked more like prisoners in uniform entering the dining room. Hmmm, had Dram told the truth? He watched Genesis until she was gone.

Inside Dram's office, another door led to a classroom. He followed Jonder and Berto into the room.

Jonder's age appeared to be late thirties to early forties. His tanned, leathery skin, bushy brows, almost black eyes and thick, bristly hair gave him a hard look. The permanent wrinkle across the bridge of his nose made him appear angry. Berto's demeanor seemed friendlier and likable with his brown eyes and short-cropped straight brown hair. He had a firm handshake.

Being a loner, he wasn't used to asking for assistance, but he needed help to escape. He had to trust somebody.

"Sit down, boys," Dram began. He leaned against his desk with his arms folded. Dram crossed his feet at the ankles.

He took a seat between Berto and Jonder. Three booklets sat on the long table.

"Take a manual. We'll cover this first," Dram said, thumbing through the pages.

"You'll have time to read and study. I'll continue the next section when I know you understand the first one. After you've passed the written test, we'll use the simulators. When you're ready, we'll fly."

Excited about the new challenge, he paid close attention to Dram. The remainder of the morning, Dram discussed the console diagrams of a cargo transport ship. Later, he went over those for smaller cruisers. He explained the instrument panels and what each dial was used for, as well as when to use them. He soaked up everything. His future depended on it.

Sim and Rosca followed Genesis, bringing up the rear. Bordon and Ethan led the group to a large cargo transport beside **The Guardian.**
Once the line moved outside, two other men she had never seen, joined them. The men stood on either side of the girls. As they boarded the ship, one man made the mistake of grabbing her.

"What's this?" he demanded, reaching for her jeweled translator.

She deflected his hand with her arm.

"Don't touch me!" she growled.

Girls near her turned to watch.

The man grabbed both her wrists. "Oh, yeah?"

She twisted her hands down and outward, freeing them. In seconds, she smacked his ears hard and he dropped at her feet.

"What did you do to him?" Sim shouted as he closed the distance between them.

Her heart pounded. She had merely used a defensive maneuver Malek had taught her *anos* ago. She didn't like being rough-handled.

Sim retrieved the man's weapon, while pointing his laser rifle at her chest. He checked the man's pulse.

She glared at Sim, refusing to answer him. After all, he was a criminal, just like Dram. She didn't owe him any explanation.

Bordon and Rosca rushed the girls through the hatchway onto the ship. The other new man grabbed her and pushed her inside. He held her against the wall, his arm across her chest. His weapon pointed at her head. Her pounding heart got louder.

"Don't touch me!" she shouted, struggling to free herself. The man's greater strength resisted her efforts to move his arm. He was tall with reddish-brown hair and green eyes. Built like a **Mica-Nulee**, he had strong, muscular arms and legs. **Tarsian** coloring marked him.

"Merka's dead," Sim announced. He reached for her medallions and the other man released her. "What are these?"

"Those are mine." She clenched her teeth, narrowing her eyes at him. She grabbed her communicators from Sim's hand and kicked him hard in the groin. She had lost her patience with Dram's men.

"Arrrgh!" he grunted, doubling over in pain. The red-haired man stunned her. The sting reminded her of her last encounter on **The Guardian** as everything grew dark when she hit the ground.

Dram stopped the pilot training for the mid-day meal break. He sent Adam, Jonder, and Berto to the eating hall. He remained to hear what news Ramen brought. Ramen had entered the room moments before. *It must be important, or he wouldn't be here.* Hopefully, Ramen had something from his contact on **Vestra Minor**.

"Did you convey my message to Z?" he asked.

"Yes, sir. I sent your apologies, boss. Then I told him he would receive a special exotic gift, as a token of your appreciation for his patience. I mentioned you wouldn't bring the shipment personally, but follow on another ship."

"Very good, Ramen. What did Z say?" Ramen had a way of wording unpleasant news to be less harsh. He liked that about him.

"I haven't received an acknowledgment yet, boss."

"Notify me as soon as you learn anything, Ramen." He turned to leave. He hoped Z took the offer otherwise he would retaliate if he felt betrayed. With one shipment already **kunnarled** he couldn't afford any more mistakes.

"Yes, sir. Oh, one other thing, boss," Ramen stepped back.

"Yes?" His eyebrows narrowed. He was hungry and this didn't sound good.

"Merka's dead."

"How the **Vaedran** hell did that happen?" Merka was expected on the transporter. He oversaw the shipments. Another **kunnarl** would force him to use plan B, an option he wanted to avoid.

"There was a confrontation when the men loaded the cargo."

He glared at Ramen, his fists clenched. He lost his patience. "Get to the point."

"The dark woman was involved. The men left with the shipment on the **Transitor** as scheduled but one crewman short."

He beat his fist against the wall. "Genesis has been nothing but trouble. First Timna, now Merka." The door hissed open at his approach. "I should have killed her back on Earth when I had the chance," he snarled. "Take care of Merka."

"All ready done sir." Ramen said, stepping out of his way.

He stormed into the eating hall. All eyes focused on him. He had to calm down or everyone would suspect something. He paced back and forth by his seat. He didn't want to stir the boy's imagination any more. Adam asked enough questions. He glanced around the table and breathed deeply before sitting.

"Well, boys," he began as calmly as he could. "Anything we need to discuss? Any problems?"

The men looked at each other. Some shrugged. Others shook their heads.

"Good, let's eat." He picked up his eating implement and dug into the concoction the cook had sent from the kitchen. Some days it was better not to ask what he had prepared.

"Hey, boss, when are we getting the new cargo transport?" Septa asked.

"It's a used one, Septa, that needs a lot of work. Rosca and Stinnet will fly the ship back," he said. *Depending on whether Z takes Genesis as appeasement. Otherwise, I'll never see that cargo transport.*

Z's promise for other business leads went with the deal. He clenched his fist, remembering Merka's death left five men to complete the mission. He glanced at Adam. He had trained his men to refer to everything as shipments and cargo. Hopefully, the boy wouldn't figure things out.

"What about us?" Ace interrupted his thoughts.

He looked at Ace and the men sitting beside him. They had worked for him a long time and deserved some explanation.

"Ace, you, Septa, Martin, and Kratt will work on the transport when it arrives. Once two operational cargo ships are available, we'll be able to alternate crews."

"Boss, all our shipments are processed at the moment," Ace said.

"Well, boys, you are officially on leave," he announced, smiling. *It was all part of the plan.* He knew he could count on them asking for time off. He hadn't given any in awhile. *This will keep everyone out of the way while I work on my scheme. The fewer witnesses, the better.*

"All right!" Septa stood.

"Can we use the cruiser, boss?" Kratt asked.

"Yes, provided you're back in three days." He noticed Adam watched the interaction. Hopefully the boy would trust him after this.

The other men left the eating hall.

"Where do the men go for fun around here?" Adam asked.

"Mostly to **Plexus**, their favorite hangout, Adam." He wiped his mouth with his **fissal** and rose from his seat.

"I've got business to take care of, boys. I'll meet you in the training room."

He headed for command. He had to know Z's response.

"Heard anything from Z?" he asked Ramen.

"No sir."

"The **Transitor**?"

"Everything is going smoothly sir. No more delays."

"If Z doesn't take the deal, I'll be leaving here in a hurry. Get my private cruiser ready, Ramen," he said. "Oh, and let's keep this conversation between us."

"Boss?"

"Yes?" He hesitated in front of the opening and faced Ramen. Ramen had helped him and Timna start the business so long ago.

"Where would you go?"

"The fewer people who know my plans, the better. If I leave this place, it's yours, Ramen. You've been a faithful employee. Besides, you're the only one who knows how to run the business."

"Uh, thanks, boss. I'm sorry about Timna."

He nodded and left the room. After today's incident with Genesis, he could only count on things getting worse. Timing was everything.

Adam got up from the table. Three girls, ages thirteen to sixteen, dressed alike in pale blue sack-like dresses, cleared the dishes. He recognized the older one from the day before. They stared at him while picking up the plates.

"I'm not Dram, okay?" he said to them as he left the room. He felt like a freak show.

"Hey, Adam," Jonder began, "How come we haven't seen you before?" He spoke gruffly, crossing his arms over his chest, like he dared him to answer.

"That's because I'm from a place called Earth. Dram brought me to **Meta,**" he said, walking toward the office.

"Against your will?" Berto asked, following him.

"The dark-haired woman mistook me for Dram. She had me in a cage when Dram came along and abducted both of us."

"So, you *are* here against your will," Berto said.

"Pretty much, yeah." He returned to his seat in the classroom. Berto and Jonder joined him. He wanted to finish the training so he could rescue Genesis and escape. One way or another, Dram would get him back to Earth, whether he knew it or not.

"How long have you two been here?" he asked, looking at Jonder, then Berto.

"About five *anos*," Jonder said.

"Four for me," Berto added.

He found Berto staring at him.

Berto shook his head. "I can't get over how much you resemble Dram. It's like seeing a slightly younger version of the man."

"*Slightly?*" Dram was in his forties.

"Why is Dram letting *you* train as a pilot?" Jonder glared at him, his arms crossed.

"What do you mean?" he asked, facing Jonder.

"Most of us started working as systems techs. We worked our way up to shipment processors, then cargo crew," he said, pointing a thumb at himself. "Being a pilot trainee is reserved for experienced men like us," he continued. "Why did he let *you* train as a pilot without going through the steps we did?" Jonder pointed a finger at him, eyebrows furrowed.

Why don't you ask *me* that question?" Dram said, as he entered the room.

The **Transitor** was on its way to **Vestra Minor**, when Genesis awoke.

"Oh," she murmured, pushing herself off the floor.

"Are you all right?" someone asked her.

She sat, knees bent, and elbows propped to hold her head in her hands.

"My skull is pounding," she said, blinking her eyes to clear the fog from her mind. The stun weapon worked on the entire nervous system, as well as the muscles. It took awhile for the effects to dissipate, depending on the victim's size. She must remember not to provoke these people in the future.

"He zapped you good," a young voice replied.

She gazed into the blue eyes of the same young blonde-haired girl from the compound.

"He sure did!" She glanced around. "Where are the men?"

"They locked us in here when we boarded," a tall blonde woman answered. "The guards are outside the door." She was older than the others, closer to her own age.

"We're going to escape," she announced.

"Oh? How do you suggest we do that?" The woman fisted her hands on her hips. "We have no weapons."

"You *know* how they'll treat us when we get to our destination," she said. She shuddered at what her mother as well as her friends and the entire village had gone through.

"Tell me," the young girl said.

"We will be slaves," she avoided the truth of the matter. A slave was the best part. She rubbed her temple, thankful her mother's jeweled translator was in place. She looked down and noticed her medallions still hung around her neck.

"Among other things," the woman mumbled, crossing her arms over her chest.

The well-built, muscular female stood about 180 centikiks tall. Her blue eyes and fair skin made her appear like the others.

"What tribe are you with?" she asked. She didn't remember seeing these girls anywhere before in her travel.

"We aren't a tribe," another girl answered. "We're **Scandin**. Haven't you studied your **Vaedran** history?"

"I know **Atrian** history," she replied. "I am Genesis, of the **Micca Nulee** tribe on White Mountain. My ancestors left **Vestra Major** to colonize **Atria**."

"Well, we're a **Scandin** clan, from the coast of **Brevin** on **Chroma**. I'm Shey," she offered her hand and pulled her to a standing position. "I taught fitness at the Academy in **Brevin's** Northern Province when they abducted us."

"We had field games that day," the young girl said. "My name is Orta," she bowed as girls gathered around her.

"Do you know of the other planets?" another girl asked.

"I've been to **Tarsius**. Those people are darker than you, with dark hair and eyes. People on **Persus** are darkest of all," she explained.

"Did you see any boys like us on **Atria**?" The tall girl asked. "I am Keentra."

"No, not on **Atria**." Adam, Dram and Bordon came to mind with skin darker than the girls. The men had been in the sun many times.

She remembered the Earth man's commitment to help her find Malek. The current situation had changed everything. She had to rescue the Earth man as soon as she figured a way out of this mess. Why did she make a deal with him? Malek must wait. *She* got the Earth man into trouble, and *she* would get him out.

"I saw some men on **Meta** that look like us. And one's on this ship," Orta said, bringing Genesis out of her thoughts.

"They're the enemies."

"Yes, two of them are."

"Which one isn't?" Keentra asked.

"The younger one. He looks like Dram." A warm, tingling went through her at the thought of him. She shook the thoughts from her mind. She would have to find him.

"We're taking over this ship," she announced.

"How?" Orta asked, taking her hand, her blue eyes hopeful.

She glanced around the space in which she was imprisoned. The thirty girls focused their attention on her.

"This is a cargo ship, right?"

"Yes," Keentra answered.

"Can you fly this ship?" she asked Shey.

"My father owns cargo ships," Shey answered. "I flew with him many times, but I can't do it alone."

"Good, I will help you," she began. "The trip to **Vestra Minor** takes days. Tonight, when they feed us, we observe what they do and count their weapons. Then, we plan."

She remembered the day Dram's men had abducted her tribe of women long ago. Only four men chased and gathered them. At least twenty mothers and twice as many children were scared as the men wielded their weapons, threatening to hurt everyone. The women made the men work hard at gathering them together to obey.

The last time she saw her mother, Herda, she'd fought Dram, trying to escape. The vision of Dram slapping her face paralyzed her. He had grabbed her medallion, ripping it from her neck. In her struggle, Herda had lost her translator. The band had signified her status as chief of her tribe when she'd lived on the **Sandren Plains.**

She paced back and forth, her hands fisted. She recalled her flight training from the I.S.P. Two pilots could fly a cargo ship. Depending on the type of vessel, though, two more might be on board, as well as a cook.

"Did we leave **Meta** after they shot me with the stun weapon?" she asked. She stopped pacing.

"Yes," another girl said.

"How many men are on board this ship?"

"At least five, since you killed one," Shey said.

She paced again. Possibly six men she had to deal with if they had replaced the dead man.

She studied her hands she used for healing. It was a gift from God. But since she had used them as weapons, would she be able to heal again after committing such a grave sin? She raised her clenched fists against the sides of her temples, her eyes closed. She offered a silent prayer and begged the Lord's forgiveness.

She was spared from her tribe's slavery for a reason. Now she was situated here. She opened her eyes and thirty faces stared at her, waiting for her response.

"We will take this ship and free ourselves." Timing was everything. Afterward, she would find the Earth man.

Adam finished his manual and simulator work. Dram left the room while he and the other two took a short break. He sat back in his seat, legs extended and fingers laced behind his head. Soon he'd fly one of Dram's ships and take Genesis away from here and help her search for her father. Besides, Genesis knew these planets. He could only guess, since Dram had showed him nothing about navigating the heavens.

To pull off a rescue, he needed a weapon. Berto and Jonder had none.

Dram stuck his head in the door.

"Come on outside, boys, and I'll show you what we'll be flying."

He followed Jonder and Berto and stopped near the landing pad.

"Here's the cruiser we'll be training in," Dram said as he pointed to **The Guardian**.

Great! At least he had some experience flying Gen's ship. This part should be easy. Dram had them board her, taking Berto into the Nav-room first. He and Jonder waited in the galley.

Jonder sat with his arms crossed over his chest and leaned forward in his seat. "Just because you're Dram's son, doesn't give you seniority."

"Don't worry, Jonder," he raised his hands in protest. "I didn't ask for this assignment, and I don't want to be here." He sat forward in his seat and closed his eyes, his elbows propped on the table.

He pictured Genesis smiling when she had worn his rain slicker. The sleeves had been too long, but she had the sexiest smile he had ever seen.

A while later, Berto returned and Jonder took his turn.

"Is this the ship you arrived in?" Berto asked.

"Yes. I've had a little practice before I arrived here. You seem to have picked up flying pretty quickly," he noted.

Berto leaned forward and spoke in a whisper. "I never told Dram I could fly. He assumed I didn't know how. I crewed for the others. Sometimes I flew when they wanted time alone with the girls."

"Girls?" He straightened in his seat.

"Never mind." Berto shook his head. "Forget I said anything." Berto sat back and crossed his arms.

He was angry and he wanted answers. He leaned across the table and grabbed Berto's shoulders. "What *girls?*" He demanded, his teeth clenched. Berto's eyes widened. Just then, Jonder returned and motioned for him to leave. He pushed Berto away. Berto held something back and he wanted to know why.

Later, he sat at the control panel while Dram reviewed the switches and levers again then let him take her up. This time around, the controls felt comfortable. He took **The Guardian** over a mountain range, pitching forward and keeping the ship low enough to view the terrain.

"Hey, what's that?" He pointed to an animal similar to a goat, though larger and without horns.

"Pull back on the throttle, boy," Dram said. "It's an **eeya.** Skittish creatures, but they make a tasty meal if you can capture one."

He yawed left and returned to the compound. The setting sun hit something shiny and metallic hidden under large bushes, several hundred yards away, causing a sharp glare. He wondered what it was, but decided not to ask. Dram didn't offer an explanation.

He thought about the way Dram had acted and the things Genesis warned him of. Dram didn't seem as bad as Gen painted him to be, but something kept gnawing at him. For one thing, Dram could've left him on Earth. For another, Dram didn't need to be so rough to Genesis. He was bossy, that's for sure, as well as rude, but murder?

Dram was wanted dead or alive, a term he had only heard in reference to the old west. Could his crimes be so despicable they didn't care as long as someone stopped him?

He set **The Guardian** on the landing pad and reversed the turbo lifters and anti-grav pulsars.

"You caught on quickly, Adam." Dram patted him on the back.

He cringed at Dram's touch. He and Dram joined Berto and Jonder in the galley.

"That's it for now, boys. We'll have our evening meal soon. Afterward, I'll brief you privately on your results," Dram said.

Dram stopped at the command room and talked to Ramen. When he got past the dining area, Jonder spoke up.

"Look, Adam, I don't like you. You come along and get pilot training while we worked our asses off. We *earned* our training." Jonder pointed a finger at him. "So don't give me any trouble!" Jonder turned and left.

"What's with him?" he asked Berto. "I didn't ask to be here. I had a life on Earth. I'm supposed to build a cabin for my boss, Jeremy, and Jonder wants to blame *me*?" He tapped his thumb against his chest.

"Never mind him. Jonder is a hothead with a short temper. Stay out of his way and you should be fine. Don't ask him any questions, either. He likes to keep to himself. Besides, he killed a man once, just for making him angry."

"If you ask me, he was *born* that way," he said, then remembered his unfinished conversation with Berto. "And you!"

"What?" Berto asked, glancing his way.

"I had some questions for you, but you didn't answer them." He folded his arms and glared at Berto.

"Later," Berto said, looking back toward the dining room doors. "Now is not a good time." Berto walked away.

He shook his head as he strode to his room. No time is good around here, and certainly not for answers. Something was up.

He glanced at his reflection in the mirror. The faint stubble from the evening before now appeared thicker and slightly darker. He rubbed his chin. The scratch of his beard irritated him. He took out his pocket knife and studied the blade. *Dull.* The thought of shaving with it bothered him.

"I'll have to itch, that's all." He closed the tool and put the knife under his pant leg. He threw himself on the bed and thought of ways to escape. The four men who'd escorted him and Genesis into the compound were gone. Another group had left earlier in the day. He would slip out and search for her. Hopefully, she'd be in the same room as the night before.

He approached the door panel button and the door hissed open.

Berto stuck his head inside. "Our meal is ready."

He stepped back. "That was quick." He walked with Berto toward the dining room.

"Where are the girls we saw this morning?" he asked Berto.

"They're history."

He stopped in his tracks, his heart dropped to his stomach. "What do you mean?" His eyebrows narrowed.

"There will be others, don't worry."

He swallowed hard. He didn't like the sound of that.

"Yes, when the men return from leave, they'll pick up more girls or women somewhere else," Berto explained.

"Where's Genesis?" His gut tightened.

"Who?"

"The dark-haired woman who arrived with me. The one who looked..." Native American would be an unknown term to Berto. His heart pounded loudly, "the beautiful one."

"Like I said, she's history."

"No!" The word came out too loudly. "That can't be."

Dram didn't say anything about sending her away.

"Where is she?" His gut instinct told him he wouldn't like what Berto had to say.

"Well, she's on her way to **Vestra Minor** with all the others."

Vestra Minor? His mouth fell open, a lump formed in his throat.

His gut tightened at the thought of her gone. He'd believed she would be here, yet Dram hadn't actually said that, had he? He should've asked more questions or paid closer attention to what Dram *hadn't* said.

"Did Dram explain the business he's in?"

"No." Adam's jaw tightened as he clenched his fists. This didn't sound good at all.

Berto glanced at the dining room doors and back at him.

"Forget we ever had this conversation," he pointed his finger at him. "Not a word to anyone."

"And why should *I* keep quiet?" He crossed his arms over his chest. He wanted answers, not lame excuses.

"Our lives depend on it."

CHAPTER SEVEN

Dram wiped his face with his **fissal**, and set it on the table. He glanced at the three men finishing up their meals. He would put Berto in charge and make Adam his copilot. Berto was a more experienced flyer than the other two and followed orders. He had the most to lose since he had a criminal history he could hold over him. Besides, he knew where Berto's sister was located, so he had another option to use.

Jonder was a troublemaker, a hothead. He **kunnarled** things worse with his temper. He only kept Jonder around because he was a good systems tech. Losing him wouldn't matter much. Berto, however, was trained by Timna. Timna had taught him ways to make their ships faster than the I.S.P. cruisers. As far as Adam goes, well, he didn't know him at all. Adam only reminded him of the love he had lost on Earth. On second thought, though, he would leave all this behind, so nothing mattered any more, as long as *he* got away.

Adam glanced up and caught Dram staring at him. He wiped his mouth with his napkin. Dram's brows narrowed, scrutinizing him. Then Dram's eyes flashed and his features hardened.

"What?" He shrugged his shoulders, both palms up. Dram's stare made him nervous.

"Explain that strange mass erupting from your skin." Dram demanded, leaning closer.

He rubbed his face all over. Did he have food smeared on his mouth? The only thing was the stubble of hair. He grew hot and his pulse quickened when he realized Dram meant his beard. All eyes focused on him.

Dram stood up, his palms on the table. "You're changing colors, too! What *is* this?"

Shocked, he jumped up so fast, he knocked his chair over. His heart pounded. He glanced at Berto, then Jonder, and back to Dram. "I didn't have anything to shave with," he shrugged again, his palms up. "I'm *not* changing colors. You're embarrassing me. What's the big deal? Haven't you ever seen a person blush before?"

Jonder and Berto stood and moved closer to examine him.

"Explain *shave*." Dram said. He glared at him, his brows furrowed.

Bordon was right. He half chuckled as he glanced at Berto, Jonder and Dram, serious expressions on all of them. He cracked his knuckles, one at a time and thought of an explanation.

"Look, on Earth, men grow hair on their faces. If they don't want it, it's cut off. Otherwise, the follicles keep growing and it's a beard or mustache." He glanced at all three of them again, mouths gaping open. "Don't you guys have any body hair?" he asked to make sure.

"The only place we grow hair is on our head," Berto tugged at his own locks and studied his face.

"Take it off." Dram slammed his fist against the table.

His mouth dropped open and he jumped back, his heart racing. "I told you, I don't have anything to shave with."

"Find something and remove it. Now!" Dram clenched his teeth and deepened his voice.

He glanced at each man again and left the table. He found the kitchen as the door hissed open. Geesh! *That* was over reacting. What was so bad about facial hair, anyway? He didn't want to imagine people without body hair.

The cook stood at the sink, running hot water. Steam rose from the large metal bowl.

"I need a sharp knife. What have you got?"

The cook glanced at him before shutting off the water. He walked to a drawer and opened it. Inside was an assortment of knives. He studied his face then backed away.

"Dram?"

"No. My name is Adam." He searched through the knives, looking for a small one. He remembered his pocket knife. Reaching under his pant leg, he pulled out the Swiss Army model he'd had since his scouting days.

"Can you sharpen this?" he asked, holding up a blade.

The cook nodded and took the knife and stuck it into a box. Without saying a word, he handed the knife back to him.

"Hmmm," He tested the sharpness against his thumb. "How about this one?" After closing the first tool, he held up another. The cook sharpened it as well. "One more," he opened a third blade and closed the other.

The cook returned the sharp knife and he closed it, wondering how he would shave without cutting himself.

"That's a cool sharpener you got there," he nodded toward the box the man had used. "I'd like one myself," he grinned.

The cook stopped him as he turned to leave.

"Where did you get that strange knife?" he asked.

"Boy Scouts," he gave the Scout salute and headed back to his cleansing compartment in his room.

When he turned the faucet on, he realized the door had been unlocked. "Hmmm."

The button above the faucet automatically dispensed soap with the water.

He succeeded in making lather from the liquid, unlike any soap he had used on Earth. He missed his shaving cream and razor.

Rubbing the light foam on his face, he carefully removed the stubble. Starting high on his cheeks he moved to his chin. He was careful, but nicked himself anyway. He held a small piece of cleansing cloth, the damp material they used for toilet paper, against his face. When the bleeding stopped, he tossed the material down the toilet. Now he understood what was meant by a straight razor. At least they had more lather.

Examining his face, he acknowledged his stubble took a long time to sprout. Was it because Dram's blood ran through his veins? Or the fact Dram didn't have facial hair?

He cleaned the sink. Afterward, he rinsed and dried his knife blade. He slipped it under his pant leg and headed to the eating hall.

When he arrived, everyone was gone. No point in telling Dram the hair would grow back in a week. Before he left, though, Dram showed up and stopped in front of him. Dram lifted his chin and inspected his face.

"What is *this*?" Dram angled his jaw to expose the small gash.

He pulled away from Dram's grip. "I cut myself shaving, okay? It happens sometimes. Normally, I don't use a knife on my face."

"Don't let that happen again," Dram said, pointing a finger at him. "By the way," Dram turned. "I've decided to make you copilot. Berto will pilot the ship and be in charge of the mission. He has more experience than you and can navigate better."

"Fine, when do we leave?" He crossed his arms over his chest. He couldn't wait to get the hell away from this place and find Genesis.

"In the morning. I'll call you when it's time." Dram left. He glanced at the double-size door to the command room. He could escape now, but he needed Berto's help to navigate. Asking for it was another matter and he wasn't used to doing that.

He tossed and turned all night and couldn't get comfortable. The day's events played in his mind like a bad movie. Things Dram had said to him crept into his thoughts. *"You're not going anywhere...I've got plans for both of you...Don't waste your time on that woman, she's nothing but trouble... Don't concern yourself with her anymore..."*

When the thoughts finally receded, he saw a clear image of Genesis' face falling against a table. She held a glass of wine in her hand. The image faded. Another came, and she was naked, lying on a bed. She wasn't alone, though. She fought someone forcing himself on her. He was a thin, wiry man, much older than Dram. He sat up, rubbing his eyes. He tried to wipe out the image. He threw the covers off his own naked body, and jumped from the bed.

Genesis wasn't here. She was on her way to **Vestra Minor**. His pulse quickened. His premonitions had always manifested after he saw them, sometimes immediately. He closed his eyes, his fists clenched tight. He tried to visualize the man hurting her, but he didn't recognize him. He couldn't let that happen, but how could he stop him?

He dropped down on the bed and ran a hand through his hair. He had to leave here and find her before it was too late. He cracked his knuckles. His only hope was to convince Berto to help him. Berto knew where **Vestra Minor** was. The location of all the planets was information Dram had conveniently omitted from training. He punched his pillow, and settled under the covers.

This time, he slept.

Hours later, he experienced three more premonitions.

The first one was a bright, shiny object that flashed, fading into a small space ship. The second was several uniformed men surrounding him and someone else. The third image was him fighting himself. Now he understood what that vision meant and he would be prepared.

Awhile later, someone knocked.

"Morning meal in five minutes," Dram called through the door.

He sat up and scratched his head. If he wasn't so tired, he might be hungry. How did they tell time around here? He had yet to find a clock and no windows existed in the bedrooms.

The **Transitor's** cargo door slid open. Genesis squatted behind the tallest girls closest to the door. Shey did the same. Several sat together in the middle of the floor, chatting. They drew attention away from her actions.

Sim stepped inside and glanced around. "Where's the dark-headed one?"

"She's not here," Keentra replied.

Sim touched the weapon strapped to his leg. "What do you mean, she's not here?"

Bordon pushed the food cart into the cargo area and glanced up as the door hissed close.

"Gone, missing, not present," Keentra explained.

"*Who's* gone?" Bordon scratched his head.

Three tall girls jumped Bordon, bringing him down. Sim spun around, his weapon drawn. She, Shey, and a third girl ambushed him. He struggled against them. She grabbed his laser and shot his thigh on half stun, paralyzing him on one side. Sim fell over, grabbing his leg.

"Ouch," he yelled.

She turned and aimed at Bordon, shooting him in the chest, on full. The girls pulled away so they wouldn't be stunned through touching Bordon's body.

Turning back to Sim, she shot him on full as well.

"Feels good, doesn't it?"

"No!" he yelled before passing out.

She leaned over his unconscious body and pulled the yav from Sim's hand. "I'll take that, thank you," she said. "Great work, girls!" She gathered the four weapons the men had carried and handed one to Keentra.

"The men should sleep for a couple of hours. When they wake, hit them once each on full stun." She showed Keentra the lock and stun sliders on the weapon.

Taking the three remaining lasers and the five tallest girls with her, she handed a weapon to each couple. "You four split up and search for Ethan," she ordered. "Shey and I will head to the Nav-room and take care of the two pilots."

"Two down and three to go," Shey said, walking beside her.

"Let's hope that's all," she said. Dwarfed next to Shey, she stood below her shoulders. That's about how tall the Earth man was.

Shey wore her long blonde hair pulled back in a thick, single braid and carried herself regally as she walked down the hallway. Glancing around, Shey stopped at the intersection of halls and grabbed her arm.

"What is it?" She looked up at Shey.

"If I'm not mistaken, this was my father's ship. His crew were attacked four years ago and left for dead on **Creton**, a moon of **Chroma**. The pirates took his transporter."

"How can you be sure it's the same one?" *Shey would be a great asset in flying a familiar cargo cruiser.*

Shey motioned for her to follow her to the Nav-room. Outside the entrance, Shey bent and retrieved a short stun weapon from an alloy beam. *Great!* Relief flowed through her. Now they had two weapons to even the score. Shey pressed the panel button and the door hissed open.

She entered first, since she was trained. She couldn't risk Shey getting hurt.

"It's about ti--" Stinnet turned and stopped in mid-sentence.

She pointed her weapon at him and fired. "Break time," she smiled. Stinnet fell over, giving her a clear shot at Rosca, so she took it. Getting even felt good especially after the way they'd treated her earlier.

"Help me with these men." She dragged Stinnet's heavy body through the entrance.

Shey pulled Rosca out the door behind her. Afterward, she slipped into the left pilot's seat. Shey took the one on the right. She busied herself with the monitor readouts, while Shey hit the intercom-link.

"Attention cargo and crew. We will take a slight detour on our trip," Shey announced. "I need Aranu and Keentra to the bridge, please."

Within minutes, the two girls reported.

"Put these two men in the cargo hold with the others and make sure they get some rest." She handed Keentra an extra weapon.

"Will do, Genesis." Keentra bent to grab Rosca's arm and glanced up at her. "Strange hair."

She nodded. Rosca's brown, matted mass of long curls looked like he had never cleansed himself.

Aranu grabbed Stinnet's arm and carried her weapon in her other hand. The two girls dragged the bodies toward cargo.

She returned to the Nav-room.

A short time later, Keentra reported on the intercom-link.

"Ethan is accounted for and all prisoners are sleeping peacefully," she announced.

"Great job, girls," she responded. She turned to Shey. "We'll triangulate our position and get you and the others back to **Chroma**." She typed her questions on the keypad and waited for the Nav-U-Com's response.

Shey did a systems check while she glanced at the monitor. In hyper speed, she could return them to their planet and head back to **Meta** in time to rescue the Earth man. She had to set things right. If not for her blunder, he would be home.

She ran her fingers across the keypad, plotting the course to **Chroma**. She reversed thrusters and flipped on the inertia canceler.

Then the thought hit her. If she hadn't made the error, she wouldn't have met him. She caught her bottom lip with her teeth, as she remembered his kiss and the excitement it had brought her the first time. The mere thought of his touch sent a warm shiver throughout her body. She wanted to taste him once more, to experience those sensations when he touched her chin. Her desire for him surprised her.

While Dram, Berto, Jonder, and Adam ate the morning meal, Ramen came from the command room. He whispered to Dram. Dram's eyes widened, his mouth dropped open. He stood up abruptly and left with Ramen.

"Something's wrong." Berto spoke softly across the table to him.

He nodded.

"I've seen that expression before," Jonder said. "Dram doesn't get upset unless..." Jonder glanced at Berto, then him. "Timna told me a guy named Derk decided to leave the business after he and Dram had an argument."

"What happened to him?" He took a bite of his eggs.

"When Dram discovered Derk had left, he searched for him until he found him," Jonder said.

Silence engulfed them as Jonder pushed his food around on his plate.

"Well? What did he do, hire him back?" Berto asked.

"No." Jonder shook his head. "Dram cut his heart out."

"My God!" This can't be the same Dram. He had the opportunity to kill him and Genesis and didn't take it. He took time instructing him on flying. There must be more to the story.

"No one crosses Dram. No one," Jonder whispered, hoarsely.

He swallowed hard as he recalled Dram's quick reflexes and his recent anger over his stubble.

Inside the command room, Dram replied to Ramen's comment in the eating hall. "What do you mean, they aren't responding?" he shouted at Ramen.

"I'm sorry, boss, but the crew didn't check in this morning. I've sent two messages since, and there is no answer," Ramen explained nervously.

An inter-planet com-link came through on the screen. The message from Z read:

"The deal is off! You are two-weeks past deadline and have failed to make delivery twice after I advanced you money. Your gift won't appease me. I want REVENGE!"

Z

He slumped into a chair, running his hands through his hair. His heart pounded and a lump formed in his throat. He had expected this, but not the accompanying feelings. The ache seized him. It was like losing Emma all over again. He loved his business more than he'd realized. He had poured his soul into his work when Emma had refused to accompany him, to help stave off the loneliness. It was years before he was able to get past her loss. That was, until Derk had killed her. Now, the emotions returned. The heart-wrenching loss of someone he loved.

Propping his elbows on his knees, he cradled his head in his hands. Things would be different from now on. He had to adjust, and he was familiar with a certain hiding place.

"You know Z, boss. He will hunt you down until he finds you," Ramen said.

"I'm counting on it, Ramen. I'm counting on it." A new plan formed in his head as he slowly rose from his seat. "Get the cruiser ready," he ordered. He returned to the eating hall.

Adam glanced up as Dram entered the room and stood at the table. This didn't look good.

"Boys, something's happened to the **Transitor.** I'm sending you three on a mission."

"What kind of mission?" Jonder asked.

"I want you to find the **Transitor**, assist the crew, and finish the original plan, which is to deliver the cargo to Z on **Vestra Minor**. Afterward, return to base with the **Transitor** and the cruiser. Any questions?" Dram asked.

"What about the other cargo transporter we were supposed to get, boss?" Jonder asked.

"I'm afraid that will wait, Jonder, since we don't know the status of the pilots or the ship. The **Transitor** is not responding to communications."

His pulse quickened. One cargo transporter had sat on the landing pad when he and Genesis arrived. Berto mentioned the girls were on their way to **Vestra Minor**, which explained the missing ship. *Oh, God, don't let anything happen to Gen.*

Berto glanced at him, then Dram. "Is the cruiser ready, sir?" he asked.

"Yes, Berto. You boys go and pack. Be back in the command room within ten minutes."

Genesis and Shey eased the controls of the **Transitor** into position. She yawed left, turning the **Transitor** on a course for **Chroma**. The warp drive stood ready.

"Prepare for hyper speed, girls," she announced over the intercom-link. She fastened her safety belt. Shey did the same and reached for the controls. The ship pitched forward.

"What was that?" Shey asked, her eyes wide.

"I don't know." Her stomach tightened with anxiety. She reached for the warp drive lever, when the ship lurched again.

Metal scraped against metal. She glanced up through the view port. Something moved above the **Transitor.**

"Look!" She pointed to the object. Her heart pounded. Please God, not pirates.

"Another ship! Why so close?" Shey asked.

Clanging and hissing sounded, while the **Transitor** wavered.

She glanced at Shey. *The I.S.P. would announce themselves. This can't be good. She* reached for the com-link, but the communications were jammed.

Louder hissing followed. "That's the air lock! Someone is boarding the ship."

Adam glanced around his room. He had nothing to pack except his jeans, sweatshirt and underwear. His muddy boots were on Gen's cruiser in the cell. Was she all right? He hoped she was safe. Dram seemed upset. Maybe this was serious. If he had known she wasn't here earlier, he could have...there wasn't anything he could have done then. But now he could. He had a way out and a plan. He had to convince Berto to help him.

He rolled his sweatshirt into the jeans and walked to the cleansing compartment and retrieved his underwear. The door slid open and a teenaged girl he had seen in the eating hall jumped at him.

"Good gosh, you startled me!" He moved back. "What are *you* doing here?"

"Take us with you," she pleaded.

"Who is *us*?"

"Me and my sisters."

"How did you know we're leaving?"

"I heard them talking. Please!" She grabbed his hand.

"Take us with you. You are different from the others. You're our only hope."

"What do you mean?"

"Something is about to happen. I can sense it. My sisters and I have been kept here against our will. We want to go home to **Tarsius**."

"I thought you worked for Dram."

"Not willingly. We were abducted three years ago." Her brown eyes glistened. "We work as Dram's house maidens during the day. At night..." The tears rolled down her cheeks. "We sleep with his men." She lowered her head, her brown hair fell off her shoulders and spilled around her face.

"Oh, God, no!" Anger consumed him. He thought of Genesis now as he drew the girl into his arms and hugged her. She appeared to be a teenager. The other two appeared even younger. Genesis faced the same fate if he didn't rescue her. Would he be able to make it in time?

"See if you can sneak on board **The Guardian**. I'll try to stall things around here. Go quickly, before they miss you."

"We have to stock the ship for you. That won't be a problem," she said, wiping tears from her face. She reached the door and turned to glance at him. "Thank you," she whispered then left.

Retrieving his underwear, he wrapped them with his other things and sat on the bed. He ran a hand through his hair. He thought of ways to stall, but he was anxious to rescue Gen. Getting the girls off **Meta** was a priority, but Genesis needed him, too.

He stood and walked to the doorway. *Lord, help me figure things out.* As the door hissed open to the hallway, Berto approached him.

"Is that all you're taking?" Berto asked.

"It's everything I own," he replied. Berto had two bags the same color as his flight suit. The small one, he carried in one hand. The other hung from his shoulder, the size of a heavy duffle bag.

"Why so much stuff?" he asked, glancing at Berto's load.

"This is everything *I* own," Berto began. "I have a feeling we won't be coming back," he whispered. "And I'm usually right about those."

Berto wasn't the only one with intuitions. He knew his visions foretold the future, but his gut instincts were just as strong sometimes. He wanted to rescue Genesis before the premonitions came true. He'd received his gift for a reason.

"I'm glad Dram put you in charge of the mission and not Jonder," he began. "I couldn't take orders from him."

"Thanks, but I don't think Jonder is too pleased with the situation. He may give us some trouble," he whispered.

He and Berto entered the command room. Ramen was the only one inside and sat in front of a large monitor. Ramen turned to face them.

"Dram should be here shortly, boys. He's putting together some maps and charts to help you locate the **Transitor** from their last known position."

He anxiously waited for Ramen's move toward the monitor. He stole a glance out the window, worried he would be caught smuggling the girls to safety. The three sisters ran to **The Guardian**, their arms loaded with stuff.

Berto glanced at him. He put his arm around Berto's shoulder and faced the monitor, blocking Ramen's view of the window.

"I wanted to ask you about these instruments." He pointed at the equipment.

"Actually, Ramen knows more than anyone," Berto said, a puzzled expression on his face.

He removed his arm from Berto's shoulders, and leaned toward Ramen.

"How do you speak to someone in space?" He caught Ramen's full attention.

Ramen pointed to the instruments and explained how he used them for communicating. He showed how messages were sent and received. Ramen perked up as he told how satellites bounced the communications across the **Vaedra** system. Sometimes a delay resulted in delivering and receiving transmissions because of satellite activity. Before he could ask another question, Dram and Jonder walked into the room.

"Here's the log book, Berto." Dram handed him a thick, leather-bound object, the size of a large paperback novel. "You know the **Transitor's** destination was **Vestra Minor**," he said as he unrolled some papers and showed Berto. "Follow the course I've marked on the charts, and you should find them." Dram handed Berto the rolled up maps.

"Yes, sir." Berto slipped the papers under his arm and shook Dram's outstretched hand. "Thank you for giving me this opportunity, sir. I won't let you down."

"Good luck, boys," Dram said. He shook their hands.

He boarded **The Guardian** with Berto and Jonder, hoping the girls had had time to stow away. He would explain their presence later. He stashed his belongings in one of the compartments, and checked the others for his bow and quiver of arrows. They were where Dram left them, along with the rope.

Hold on Gen, I'm coming. He wished he could communicate with her.

Berto and Jonder stashed their gear before Berto locked everything and closed the hatch. He followed Berto into the Nav-room, while Jonder sat at the table in the galley.

"So far, so good," Berto whispered after the door hissed closed.

"What do you mean?"

"No complaints from Jonder is a good thing."

"Tell me, Berto," he said, his arms crossed over his chest. "Are those girls I saw yesterday, on the **Transitor**?"

"Yes, along with our crew."

He didn't care about Dram's men. He cared about Genesis. If she accompanied them, she could be in danger. He dropped into the seat beside Berto. He hoped there was time. *Hang on, Gen.* This could work, whether Berto helped or not. Once he found her, he would take over. He glanced at Berto, while he readied **The Guardian**.

Berto had the engines on and eased her off the pad taking her up a hundred feet, or 300 centikiks. The glare from the shiny metal object he had seen yesterday blinded him.

"What the **Vaedran** hell?" Berto said. He yawed left to avoid the sharp blast of light.

"The same thing happened to me yesterday, when I landed," he said.

"Let's check it out." Berto pulled the ship around and returned from a different angle.

"A small space cruiser? I thought we had the last one on **Meta**," Berto said.

"Do you suppose it belongs to Dram?" he asked, remembering his premonition.

"Oh, I *know* it does. I helped him steal the damn thing." Berto glanced at him. "He told me he'd sold the cruiser some time ago."

"Something's wrong," he shook his head. His gut instinct kicked in. "It's almost too...easy." He couldn't say more or Berto would be on to him.

Berto glared at him. "We've been set up!" He pulled back on the throttle and **The Guardian** lifted.

"Set up, how?" He cocked his head.

"Dram was personally supposed to deliver the shipment to Z."

He raised a brow, puzzled.

"Two weeks ago, the crew on the **Transitor kunnarled** and missed the rendezvous point. Z was **pizood,**" Berto explained.

"Who crewed?"

"Ace, Septa, Kratt, and Martin. Jonder and I were in charge of cargo. When Dram came back with you, he changed plans and sent Stinnet and the others to take the shipment. Now, something might be wrong with the **Transitor,** and maybe not. If Z is **pizood** even more, he's going to make Dram pay. Only Dram won't be here, *you* will."

All his thoughts merged into one. Everything that had transpired since he'd met Dram, now made sense. His stomach knotted as if sucker punched.

"Dram flipped out when he saw hair on my face because I no longer looked like him." His heart pounded.

"Exactly!" Berto nodded.

"He was so nice and convincing," he added. Dram's words came back to him. *'I've got plans for both of you.'*

"Yeah, and that's why we got a short course in flying," Berto said.

He glanced at Berto. "Dram told me Genesis interfered with a big shipment of his."

"The transaction with Z," Berto said. "Dram didn't give the coordinates to the crew on time. He left **Vestra Minor**, in a hurry, to lose the bounty hunter."

"Genesis."

Berto nodded. "She works for the I.S.P. I'm sure they'll be looking for her. I heard Dram tell Ramen he had to deliver the shipment in person. Z will seek revenge if he feels betrayed."

"So, this is a suicide mission."

"If Z kills you, thinking you're Dram, Dram is off the hook. He can go anywhere in the universe and start over."

He ran a hand through his hair. "We can deal with Dram later if we can keep him here." He waved his hands in the air for emphasis.

"I've got an idea," Berto began. "You and Jonder go below and find some weapons. I'll keep the cruiser up here so Dram won't suspect anything. If you find any weapons, we'll blow his cruiser so he can't escape, buying us time. At least he's stuck until Ace returns the other ship."

"Got it," he jumped from his scat and left the room.

"Jonder, I need your help to locate weapons," he said.

"What for?" Jonder's bushy brows furrowed, his arms crossed over his chest.

"Berto thinks we've been set up. Come on, and I'll explain."

He found the hatch near the galley on the floor. He and Jonder slipped down the metal steps to the engine room as he explained Berto's theory. He and Jonder searched for the weapons.

"Berto, this is Adam. Can you hear me?" He spoke through the intercom-link located beside the turbo lasers.

"Yes, loud and clear. What have you got?"

"Jonder says one ion cannon and four turbo lasers. There's a cache of rifles and small laser weapons."

"Use the turbos," Berto said. "On my signal, go for it."

He positioned himself at a weapon and opened the view port. He found the headset and put it on.

"I can't believe Dram set us up." Jonder sat at another turbo and sited his weapon. "That explains why he's been nice lately, and why he made you copilot. Dram was always in the Nav-room."

He felt the ship yaw left. Stars shone above as **The Guardian** swung into range. His heart pounded and the adrenaline pumped through his veins. He was mad. Dram had used him. They approached the target.

"We'll be in position any minute now," Berto came across the intercom-link.

He held his hand on the trigger. He had never shot a gun before. Larger than anything he had seen, the gun resembled something on an Army tank. Dram's cruiser, straight ahead.

"Hit it!" Berto ordered.

He pulled the turbo laser's sensitive trigger a second ahead of Jonder. The cruiser blew up instantly.

Relief washed over him. Dram couldn't do much damage now.

He wondered if Dram ever had premonitions. He knew the other visions would manifest in a matter of time, unless he could prevent them. He and Jonder returned to their seats above.

The noise was deafening, as Dram ran in to the command room. "What happened?" He demanded.

Ramen stood in the doorway, looking at something. He shook his head. "Your cruiser, boss. I guess they figured out your plans."

Dram moved beside Ramen. "Damn!" He crossed his arms over his chest and watched the **Talisman** burn. His means of escape vanished. He would wait until the other crew members returned, merely a delay. He heard the cook as he entered the room.

"Boss? The house maidens have disappeared."

CHAPTER EIGHT

"What's happening?" Shey looked at Genesis.

"Someone is boarding the ship." No use trying the controls. Once the air-lock was connected to another vessel, the controls were locked. The com-links were jammed also, though that wasn't common practice. She had a bad feeling about the whole thing. This had never happened to her before, but the I.S.P. had informed her of the procedures when they boarded another ship. This was definitely someone else.

"Prepare to surrender your vessel," a gruff male voice announced over the intercom-link.

Anger mixed with fear as she pressed the com-link to respond, but communications was stilled jammed on her end.

"Who was that?" Shey asked, her eyes wide.

"I don't know. He doesn't sound like anyone at the I.S.P." She tried to calm her emotions. She had to get her mind on something she could deal with. If not the Space Patrol, then who was he? She pulled her hands off the controls to keep Shey from seeing them shake.

"What is the I.S.P.?"

"I work for them as a bounty hunter. It stands for Interplanetary Space Patrol. My father, Malek, and I were on a mission to find Dram and his slave traders after they abducted all the women from our village."

Shey stared at her. "*You* are a bounty hunter?"

She nodded. "I planned to contact them for an escort back to **Chroma** once we turned the ship around, but it's too late. I'm sorry." She wrung her hands. She was helpless yet responsible for all these girls.

Shey looked puzzled as she leaned on the console, holding her head. "This is too much," she said, finally.

She put her hand on Shey's back. "I'll figure something out, Shey. We'll get through it." Now if only she could convince herself of that.

There was a commotion in the center of the ship. She and Shey left the Nav-room, weapons drawn. She flattened herself against the corner wall, and held Shey back with her arm. The Earth man and Malek would have to wait. The girls and their safety were her first priority now.

Men poured in through the opening, down the ladder, and carried laser rifles and smaller weapons. She set her weapon on stun and shot several of them before they returned fire. She ducked, tensing her leg muscles, ready to spring as sparks sprayed along the corner wall she leaned against. Shey reached over her head and took out a few men off the ladder.

Someone returned shots, and she jumped back. "They're not using stunners," she whispered to Shey.

Three large men leapt out from the corner, startling a gasp out of her.

"Drop your weapons!" One of them demanded, pointing a laser rifle at her. Her heart thudded.

She did as she was told, remembering the pain last time she was shot. She wasn't good at defeat, but she wouldn't provoke him. Shey dropped her weapon on the floor, beside her own.

Another man prodded her with his laser rifle then pushed her and Shey toward the intruder.

A thin, wiry man came toward her. His pale skin and off-white calf-length tunic, gave him a ghostly appearance. Pant legs billowed above the top of his black boots and around his waist he wore a wide, tulin-colored belt. His evil glare and vicious smile made her uneasy.

"Where are the men on this ship?" he demanded.

"They are my prisoners." She folded her arms across her chest. "And who are *you*?" She glared back at him and tamped down her anger and fear. Now to calm her pounding heart...

His eyes scanned her body before he spoke. "I am Z, master harvester on **Vestra Minor**. You are now *my* prisoners, and this is *my* ship." He gestured with his hands.

She clenched her fists and tensed her jaw. *How dare he say that to her?*

"Oh, no it's not!" Shey straightened to her full height, crossing her arms over her chest. One of Z's men pointed a laser at Shey.

She threw her arm out to protect Shey. "Don't touch her, or I'll report you to the I.S.P." She glared at Z.

He cocked his head and gazed at her. "So, you must be the one Dram spoke about." Z crept around her and Shey, regarding them like a bird homing in on its prey.

What had Dram told him?

"Nice. Very nice." He tapped his chin with long narrow fingers.

She was nauseous. She sensed the evil nature oozing from the man's pores.

"What do you want?" she demanded, her fists still clenched. Her nails dug into her palms.

"I have come to claim my ship and all that's on it." He turned to his men. "Take them."

"No! This transporter belongs to her father," she pointed to Shey. "The men here are *my* prisoners. And you, sir, are interfering with an I.S.P. agent," she poked his chest.

A man grabbed her from behind, her arms pulled back. She struggled until she remembered how her last confrontation had ended. Another man restrained Shey the same way.

When the guard pushed her toward the ladder, the **yav** fell out of her sleeve. Z bent to retrieve the item.

"Well, this is interesting," he said. "I love **yavs.** They seem to unlock so many secrets." He moved to the ladder and stood before her. Then, he slid his finger under her chin.

She pulled away. His icy touch gave her cold chills. The evil presence surrounding him was greater than what she had sensed with Dram.

"Find out where this belongs," he handed the **yav** to one of his guards. He turned to the men holding her and Shey. "Take the two females to the cell," he ordered.

Forced up the ladder and into the other ship, the men led them to a small, empty room the size of the sleeping compartments on **The**

Guardian. The men clamped wrist restraints on Shey and her before leaving. Unlike the cage on **The Guardian,** this one had four solid walls and a door.

She fell to her knees and lowered her head, offering up a silent prayer. And for the first time, instead of calling out to Herda, she thought of the Earth man. Would he come for her?

"Adam," she said aloud. If only she could communicate with him.

"I can't believe this is happening." Shey leaned back against a wall, her eyes closed. "It took me a long time to calm the girls down after we were abducted the first time. And now, this happens."

"Don't give up," she said with a sigh, standing. She needed to believe that advice herself. Shey's frustration showed on her face. Anxiety gripped her, while inadequacy crept in. She understood Shey's pain.

She did the only thing she knew to do, hoping it would work.

"Adam, we are held captive. Please hurry," she said aloud. She concentrated on those words in her mind.

Shey stared at her. "Who's Adam?"

"I'm communicating with the Earth man."

Shey's eyebrows narrowed. "How can you do that?"

"Telepathy. He will come for us." She had to be positive. Just like her healing gift, she believed he heard her, so it would manifest. She swallowed all doubts and held on to his promise to help her escape and rescue her father. Then the thought of his lips pressed against hers sent a shiver through her body. He *had* to find her, she almost tasted him.

"Z is evil," Shey clenched her teeth. "He'd better not hurt those girls."

"Be strong," she said.

"What do you mean?"

"Do not let the girls see your fear. They get their strength from you."

Shey nodded. "You're right."

Silence grew until the door hissed open. Two tall guards entered the room.

"You come with us," one man ordered Shey. The two of them

escorted her out. Shey looked over her shoulder at her.

"Be strong," she whispered.

Shey nodded as she left.

She closed her eyes and prayed for Shey's safety, as well as the safety of all the girls. When she lifted her gaze, Z stood before her.

The sight of him shocked her so, she stumbled and fell on the floor, her hands still bound behind her. Z reached for her, but she pushed herself away then sprang to her feet.

"Don't touch me!" she snarled at him. His features were drawn and wrinkled. Why was he here? What did he want? The sight of the man repulsed her.

"Well, I like that. You have such a spirited demeanor. It intrigues me." He walked around her. She turned so Z would have to face her. Her skin crawled at his nearness.

"You don't trust me?" He clasped his hands. "I suppose that's normal under the circumstances." He glanced over her body as he paced. "Hopefully, that will change."

"I want to be with the others," she demanded.

"Oh, I'm sorry," he gestured, "but that's not possible."

"Why not?" Annoyed, she didn't like where this led.

"The others are here to harvest the crops. You are here for another purpose." Z backed her into a corner. "My personal needs, you might say." He put a hand on either side of her, pinning her against the two walls.

Her pulse quickened at his nearness and a lump formed in her throat. His evil stare and foul breath made her nostrils burn and her gut tighten.

"Whatever my heart desires." he leaned close.

Adam and Berto sat at the controls of **The Guardian,** taking her into space.

"Now, are you going to tell me what business Dram is in?" he asked Berto. Berto either lied, or he was keeping something from him. He was tired of this game Berto played. He wanted answers and Berto had no more excuses. Berto had sealed his fate the moment he'd ordered the destruction of Dram's cruiser.

Berto scowled at him as he slid the lever into place.

"He's a slave trader."

"A what? His mouth dropped open as he stared at Berto. Berto glanced at him, nodded, and then looked away, his jaw tensed.

"My God! Slavery was outlawed after the Civil War." His focus remained on Berto.

"Maybe on your planet, but it was never legal in our system," he returned the glance.

"Why does he do it?" He ran a hand through his hair, as he gazed out the view port. Disgust crept in.

"The pay is excellent, actually. When Vestra Major sent out the first colonists, they had to explore the planets and do all the work themselves. Some of the missions barely survived because of the need for more workers. Dram supplied a labor force to those who wanted one and were willing to pay for it." Berto sat back in his seat, his arms crossed over his chest.

"And where does he get this labor force?" He raised an eyebrow.

"He sends us out to locate males or females, depending on what is requested."

"And how do you find these people?"

Berto lowered his eyes and then glanced away. "We abduct them and bring them to the complex for processing." He gazed out the view port. "When the shipment is ready, we deliver it."

He glanced at him. "What do you mean by processing?"

"We clean, clothe, feed and lock them up until Dram has a buyer."

"And that doesn't bother you?"

"Sometimes," Berto said, looking out the view port and tensing his jaw.

"*Adam*." He heard Genesis call him. He glanced around the Nav-room, but no one was there besides Berto and himself.

"Did you hear that?" he asked.

"Hear what?" Berto turned to look at him.

"She called me."

Berto looked puzzled. "Who did?"

Was it his imagination? Genesis distracted him, especially the reoccurring thoughts of kissing her sweet lips. Maybe he just wanted to hear her voice so bad, it sounded real to him. Was she telepathic?

"Uh, never mind." He needed to get back to the business at hand. "How did you get into this mess with Dram?" He tried to shake the thoughts of her out of his mind, but he wanted to know the truth. While Berto was in a confessing mood, he would pump him for more information.

"I was caught trying to steal a transporter. The **Transitor,** actually."

"You stole a space ship?"

"Bordon and I confiscated it. When Dram and some of the others came along and found us, he threatened to turn us in unless we worked for him."

"So, he stole from you and made you work for him?"

"Something like that," Berto said.

"That's blackmail." He shook his head. "Well, now's your chance to make everything right, Berto." He had to convince him to help. He needed an ally to rescue Genesis and the other girls. There was no way he could do it alone. Berto was an expert in navigation.

"What do you mean?" Berto frowned.

"We've got to make a stop on **Tarsius.** How close is it to the **Transitor**?"

"**Tarsius**? Why?" Berto raised an eyebrow, suspicious.

"I promised the house maidens I'd take them home," he dared Berto to say anything.

"You did *what*?" Berto glared at him, tightening his fists.

"Hey, we don't work for Dram anymore, remember? And neither do the house maidens. Besides, it's on the way, isn't it?" *According to the charts it was.* Berto couldn't argue or deny that fact.

Berto shook his head and cursed under his breath.

"Dram will kill us for sure."

"Dram has more to worry about right now than chasing us across the galaxy. Besides, after we drop off the girls, we'll rescue Genesis and the others."

"Adam. We are held captive. Please hurry."

Adam's eyes widened as Gen's voice sounded in his head and he jumped out of his seat. Turning, he looked at Berto.

"My God! Tell me you heard that!"

Berto frowned at him. "You're hearing things," he said, pointing a finger at him.

"No! It was Genesis. They've all been captured."

Berto's mouth dropped open as he scowled at him. "You *are* crazy. Besides, why should we rescue them? We have the chance to escape ourselves. There's no point in following through with Dram's orders."

"Because you know it's right." He pointed at Berto. He hoped it wasn't too late for Genesis. He still tasted her last kiss as he licked his lips. He slowly sat down in his seat.

Berto shook his head, while pulling out the charts Dram had given him. He checked the coordinates for the last transmission from the **Transitor** and then referred to the maps.

"I don't know *why* I'm doing this. It makes absolutely no sense," Berto mumbled as he moved the papers around to study them.

He fought back a smile while he assisted Berto. He was thankful for the help.

"According to these coordinates," Berto began, "the **Transitor** was near **Tarsius,** and was last heard from here," he pointed to a spot on the map beside the planet **Tarsius**.

"Good," he looked to where Berto motioned. "Since the sisters are safe for now, we'll rescue Genesis and the girls first then take the others to **Tarsius** afterward."

He typed in the coordinates on the keyboard. The route flashed on the monitor. At least the **Transitor** wasn't far.

"Hold on, Gen, I'm coming," he said aloud.

Berto stared at him. "She can't hear you, you know."

"Well, if I can hear *her* then maybe she *can.*"

Berto shook his head and moved the controls for **Tarsius,** while he set the warp drive for hyper speed.

"There's another thing, Berto," he began. He might as well warn him, since Berto was involved.

Berto rolled his eyes and glanced at him. "I'm afraid to ask what it is."

"I have premonitions."

"And?"

"Well, the first one was the space cruiser we blew up." The events had unfolded so quickly he hadn't realized what had happened until it was over. "The premonition afterward was a bunch of uniformed men surrounding me and someone else." He was pretty sure now it involved Berto, but why tell him? He would find out soon enough.

"Uniformed men?" Berto's eyebrows narrowed.

"Yes, uh, you call it unicrin. I thought I'd warn you ahead of time, although I don't know what it means."

"I hope *that* premonition doesn't happen." Berto looked out the view port.

He swallowed hard. *Should he tell him all his visions came true? Would it make a difference if he did?* "I had a few premonitions about Genesis, too," he continued.

Berto's attention snapped toward him.

"Someone wants to hurt her, and I can't let that happen." He didn't need to give Berto all the details just yet. He'd fill him in later.

"What is so special about her anyway? Dram said she was nothing but trouble."

"I promised her I'd help her find her father, if she would return me to Earth."

"You know, your promises will get us killed." Berto shook his head. "Besides, you don't need her to get back to Earth."

His heart skipped a beat. "What do you mean?" He narrowed his brows.

"This is the ship you arrived in, isn't it?"

"Yes."

"The coordinates for going to and from Earth will have been recorded in the database. We can go to Earth now, and forget everyone else."

He could go to Earth? Return home? But he had made a promise to Genesis.

His parents had promised to come home from the party the night they died. They'd never fulfilled that promise and it took him a long time to realize it wasn't their fault. He vowed to himself to always keep his promises. How could he let Gen down now when she needed him the most? He wouldn't be able to live with himself if he did. Who would help all those other girls and the three sisters? Too many people counted on him. And the thought of that old man raping Genesis sickened him.

No, he had promised Gen, and she gave *her* word to take him home. She counted on him. *His* needs would have to wait. He glanced at Berto.

"I can't. I promised her."

Berto shook his head. "I think you're making a big mistake."

"Maybe. I'm going to check on the sisters." He left the Nav-room. Breathing deeply, he knew he'd made the right decision.

Jonder was nowhere in sight. He looked in the first compartment and found Jonder asleep on one of the bunks. The three sisters were in the second room. Two sat on the bottom bunk, talking. One lay on the top, resting her head on the pillow.

"Are you girls all right?" He asked.

"Oh, yes." The smallest one said, jumping up. She grabbed his hand.

"Thank you for rescuing us from that horrid place!" She kissed his fingers.

"Uh, you're welcome." Uncomfortable with the attention, he gently pulled his arm away.

"We're on our way to **Tarsius**, but first we need to rescue some other girls who are captives. You'll be fine a little longer, won't you?" He glanced at all three of them.

"Yes, as long as we don't have to go back to that prison, we're good."

"Are you getting hungry?" His own hunger caused his stomach to growl as he asked the question.

"Yes!" The brown-haired girl with the ponytail jumped up from the bed. "We'll prepare something for you," she grabbed his hand.

"Yes, that's the least we can do," the one sitting on the top bunk said. In one motion, she leapt off the bed and landed on the floor beside the other two. "I am Kinya, and these are my younger sisters, Anya and Moya," she straightened to her full height. Anya and Moya bowed at the sound of their names. While all three girls looked similar, he recognized Kinya as the one who'd approached him about taking them away from **Meta.** The two younger ones could pass as twins. Kinya was a full two inches taller, but she was shorter than Genesis.

"My name is Adam, the pilot is Berto, and Jonder is asleep in the next compartment. If you want to fix something for all of us, that would be great, but all we have is space food." The thought of eating that stuff didn't appeal to him at all, but he was hungry.

Kinya moved close to him and put her hands on his chest.

"We would be pleased to do so," she gently pushed him back. "Now go. We will bring it to you when we finish."

"Thanks," he shook his head. A smile slipped past his lips as he left the compartment. A light shone in the girls' eyes as they expressed their gratitude. It made him feel good, like he had done the right thing. He had to convince Berto it would all be worthwhile.

The door to the Nav-room hissed open.

"So, how *are* the girls?" Berto asked.

He slid into his seat beside Berto and looked over at him.

"Kinya is so grateful, she's preparing a meal for us right now." He half smiled.

"Really?"

"Kinya said that was the least they could do. They were so relieved to get away from **Meta.**" He leaned back in his seat and laced his fingers behind his head. He wondered what Genesis was doing now. Was she all right? Had the old man touched her?

"Who is Kinya?" Berto asked, glancing at him.

He sat forward and stared at Berto in disbelief, his brows narrowed.

"You're kidding."

Berto looked puzzled.

"The three of them had to sleep with Dram's men at night as part of their job," he said. "I would think you'd want to know a woman's name before you took her to bed." He leaned his elbow on the arm rest.

"Who said I slept with them?" Berto demanded.

"Didn't you?"

"No! Until you came along, I was the youngest one there. Age has its privileges when it comes to women and working for Dram. I was never alone with any of them to learn names. Besides, I saw the expressions on their faces after the men took them. At first they looked horrified. Later, they became withdrawn, like there was no soul left, as if a part of them died." Berto gazed out the view port, quietly reflecting on something.

"I killed someone once for doing the same thing to my sister," Berto confessed.

He quietly studied Berto, but didn't speak.

"He and two others, in mid youth, attempted to rape my sister." Berto glanced at him. "Mari was only seven, I was fourteen." He turned his gaze toward the view port and then studied his hands.

"I discovered I had some kind of power I never knew I had."

"What kind of power?"

"I was so angry I wanted to squeeze the life out of that **skunt**," he gestured, his hands around some invisible neck.

"When I lunged for him, I had my arms outstretched, he flew off my sister and slammed into the wall of the cave behind him, cracking his skull open." He clenched his jaw. "Then I stretched one hand out to another of the boys, and threw him at another rock." Berto studied his hands.

"Did you kill him, too?" He asked.

"No. He was knocked unconscious. The third boy ran away. Berto propped his elbows on his thighs and held his head in his hands. "I haven't told anyone that story since it happened."

"What happened to your sister? Was she all right?" He swallowed, wondering how he would react if he had a sibling.

"She was traumatized," Berto shook his head, "but I found a healer who helped her." After a few minutes, Berto glanced at him.

"If I sleep with a woman, it will be someone I love, who willingly gives herself to me," Berto touched his chest. Then he crossed his arms and turned to gaze at the stars.

He shared Berto's thoughts as well, but he'd never believed he would meet anyone he cared enough about until Genesis. He'd spent a lot of time guarding his heart and keeping his emotions in check. He wouldn't allow himself the heartache of losing somebody again like when he'd lost his parents. Yet, Genesis had managed to crack the invisible wall he had built.

Too often now, he thought of her. Concentration on tasks became more difficult.

"We're doing the right thing, Berto."

Berto nodded.

The door hissed open. Anya and Kinya came into the Nav-room. They carried bowls, handing one to Berto and one to him.

"Mmmm, something smells good," he said. "Did you make this with food paste?"

"Yes. We call it creative cooking. Hope you enjoy the trew," Kinya touched his shoulder.

"Thanks," he glanced up at her.

Anya waved as she left the room. Kinya bowed and followed her.

"The trew is quite tasty," Berto looked up from his bowl.

He sipped his own pasty concoction. The texture was more like thick pea soup, but tasted similar to stew, without any chunky vegetables or meat.

"Mmmm, I didn't know space food tasted this good."

"I've never had it prepared this way, either," Berto slurped his food.

Inside the command room on **Meta**, Dram spoke to Ramen and the cook.

"Boys, I'm afraid our location has been compromised." Dram ran a hand through his thick hair. "The others should have returned by now." He could easily take all of them on the cruiser and be far away from **Meta**, but they weren't answering communications. It wasn't like Ace to ignore him, unless something had happened. And he had a bad feeling about the whole thing. Everything had gone wrong.

"What do you mean, boss?" The cook asked.

"I feel we need to leave this place at once. The I.S.P. will look for us."

"Where would we go? All our ships are gone," the cook said.

"To the mountains," Ramen responded.

"How much food do we have on hand?" Dram asked.

"I guess if it's just the three of us, plenty to last a couple of weeks. But how will we take all this stuff to the mountains?" The cook asked.

"Leave that to me," Dram said. "Right now, start packing your survival gear."

The cook left the room.

"Boss, what about our files?" Ramen asked.

"I suggest you save everything onto something portable and delete anything off the processor that can implicate us."

"This is it, isn't it?"

"Yes, unless the boys return from **Plexus** before sunset, Ramen."

His plan would have worked, too, if it hadn't been for the ship incident. He'd thought it was well concealed. No one knew about it but him and Ramen and he would bet tulin Adam had something to do with it. He could have lived out his life on Earth. No one would look for him there, except a handful of pirates. In fact, only the ancient ones knew the system existed.

Thoughts of Emma came back to him. She had long blonde hair. Her blue eyes sparkled when she smiled at him. Then, that damn premonition of hers got in the way. The very reason she refused to go with him was because she thought he and their son would one day fight each other. He had lied to the boy, but who cared? The face-off between the two of them would leave only one survivor.

Inside Z's small holding compartment, Genesis ducked under Z's arms and ran from him.

"Oh, you like to play? That's fine. I love a good chase. Know this," he pointed a scrawny finger at her. "I always get what I'm after, one way or another." He walked past her and exited the room.

She remained inside the small compartment, relieved that Z was gone, and eventually drifted to sleep. Later, she woke to the noise of the door hissing open. The guard led her off the ship, gripping her upper arm. Her hands bound behind her, she clenched her jaw and thought of ways to escape.

Outside, she squinted at the brightness of **Vaedra** in the afternoon. She stood in front of the grandest house she had ever seen. Her skin warmed as **Vaedra's** rays touched her face. The feel of solid ground beneath her feet and fresh air in her lungs reminded her of **Atria**. God, she missed her home and the life she'd once had. She inhaled deeply as the guard pulled her toward the three tiers-high building. Several balconies poked out on the second and third levels with great windows leading onto each.

The rose colored stone work on the exterior of the house appeared smooth to the touch, yet in the design, cracks and swirls of gray and black ran throughout. She had never seen rock like that.

She and the guard boarded a vertical people mover, and got off on one of the higher levels. They stopped inside a large room where fabric draped every wall so no doors or windows showed. In the center was a huge bed. It was larger than any she had seen. Several people could have slept on it comfortably. Steps on both sides led to the bed. Four posts rose up, one at each corner. They looked like trunks of trees with the bark removed. Intricately carved scenes of wild beasts and fowl decorated the columns. Fabric stretched across the posts and flowed in **quastic** fashion. It reminded her of the shelters set up when tribes traveled to new places.

"Here!" Another man stepped out from behind the drapes, holding some flimsy blue material.

The man who escorted her removed her restraints. "Put that on," he pointed to the fabric.

The second man shoved the transparent cloth into her hands. "Z will be back to check on you shortly."

She caught the material and made a tsking sound, in disgust. "I will not wear this thing," she threw the object on the floor.

"Fine, Z can dress you himself, then." The two men left. She heard them bolt the door. That sick, anxious feeling came back. She sat on the steps near the bed, propped her elbows on her knees and sighed deeply. Her fingers barely touched the jeweled band. She had to escape. The girls and Shey depended on her. She'd have to find them and make sure they were all right. Would the Earth man come for her? If only she could hear his voice.

Moments later, the bolt on the door clicked before hissing open. She was trying to locate the source of the sound, when Z appeared in front of her, near the drapes, his hands behind his back.

She glared at him, anger welling up inside.

"Well, I see you are not pleased with my gift." He glanced at the fabric on the floor.

She sneered at him, her fists tightly clenched. I refuse to wear that piece of cloth." she said, disgusted. "There's nothing there but a mere fragment."

"Here are others from which to choose." He pulled more from behind his back to show her. There was red, purple, and deep blue, along with shimmery silver and black outfits.

On **Atria,** the men wore loin cloths made of animal skins, while the women covered their torsos with the same. It had been a long time since she'd returned home, much less worn her native clothing.

She allowed herself to look at what he had in his hands, the colors fascinated her. Never had she seen such beautiful fabrics. Then she remembered who he was, a sludge of human waste.

"I am not interested in you or anything you have." She turned away from him, her jaw tense and arms crossed. She tried to tamp down the skin-crawling feeling she got when she was around him.

"Oh, you will be, my dear, in time. You must be hungry. I have brought you some food and drink." He stepped aside while two men entered the room carrying a round table and two chairs. She watched as they set the table with a white cloth. They placed a platter of roast bird on it, the aroma made her stomach howl in pain. How long had it been since her last meal? One man brought bowls of steaming hot vegetables, while another carried a large bowl of exotic fruit. The two men set down fancy plates and glasses, filling the containers with a pink beverage. She was hungrier than she realized, and roast bird *was* her favorite meal.

She licked her lips. Maybe just a taste. She found herself moving toward the table, reaching her hand to sample the fruit. A great feast was something she had not seen since her childhood, and the succulent food drew the growling noise from her belly.

"Have a seat, my dear," Z said, pulling a chair out for her.

The wafting scent of the hot meal pulled her like a magnet. With nothing to eat or drink since her latest captivity, her mouth was dry and her hunger great.

"You are indeed a beautiful young woman," Z sat across from her.

She ignored him, licking her lips once more, while gazing at the elegant morsels.

"I shall treat you like a princess," he picked up a glass and handed it to her.

"Have some. It's a special vintage, and will make your food taste heavenly."

Taking the container of pink beverage, she narrowed her eyes at him in distrust. He was up to something. Why was he nice to her? She was thirsty, though, and her throat was parched. She looked at the drink in the beautifully cut goblet as Z picked up his vessel, lifting it to her.

"To you, my princess," he took a sip.

When nothing happened, she sipped from her own glass. The liquid was sweet on her lips, like nectar and cool on her tongue. She swallowed the smooth drink. A bigger sip this time, she savored the flavor.

"Very tasty," she licked the beverage from her bottom lip.

Z smiled at her as he sat his half-empty container down.

She took another big sip, and as she swallowed, a warm sensation ran through her body at light speed.

"Your glass was laced with **senqua,** it'll make you very relaxed. On an empty stomach, it seems to work...instantly." Z waited expectantly, his hands folded on the table.

Suddenly, she felt strange all over. Her arms and legs were heavy like the precious metal, tulin. The room spun around her, making her dizzy. She dropped her glass and fell into her plate of food.

Adam thought about Genesis when a piercing scream brought him to his feet. Berto glanced up at him, his brows raised.

He shrugged then dashed out of the Nav-room, while Berto remained at the controls.

Jonder dragged Anya toward the sleeping compartment he used.

"No!" she screamed again, pulling away from him.

He clenched his fists. "Let her go, Jonder!" he demanded.

"Stay out of this, boy. These girls are ours to use as we please."

"We no longer work for Dram, and neither do they. Let her go!" he shouted in anger.

Jonder jerked Anya once more, knocking her off balance.

He dove for Jonder's legs, taking him down in a move he had often used during his high school wrestling career.

Within seconds, he pinned Jonder's shoulders to the ground. Their faces inches apart.

"So help me, Jonder, you touch one of those girls again, I will lock you in the cell for the rest of this trip. You got that!" He spoke with a harsh voice he didn't know he possessed.

Jonder's eyes widened as he nodded. Anya ran back to her sisters.

A loud alarm sounded in the Nav-room. He pushed off Jonder's chest to get up.

"Hey, you two get in here, quick!" Berto shouted from the controls.

"This is the Interplanetary Space Patrol. Transmit your I.D. now." A voice came over the com-link.

Stunned, he didn't remember learning anything about I.D.s in training.

"What I.D. number?" Jonder glanced at Berto.

Berto shrugged.

"This is Malek's ship," he began. "Genesis and her father, Malek worked for the I.S.P." He reached over Berto and hit the com-link.

"Adam Davis here. Dram captured Genesis and Malek and sent them to other planets. We have escaped from Dram ourselves and are searching for Genesis."

"Prepare to be boarded," replied the voice.

"What are you doing?" Berto demanded, glaring at him.

"He's going to get us killed!" Jonder shouted as he threw up his hands.

"We're telling the truth. It's the only way out of this mess," he tried to reassure them.

"Yeah, if you want to go to **Plumaris** for the rest of your life,"

Jonder spat out. "I have arrest warrants out for my ass."

"I've got a record, too," Berto mumbled.

"Well it's time to make things right. Maybe they'll bargain with us if we tell the truth."

There was a noise above the ship.

"How will they board us in space?" he asked.

"Two docking bays are built in every cruiser and transporter above and below for emergencies," Berto explained.

"I'm not going to let them take me," Jonder announced as he grabbed Berto's laser weapon and ran out of the Nav-room with it. While Berto remained at the controls, he ran after Jonder.

Jonder let off a shot at a pair of feet descending the hatchway.

He tackled Jonder and knocked him down.

"Hold your fire!" Berto shouted, coming from the Nav-room.

He struggled to keep Jonder pinned.

"We've got him under control," Berto said.

"Yeah? That's easy for you to say," he said, holding Jonder's arms at his side, while prone on the floor, his knee in Jonder's back.

Uniformed I.S.P. agents entered the ship through the hatchway with weapons drawn and aimed at all three of them. They were surrounded, just like in his premonition. He pulled Jonder up off the floor into a standing position, tossing the laser weapon to an agent. He and Berto exchanged glances, as he swallowed hard. He didn't remember seeing all those weapons.

"This ship belongs to the Interplanetary Space Patrol and was loaned to two bounty hunters. I'm Captain Luc. What have you done with Malek and Genesis?"

CHAPTER NINE

"**I**'m telling you the truth! You have to listen to me," Adam pulled against the restraints binding him to the chair. He was locked inside some interrogation room at the I.S.P. Headquarters on **Tarsius**, where no one believed him.

"Genesis is in trouble, and if we don't get to her soon, it'll be too late," he pleaded with Captain Luc. Why couldn't he understand? He tightened his fists.

The Captain, at least six feet tall, walked around his chair and stopped in front of him. His hands clasped behind his back. Luc had blond hair and blue eyes. His fair skin made him appear like all those girls he had seen on **Meta**, with the same regal look. Could Luc be related to them?

He tensed his jaw. The Captain had to believe him, for her sake if nothing else. If she worked for the I.S.P., that should count for something.

"If only you had proof," the Captain said, pacing back and forth.

He looked like Dram, except the eighteen- years difference in their ages. Was that enough to convince them? *No.* He'd informed Captain Luc of everything, yet Luc still questioned him.

"She told me about the abduction of the women from her village, and how she and Malek had been searching for Dram for ten years—uh, anos," he tried again, hopeful.

"Go on," the Captain stopped pacing and faced him.

"She said Dram and his men landed in her village and rounded up all the women and children. She ran to get help, but when she returned, they were all gone." He glanced up at the Captain, hoping he would finally release him.

"She has the gift of healing," he added.

"Yes, I know all about Genesis. She's a princess as well, and next in line to be chief if anything happens to Malek," Captain Luc replied.

"A princess?" She *did* look like one. The memory of her being ushered out through the eating hall doors came back to him.

"What I need is proof of who *you* are," the Captain said, crossing his arms over his chest.

He pulled at his restraints in frustration, pinching the hairs on his arm under his suit.

"All my identification is on Earth. What kind of proof do you need?"

"Anything to prove you aren't Dram," the Captain said.

His facial hair should be noticeable by now. He cocked his head. "Look at me, at my face."

Luc moved closer to study him. His brows narrowed.

"Do you see it? I have facial hair and Dram does not."

"Facial hair?"

"Yes! I have hair on other parts of my body as well, like my arms and legs," he explained. He hoped it wouldn't get more personal than that, but he had to try something.

"Show me."

"You'll have to lift up my sleeve." *This had to work.*

The Captain peeled the top of the flight suit off him to expose his chest and arms by releasing the magnetic strips across the shoulders. He left him bound to the chair.

Not much hair compared to a couple of the guys he worked with back home, but his fine, blond curls on his forearms and chest should be more than adequate proof. Captain Luc stared at his chest then walked behind him, where he ran his hand across one of his arms.

"Are all your people on Earth like this?" Luc asked.

"Some men have hair on their chests, but women don't. Women just grow hair on their legs and arms."

Suddenly, the restraints fell away from his hands.

"You can get dressed. I believe you."

"Thank you, sir," he rubbed his wrists, relieved. He remembered the burns he had once endured when Genesis had restrained him. He refastened his flight suit and stood up.

"If you've spoken the truth, then we don't have time to waste," Captain Luc ran a hand through his hair.

"That's what I've been trying to tell you!" He gestured with his hands. *Hold on, Genesis we're coming for you.*

Luc pressed a button on the wall and another agent entered the room. The two of them spoke together quietly before the Captain turned back to him. The other agent left.

"Anya, Kinya, and Moya will be returned to their home on **Tarsius.** You have my word," Luc began. "As for Jonder, well, I'm afraid he was very uncooperative. Since he has an extensive criminal record, we will detain him."

He nodded. Fine with him. "What about Berto?"

"Berto is a different story. He admitted to stealing the **Transitor,** but since he was coerced into working for Dram, we'll let him work off most of his punishment."

"How?" He was curious. Berto must not have told them everything.

"He will assist us in locating all the people who had been abducted by Dram and his men," he explained. "Berto also gave us a location of a hangout for Dram's workers on **Plexus**. We had some agents in place on another assignment and they were able to capture four of Dram's men."

"Did Berto volunteer to help you?" he asked.

"Yes, as a matter of fact. He said he knew Ramen's passwords on the processor and could access the files we need. He also remembered some of the locations for pick ups and deliveries. That should help us locate these people much quicker."

He nodded. Deep down Berto knew to do the right thing, but if they knew about the boy he had killed, would they let him work that off?

"When can we get started?" He was anxious to find Genesis. *Hold on, Gen.*

"Right now. Follow me."

The Captain led the way through the door and down a hallway. "I've already launched a team to search for the first group of abductees Berto gave us," the Captain said as they walked. "You and Berto will fly **The Guardian** to **Vestra Minor**, along with a small contingency of I.S.P. agents. On **Vestra**, another I.S.P. transporter is on standby. Rescue the **Chromian** girls and Genesis and leave on the larger ship. The other crew will raid Z's headquarters."

"What about **The Guardian**?" he asked.

"My agents will return her to headquarters where I'll brief you on our attack of Dram's hideout." The Captain stopped in front of a door. Another agent stood at the entrance.

"Thank you, sir," he said, offering him his hand.

"I should be thanking *you*. This slave trading business has been going on for over 25 anos. We've had teams looking for him all over the galaxy. We will finally put an end to it and return everyone we can find back to their homes and families. It's a huge accomplishment." Captain Luc shook his hand, saluted the other agent, and stepped inside the room.

"Follow me," the agent said, closing the door behind the Captain. He walked down the hall toward a docking bay.

"You will board **The Guardian** now for your mission. Good luck!" The agent saluted him and left.

The door slid open and Berto stood in the hatch way.

"Adam, telling the truth *was* the right thing to do. I feel like a huge weight has been lifted off me." Berto offered him his hand, and when he took it, he drew Berto into a brotherly hug. He was happy for Berto.

"I'm glad we're working together on this," he grabbed Berto's shoulders. "I just hope it's not too late." He gave Berto a slight squeeze and turned him around, heading inside the ship.

"Did you tell the Captain about your past?" he asked.

"I told him everything. Since I was so young when I defended my sister, he said he would get me a pardon in exchange for my help in locating the slaves, but I am indebted to the I.S.P. until everyone is found however long that takes."

Two I.S.P. agents remained in the Nav-room, while he and Berto took the controls. He was glad to be flying again.

Four others set up some elaborate equipment for scanning buildings, as well as storing extra weapons.

En route to **Vestra Minor**, his premonition of Genesis falling into her plate of food came back to him. This time the vision was more vivid.

She had a drink in her hand and an old man hovered over her. Oh, Lord, don't let me be too late, he prayed.

Genesis woke with a start. She sat up, rubbing her temples, her eyes closed from the pain. Her head hurt, like someone had hit her hard. She blinked and gasped to see she wore one of the fabric pieces Z had shown her. She didn't remember putting it on, though. With thin straps and a deep plunging neckline, the silky, red material was nearly transparent.

"Oh!" She was mad at the thought of Z dressing her. How dare he touch her! A shiver of disgust ran through her. She glanced around. She was on the large bed in the middle of room, alone. The bed was still made up. Relief swept over her. Then her stomach churned with hunger. She had not eaten in two days.

What had happened to her? She rubbed her head once more at the temples, trying to clear the fog from her mind. She drank something sweet and tasty but afterward, her memory failed her.

She climbed out of the massive bed and searched for her clothes but they were gone. She felt along the fabric draped walls until she found a panel with buttons. She pressed the blue knob and lights went on and off in different parts of the room. The red knob opened the ceiling to reveal a massive mirror centered over the bed. Her mouth dropped open. She hit the knob again until the ceiling closed. She had to get out of here. Z could show up at any moment and time was running out.

Continuing along the wall, she felt a door panel. She separated the fabric and pressed the release and it opened. The hallway was clear.

Quietly, she slipped out, going right, until she came to an intersection. Her heart pounded, while the cool air chilled her bare skin. No one was around. *Good.* On the far right was a large window at the end of the hall, leading to a balcony. She ran toward her freedom. She reached the window and two arms grabbed her waist from behind.

"Where do you think you're going?" the huge guard asked. He stood almost 210 centikiks, thirty centikiks taller than Shey.

"Let me go!" she shouted. She twisted in his arms but he managed to pry her fingers loose from the window facing and carried her back to the room in one arm.

She kicked, scratched and pounded him, but he only tightened his grip around her waist. The red garment barely covered her body.

"Look what I found, boss," he said to Z as Z approached her.

Oh great!

"Take her to my room," Z ordered. "And this time, stay at your post!"

Adam looked through the view port. Z's compound on **Vestra Minor** was massive, yet elegant like some Italian villa he had seen in a movie. It sat three stories high in the middle of a beautiful garden. Rows upon rows of vegetables and crops grew green and lush in fields behind the palatial-looking building.

A walled patio surrounded by flowering plants sat in back of the palace.

"Take her down above the building," one of the I.S.P. agents ordered. "We can scan from there."

It was dusk. No one was outside. He and Berto lowered **The Guardian** over the villa about twenty feet above the roof. The I.S.P. agents engaged their equipment, while they hovered.

"Here, you take the controls for me. I want to check out the monitor on the scanner," he said to an agent, leaving his seat.

He joined the others in the center of the ship, cracking his knuckles, one at a time, while the schematics of the building showed up.

Hold on, Genesis. I'm coming for you. His pulse quickened and he tamped down his excitement at the thought of seeing her again. He wanted his arms around her, to kiss her once more.

Berto joined him, while Agent Tremol took over in the Nav-room.

A piece of equipment spat out several sheets of paper. He watched Lieutenant Howell as he studied the printouts, then motioned for everyone to look at the monitor.

"The top level has no body readings," he began. "We will

concentrate our rescue efforts on the mid level, where a significant number of people are located," he pointed to the screen. The image he looked at changed to show the schematics.

Two rooms appeared to have about fifteen bodies in each.

"Thirty girls were captured from **Chroma**," Berto said, his hands behind his back.

"That's where we'll go," Lieutenant Howell said.

"And Genesis?" he asked.

Howell looked at the monitor again. Other rooms showed three or four people in them. A movement on either side of the hallway showed an elevator bubble. One moved up, while the other went down. People were in each bubble.

"Those could be guards," Berto pointed at the monitor.

But something caught his attention. "Look at this," he indicated a room with one person in it. His heart raced and anxiety welled up as he thought of Genesis. Three figures got off one of the elevator bubbles and moved to the room. Two bodies remained outside, while one entered. A bad feeling hit him in the gut. One of the figures was female, the other, male and much thinner. The two figures struggled with each other. The **Chromian** girls were down the hall.

"Gen's in there," he said, fisting his hands. He wanted to pound the old man.

"How do you know?" Berto asked, staring at him.

"I felt it." He kept his eyes focused on the monitor, while Howell gave out orders and headsets. After being briefed of the procedures, he, Berto and four agents dropped silently onto the balcony. **The Guardian** hovered near the window on the second floor.

Lieutenant Howell and Agent Tamlin led the group carrying laser rifles, followed by him and Berto, with stun weapons. Danner and Spencer had rifles as well.

"Why did we get stun weapons?" he whispered to Berto. He turned the weapon over in his hand to study it.

"A matter of trust, I believe," Berto said.

He adjusted his bow and quiver of arrows, on his shoulder, as he thought about how deadly his aim was with his weapon of choice. He had never used a stunner, much less a gun on Earth, but he knew his bow well from spending hours a day practicing.

Howell and Tamlin stopped in the intersection of halls and fired on the guards on the side hallways.

"Let's go!" Howell ordered, as he positioned himself back to back with Tamlin, to catch any action in either direction.

He and Danner turned right down the hall and went to the door on the left. Berto and Spencer headed for the one on the right.

He shot the door panel and the door sprung open. Fifteen startled girls jumped at the sound.

"We came to take you home," he announced, gesturing for them to follow. If he had the choice, he would have searched for Genesis first, but Howell called the shots and he could only follow orders at this point.

The girls followed him down the hall. Danner brought up the rear and kept watch for guards, while he led the girls to the window. Once on the balcony, he helped them get onto the transporter.

He didn't see Berto and Spencer. He ran back to check. They were in the hall, arguing with someone in the room. Could it be Gen? He moved to the doorway.

"What's the problem?" he asked, looking at Berto, then at a tall blonde, her hands on her hips.

She pointed at Berto. "He's the one who abducted us from the academy."

He looked at Berto whose jaw was tensed and his brows furrowed.

"Well," he shrugged. "If you don't want to go back to **Chroma** with the other girls, we'll be on our way." He put his arm around Berto and turned him away from the door, ushering him and Spencer out into the hall. Berto scowled at him.

"Wait!" she called out. He gave Berto a wink then faced the woman.

Berto moved toward her, getting in her face. "You've got one minute to get your ass on that ship before I change my mind," he whispered harshly.

She swallowed hard, her eyes widened as they glared at each other.

"Come on, girls," she said ushering them past Berto while her gaze locked on him.

His chest tightened, as he heard Gen's voice in his head.

"Help me!"

"Gen, I'm here!" "I'm going after Genesis," he said, running down the hall past Tamlin and Howell. Berto had the girls to the window, and Spencer brought up the rear by the time he was at the door.

"Hurry up!" Howell whispered. "Someone's getting on the people mover on the bottom level," he said, touching his headset. Several guards poured out in the hall at the opposite end. Spencer came back to help shoot, and Howell and Tamlin took refuge at the intersection of halls.

He shot at the lock mechanism with his stun weapon and the door slid open. He holstered his laser and fixed an arrow to his bowstring. Fabric hung from the ceiling.

"No!" she screamed.

Genesis! His heart pounded wildly, anxiety washed over him and adrenaline pumped through his veins. He tightened his jaw and pulled back on his bowstring. One good shot was all he needed. He found an opening in the drapes and kicked them apart.

In the center of the room was the gaudiest looking bed he had ever seen. Lying on top was Genesis, struggling against the weight of the man in his premonitions, and he was naked.

"Get off her, you bastard!" he yelled as he released the arrow. It stuck in the man's shoulder. The man gasped as he turned to face him, while grabbing his arm. He nocked another arrow, releasing it deep into the man's chest. He never saw it coming. A shocked expression marked him as he fell on Genesis.

Genesis screamed once more as he slipped his bow over his shoulder. His long strides brought him to her side. His heart pounded so loudly he heard it. *Oh, God, let her be okay.* He lifted the dead man off her, pushing him aside. Gen's eyes were wide with surprise and her mouth open as she looked at him.

He scooped her up in his arms, allowing himself to briefly see her beautiful, naked form. He hardened at the sight of her deeply tanned flesh. Berto had been right, no body hair.

His lips brushed hers momentarily then he claimed her mouth, devouring her. She reached her arms around his neck, pressing herself against him, opening her mouth and allowing him access.

He hadn't realized how much he missed her until that moment. All the heat from the kiss coursed through his body at a dizzying rate. He set her on the ground, pulling away reluctantly. He reached for the sheet, yanked it off the bed, and gently wrapped her in it. He pulled her into his arms.

"Genesis," he whispered in her ear, kissing her once more.

Her hands and fingers caressed his head, her touch weakening him momentarily, until he heard shouting from his headset.

"Get out now, we can't hold them much longer," Howell ordered.

"I've got to get you out of here," he pulled away and handed her the stun weapon. He bent down and lifted her over his shoulder like a sack of potatoes, so he could run faster.

"Shoot anything that shoots at us, Gen." He was out the door and ran toward Howell and Tamlin. He passed the two men and they backed down the hall behind him, shooting at the guards. Spencer and Danner were on the balcony taking shots at men below on the patio.

"There's a half-dozen of them," Tamlin said, crouching to get better aim.

He made it to the window and lowered Genesis to the floor. The transporter was missing.

"Another people mover is approaching the second level with four more guards," an agent on **The Guardian** announced into his headset.

He retrieved his bow off his shoulder and nocked an arrow to the bowstring. "I'll shoot high, you guys hit low," he said as he released an arrow, watching it bury itself into a guard's chest. More guards came down the hall.

"Good shot, Earth man," Gen said, as she hit another guard using the stun weapon.

He swallowed the compliment and exchanged glances with Genesis, raising an eyebrow. She knew his name--why did she call him Earth man?

"Get her on the ship!" Howell yelled.

He turned to see the transporter now hovering out the window.

He slung his bow on his shoulder and scooped her over the other. As he reached for the rope dangling above the balcony, something stung his leg. A stray shot had caught him in the left calf muscle. Pain seared his leg, causing him to lose his balance and his grip on Genesis. His leg was on fire, burning his flesh. Genesis slid down his front and had one arm tight over one of his shoulders, and the other under his arm.

"Hang on, Gen," he grunted as he righted himself. He wrapped the excess rope around his arm and let Berto pull him up into the transporter with some type of winch. Once safely inside, he balanced on his right foot as he lowered Gen to the floor.

She desperately clung to her sheet with one hand, while she handed the stun weapon to the I.S.P. agent who came to assist her.

He hobbled over to the side of the transporter, easing himself down on the floor, his back against the wall. The movement exacerbated the pain. Berto helped Howell, Tamlin, Spencer and Danner onto the ship. Genesis pulled her sheet up with both hands and joined him. People sat everywhere, in close proximity, crowded into each other.

"You're injured," she said, kneeling before him.

He clenched his teeth. "I'll live," he grunted in pain. It hurt like hell, but he wouldn't admit it, not in front of all these people and I.S.P. agents looking on. He watched as the hatchway closed. The transporter lifted higher in the air. Then he shut his eyes briefly. If only he wasn't in so much pain. He wanted to be alone with Genesis right now, kissing her senseless and exploring her body, caressing her skin, and running his fingers through long, silky black hair. His groin tightened at the thought of her.

Suddenly, a warm sensation ran through his leg and he opened his eyes. Genesis held her hands on the open wound and uttered some prayers.

He kept still while her soft, soothing touch sent another scorching fire through his loins. He clenched his jaw tight, trying to control his reaction to her. The pain in his leg was forgotten, as he watched her sheet slowly slide down her chest.

"Genesis, wait!" He leaned forward, grabbing her ribs under her breasts and pulled her onto his lap. He turned her to face the others.

"Hey!" She tried to wriggle loose.

"Gen," he whispered in her ear, low enough so no one else could hear. "You were about to lose your sheet. My leg can wait."

She glanced down and grabbed her covering, then settled into his arms. He leaned close and whispered, "Thanks Gen."

Her long, blue-black, silky hair was loose on her shoulders. He wanted to kiss her neck and work his way down her back, but he had an audience to consider, so he restrained himself. He allowed his senses to soak in her fragrance, while his chest enjoyed the warmth of her body.

He ran his fingers across her forearm, caressing her bare skin, and wondered how sensuous the rest of her would feel. But the thought hardened him more and he felt her butt tense against his shaft.

Sitting on Adam's lap, Genesis ran her fingers through her hair. The excitement of the past few minutes had shot her heart rate up. The Earth man had one arm around her waist. When she let go of her mane, he gently brushed his fingers against the flesh of her arm. She enjoyed his touch.

When he stopped caressing her arm, he moved his hands around her waist. A tingly sensation flowed down her body to the place where her legs joined together. A strange ache started, one she had never experienced before.

A movement against her butt told her he felt the same sensations. Did he enjoy them as much as she did? She could get used to this. She wanted more of his touch, without the others looking on.

She relaxed a little. His body was warm against hers. She remembered how he held her in one arm, clinging to the rope with the other. Never had she known a man this strong, not even from her own village. She leaned onto his chest and closed her eyes, and felt the steady pounding of his heart. She imagined him kissing her again. She was safe here.

After a few minutes, his fingers ran down her back. He gently pulled her locks out from under the sheet. He breathed close to her ear. Too close. She shivered at the feel of his breath against her skin as he let her hair fall freely around her shoulders.

"Gen," he whispered. "Did he...touch you?" The warmth of his breath sent an intense surge of heat throughout her veins, pooling between her legs. She drew her knees up and turned her body toward him, her hand fell on his open palm.

He laced her fingers with his. She gazed in his pale blue eyes. This man who looked so much like Dram was so different in every way.

"If you hadn't come when you did, he would have succeeded," she whispered.

He kissed her temple, sending another shock wave throughout her body. *If only the others weren't here.*

"Don't worry, Gen, I won't let anyone hurt you again."

Then she noticed them-the small, hair-like projections coming out of his face. What was that? She reached up and touched his cheek, running her fingers across the fuzzy mass. It tickled. He put his hands over hers and closed his eyes.

"Is that hair coming out of your skin?" she asked.

He gazed at her, his eyebrows raised.

His full lips were so close, so tempting. He tightened his jaw, as he took her hand away and held it against his wildly beating heart.

"It's called stubble. I've decided to grow a beard..."

She raised both eyebrows as she studied him.

"...so I won't look like Dram anymore," he whispered, pulling his injured leg up into a bent position.

She turned slightly and opened his pant leg to access his injury.

"Whoa!" He stopped her.

"I must finish your healing," she said, their gazes locked. His jaw tensed again. He let go of her hand. She reached inside to his injured calf, the skin blistered and open from the laser wound. How could he stand the pain? Most men would cry out. As she touched him to pray, she noticed he had hair on his legs as well, and the fact his calves were well-formed and muscular. Briefly she thought of exploring more of his body, but she remembered she was in a cargo hold with young girls and other I.S.P. agents with whom she had worked.

She closed her eyes and tried to concentrate on his healing rather than her pleasure. While she prayed, she felt the wound close up. She continued praying until his skin and the deeper muscles were whole again.

"What did you just do?" someone asked as she finished closing Adam's flight suit.

Curious, she turned to look at him. The man had been propped up against the opposite wall. Sitting next to him was Shey. The two of them were surrounded by Shey's students.

"She healed my leg," Adam explained.

She turned to look at Adam and he winked at her. Happiness overwhelmed her and a smile escaped her lips. She pulled up on the sheet she wore before she faced the man beside Shey.

"You can do that?" Berto asked.

She nodded but Adam answered once more.

"She has many talents, Berto," he said, then reached for her arm and pulled her toward him. She sat next to him on the floor and he put his arm around her.

"Unlike you," Shey tapped Berto in the chest with the back of her hand. Berto and Shey glared at each other before Berto spoke.

"How do you know what I can do? I have gifts," Berto said to her. "Besides, you don't even know me."

"I know enough about you to own an opinion," Shey crossed her arms.

"Yeah, right," Berto mumbled and turned away from Shey.

Adam tightened his grip around Genesis and kissed the top of her head. She reached behind him and hugged his waist. If only they were alone, she would show him how grateful she really was.

Captain Luc greeted them at the Interplanetary Space Patrol

Headquarters on **Tarsius.** Genesis and the girls had all been taken to the eating hall before the long trip home to **Chroma**. He didn't know if he would get to see Genesis again until he returned from his assignment to capture Dram. He wanted to get her alone and show her how much he had missed her.

If she had touched him once more on the transporter, he would have lost all self control. Her touch burned him with a desire for her he had never felt for another woman. He hadn't realized how much he'd wanted to find her and the impact it would make on him when he did.

Maybe he should have told her he heard her voice calling him while they were separated. Thoughts and anger seared him at the sight of Z on top of her. He'd reacted swiftly. Thank God Z hadn't succeeded. He'd never felt that kind of anger before coupled with a strange and overwhelming sense or need to protect her. All these new feelings and emotions confused and bombarded him. And today, he'd killed a man.

It was hard to get Genesis out of his head, but he had to. The new mission required more concentration on his part. After all this was where he and Dram would face off. Only one of them would survive.

The Captain had been speaking to Berto about finding Dram's men on **Plexus**, when he realized how much of the conversation he had spent thinking of Genesis.

"What are your plans for us, Captain," Berto asked, crossing his arms.

"We're sending two crews out to **Meta**. One will gain access to Dram's compound and search through his processing unit to uncover any information about the pick ups and deliveries he's made over the past twenty-five *anos*, and then look for Dram. The others will serve as back up, ready for any attacks he may make. You two will be on the first ship," Luc said.

"When do we leave, sir?" Berto asked.

Captain Luc gestured he was getting a message through his headset.

"They're preparing the ships now. You leave in thirty minutes. Agent Tamlin, escort these men to the docking station." The Captain left the room.

"We've got some time, if you two want to grab a bite to eat before we leave," Tamlin said.

He glanced at Berto, thoughts of Genesis flooding his mind. "I know what *I* want to do," he said, raising an eyebrow.

Berto looked back at him, his eyebrows furrowed. "Let's get something to eat before we leave. I'm starving!" Berto left.

"Eat?" He liked his idea better, but Genesis wasn't here.

Tamlin escorted them to the eating hall, where the girls were lined up to leave. He visually scanned the area, but didn't see Genesis anywhere.

Berto nudged him. "You've rescued her, now you're done," he said, pulling his attention back to their conversation.

Disappointment crept in. "No, I'm not," he began. "I promised to help her find her father."

"Well, that will have to wait. Our job now is to locate Dram before he tries to escape, remember?" Berto said.

"I've got to tell her we're departing," he said, turning to leave.

Berto grabbed his arm. "The Captain will inform her, I'm sure. She works for them, remember?"

He nodded. That didn't change the fact he wanted to see her again. There was so much he wanted to say to her. Hell, there was a lot he wanted to *do* to her. He would have to wait. After he and Berto captured Dram then he would *show* her how much he'd missed her, that is, before he helped her find Malek.

About twenty minutes later, Tamlin escorted Berto and him to the docking station, where **The Guardian** sat. Inside, he was greeted by Lieutenant Howell, Danner, and Spencer. Tamlin joined them inside as the ramp closed.

"Didn't we just do this scene a few hours ago?" He looked at each man.

"We worked so well together the last time, Captain Luc decided to make us a team once more," Howell said.

The six of them sat or stood at the table in the galley, while Howell explained the mission.

"How many are left at the compound, Berto?" Howell asked.

"Only three, Dram, Ramen, and the cook."

"This shouldn't take too long, then," Howell said.

"Dram won't be waiting for us at the compound."

"What do you mean?" Howell asked.

"When Dram realized the others weren't coming back, he'd head to the mountains."

Genesis triangulated their position and set the course for **Meta**, after giving **The Guardian** her verbal orders. It felt good to be in control again. She had actually missed flying. She looked over at Agent Tremol, who sat next to her in the Nav-room.

He was stunningly handsome with his black hair and dark brown eyes, but he held no appeal for her. It was the Earth man she longed to be near. After this mission, she would take the time to let the man know how she felt. Adam was just beyond the Nav-room, yet she couldn't speak to him. Did he realize she was part of this assignment?

She hadn't had a chance to talk to him privately before she was whisked off in another direction for her briefing. She wanted to tell him she had heard his voice in her head, especially when Z forced himself on her. She had never been more relieved to hear him utter the words, *"I'm here,"* in her mind. Did he know he had the gift of telepathy?

For her to communicate, she had to wear the translator, touching it while speaking out loud. But he had the ability to communicate through his mind only.

"I bet you're glad this mission is coming to an end," Tremol said.

She had waited ten long anos to capture Dram, and now it was finally happening.

"I hope he gives up the location of my father and my people," she said. To be reunited with her mother was her dream. She had so much to ask Herda about men, especially the Earth man. The thought of him being on **The Guardian** excited her, but she controlled her emotions.

During the trip to **Meta**, Tremol spoke to her many times, but her thoughts kept drifting back to Adam.

Following the orders of the I.S.P. was her job now. She had plenty to think about. Hc had affected her, that was for sure. Adam had her thinking of things she had never thought of before. And she wanted to see him again.

"I heard if we capture Dram, we will take his base as a training camp for the I.S.P.," Tremol said.

"Really?" Her thoughts were on Adam as she remembered herself sitting on his lap, touching his prickly face. When he took her hand away and held it against his chest, his heart pounded. Did she affect him that way? Her heart beat harder thinking of him. Did he think about her now?

She adjusted some levers on the control panel and smiled at the fact Adam had rescued her. He didn't have to. And he had seen her naked. No other man had looked at her that way except Z, and he wasn't a man. Z was the dirt that clung to her boots.

Licking her dry lips, she remembered the sweetness of Adam's kiss before he'd draped the sheet around her and carried her to safety. She smiled at the thought.

"After the mission, will you continue on with the I.S.P.?" Tremol asked.

"When this is over, I will search for my father and the people from my village," she said.

If Adam kept his promise to help her find Malek, though, she was obligated to return him to Earth. Then *he* would be gone. That was the bargain. Besides, Adam was not of her race and the edict made it illegal to take a mate of another race. That was the whole basis for each race colonizing their own planet—to keep the races pure.

Why was she thinking of a mate? She'd never entertained the thought before. She had been consumed with finding Dram. On **Atria**, she would be considered too old, since most took mates in their eighteenth ano. Had the men of her village waited? If they went beyond the borders to seek mates, there would be no village. Life as she knew it was not the same. Her thoughts drifted back to Adam. He certainly had some qualities she admired.

She put thoughts of him aside as **Meta** came in to view. Soon, she needed to land **The Guardian** and search for Dram. She had to find him and end the terror he'd created. It may take anos before everyone was found and returned to their planets. Would they want to go back since so much time had lapsed? Could she find Herda or Malek? Would Adam remember his promise?

She landed **The Guardian** on the platform for space cruisers, the same spot Dram had used. She remained inside the Nav-room, waiting for her orders.

The door hissed open. Lieutenant Howell stepped into the room and she turned to face him.

"The first search party has left to check out the compound. I want to be sure no one is here before we move on," he said.

"And what will you have me do?" she asked.

"Take a small group to the far side of the mountains, scan for life forms, and search for Dram and his two men. Tremol, you take a party and begin your search on the other side of the mountain."

"And after we find them?" Genesis asked.

"They're all wanted dead or alive. It's your call."

CHAPTER TEN

The search of the compound turned up nothing but evidence that Dram had left. All food was gone. Bedding and pillows were missing from three rooms, as well as emergency items.

Berto worked on the processing unit, when Adam entered the command room with the I.S.P. agents who helped in the search. Agent Tremol stood near Berto.

"I think you were right about them going to the mountains, Berto," he began. "Camping supplies are missing." Curious, he moved behind Berto, looking over his head. "Any luck with the processor?"

"No. Ramen has cleared the unit. I'm trying to recall the information now but I haven't been able to get it back." Berto studied the monitor while talking.

"Smart move," he said.

Tremol glared at him.

"He's covering his tracks," he shrugged. "Did Ramen keep any paper files on business dealings?"

"I've already thought of that," Tremol replied, arms crossed over his chest. "I searched the entire room while you were gone. There's nothing here."

"Who worked with Dram the longest, Berto?" He paced. There had to be something or someone who might have the information Berto was seeking.

"Well, since Timna's death, Ramen has been here the longest. Then there's Ethan and Merka. But Genesis killed Merka, remember?" Berto said, punching keys.

"What?" His mouth dropped open in surprise.

Berto glanced at him. "You mean you didn't know?"

He shook his head slowly. Why had Genesis killed someone? He recalled his first meeting with her. He ran his hand around the back of his neck. How could he forget? But she had thought he was Dram.

Merka had threatened her in some way. She *was* angry at the time. Until he'd met her, he had never known anyone with that much hate for another human being.

He remembered how he'd felt when Z forced himself on Genesis, and he understood.

"When did she kill him?" he managed to ask in his confusion.

Berto glanced at him, his hands poised over the keypad. "The day before we left **Meta**. Ramen told me." Berto said.

"Isn't Ethan one of the men you apprehended when you raided Z's compound?" Tremol asked the agent who stood next to him.

"Yes. We found five of Dram's men held in a room on the first level. Let me talk to Lieutenant Howell and see if he can get some information for us." The agent left.

Berto worked on the processing unit a few more minutes. "I'm afraid this is hopeless," he said, slamming his fists beside the keypad.

Tremol pressed his hand against the headset as he received information. "We're moving out, everyone to **The Guardian**."

Outside the ship, on the landing pad, Lieutenant Howell explained how they would split into two groups to search the mountains. Each group would approach on opposite sides from behind the range of mountains and make their way to the front. The transporter offered protection from the front, while **The Guardian** would cover the back.

"You three will be dropped off on the right side," Howell pointed to Tremol and the two other agents who had helped him. "And you start on the left." He glanced at him and Berto. He looked over his shoulder to see who the third man was, and did a double take. Genesis stood behind him. His pulse quickened. He was glad to see her.

"Gen, when did *you* get here?" he whispered.

Howell cleared his throat. "Tremol, you're in charge of your group. Genesis heads up the other. I will feed you information as I get it since we'll be scanning the mountains. Any questions?"

"What are you doing here, Gen?" He was concerned now at her part in the mission.

"I'm following orders, same as you," she folded her arms under her breasts.

"This is too dangerous, Gen. You shouldn't be here." He couldn't bear to see her get hurt.

Her eyes narrowed as she glanced up at him.

"Have you forgotten how we met, Earth man? I've been searching for Dram for ten long anos and I'm not about to give up now, not when he's this close." She tensed her jaw and glared at him.

He understood her reasoning but his concern for her safety overwhelmed him. He ran a hand through his hair.

"...our communications headquarters will be here," Howell finished answering someone's question.

"Sir?" He spoke up. "Don't you think this mission is too dangerous to involve Genesis?" He glanced at her, his heart beating fast. She glared at him, her brows narrowed. He looked at Howell. He couldn't watch her get hurt, especially after what she had been through with Z. And the way Dram had treated her, well he didn't want to think about that. The thought of losing her frightened him.

"I have every confidence in her abilities," Howell said. "After all, she's been working for the ISP for ten anos and is trained and experienced."

She saluted Howell, turned and glared once more at him.

"Thank you, sir," she said.

"Pick up your headsets and climbing gear at the transporter," Howell directed them before leaving.

"You'll slow us down, Gen. I really don't think you should go," he said to her, still worried about her safety.

"*I'm* leading this crew, and if you want to be part of it, you'll follow *my* instructions." She turned and walked away.

He wasn't used to taking orders. He had been his own boss since he left the orphanage and became Jeremy's foreman on the cabin building crew. He glanced at Berto who had his arms crossed. Berto smiled while shaking his head.

"What are you looking at?" he demanded, embarrassed at Gen's rebuke.

"You two. Now I *know* why she's so special."

"What are you talking about?" he asked, confused.

Berto leaned closer and whispered, "You're in love with her."

"Me? I barely know her," he said, shocked. His brows furrowed. Besides, he'd never loved anyone before and he didn't know how that felt. He shook his head and walked to the line where all the I.S.P. agents and Genesis stood ready to pick up their survival gear.

After Berto picked up his equipment, the three of them climbed aboard **The Guardian**. The other team was already inside. He sat between Genesis and Berto on the floor, anxiety washing over him.

Agent Tremol leaned close to Genesis and spoke loud enough for him to hear. "Good luck with your mission." He offered her his hand, and she shook it.

"Thanks," she said.

Soon after, Tremol's team was dropped off on a rocky cliff jutting out from the mountain.

Genesis's group disembarked at the base of the barren outcropping. He swore silently. While he'd lived in the Smoky Mountains all his life, he had never needed climbing equipment since the Smokies had plenty of vegetation and trees to use. This place was treeless. Not even moss grew on the rocks. When he hiked, he had always felt refreshed after being in the coolness of the mountains. Here, it was hot and dry.

"We're a team now, so don't you two give me any trouble." Berto looked at him and Genesis.

"I wouldn't think of it." He scowled.

Genesis put her hands on her hips. They were nice, too, he remembered.

Genesis raised an eyebrow. "*I'm* leading this crew."

"Well, you may be in charge, Genesis, but I know this mountain. Or would you like to lead the way?" He gestured with his arm to let her pass. The two of them locked gazes. She narrowed her eyes at him.

"I call the shots, Berto. You can be our guide. Lead us up," she motioned with her hand.

"Fair enough," he conceded. "But I'd like to make a suggestion."

"And that is?"

"I suggest *you* follow me and Adam goes behind you."

"And why is that?" she asked, her hands on her hips.

"If something happens to you, I can pull you up. But it'll take two of us to help Adam up."

"What if *you* have problems?" he asked Berto, curious.

Berto glared at him. "*I* know how to climb," he touched his chest with his thumb.

"I hope so," he mumbled, but he had a bad feeling about it.

"We have plenty of handholds or crevices at this point," Berto began, "but once we get past that spot up there," he pointed, "we'll have to use our gear. You two follow my lead."

Berto reached up into a crevice and pulled himself up, stepping onto an outcropping of rocks as he went. Genesis gave him some distance before she followed. He did the same for her. As long as the mountain didn't give him any trouble, he would be fine. The hard part was concentrating on what he had to do when he had a fabulous view of Gen's perfect bottom above him, all day, without underwear. He shook his head. She wore her white flight suit, like all the other I.S.P. agents, while he and Berto still had the blue suits on.

Genesis moved steadily up the mountain behind Berto. Maybe he'd misjudged her. Why hadn't she made herself known on **The Guardian**? She must have piloted the ship. He'd had no time to talk to her alone, though, with so many people around. Besides, it wasn't so much that he wanted to talk but to kiss her. She certainly reciprocated at Z's place but he didn't have enough time to explore her mouth fully.

Berto reached a small plateau and pulled out his harness and ropes. Genesis came up from behind and got out her gear as well. Berto showed her how to use the equipment, while he caught up to them. After receiving his instructions and tying his ropes together, he followed the other two up. The sun set lower in the sky. Each time he pushed off with his foot, reaching for a handhold became more strenuous and they were farther apart.

As they moved up the mountain, rocks fell on his head. Puzzled, he looked up to see a loose place in the bedrock as Gen strained to push off. He cautiously placed his hand in the rocky crevice. It seemed solid. Sighing, he braced himself to make the next climb. He gingerly put his foot in the indention and pushed off when the bottom gave way. He lost his balance scrambling to clutch the remaining hold.

"Gen!" he cried out. His adrenaline kicked in as the rocky knob wasn't large enough for both hands. The thought of falling to his death flashed through his mind. His feet dangled as he tried to gain purchase in another spot with his foot. He couldn't die now, he had to fight Dram. His arm strained to support his weight.

Genesis had glanced down to see how Adam was doing, when she heard him call her name. He struggled to hang on to the cliff with one hand.

"Berto! A little help here," she called out as she flattened herself on the ledge. She dropped her coil of rope over the side, her heart pounding. She couldn't let him fall. *Hold on, Adam!* She spoke to him in her mind. "Grab the rope," she shouted.

"Wait!" Berto said as he moved back down the mountain and toward the ledge.

"You'll go over, Genesis!" Berto braced himself against the rock behind him and grabbed her around the waist. She lowered her rope once more, holding on with both hands. She prepared herself for his weight. She couldn't let him fall, not after he had rescued her from Z. She was determined to hold him to his promise to help her find Malek. Besides, she owed him for her blunder of mistaking him for Dram. It was her fault he was even here.

Adam swung and grabbed the dangling rope, pulling up enough to reach the next handhold with his foot and other hand. Then he let go. Breathing hard, he hoisted himself onto the ledge. She noticed his arms shaking from the strain. She and Berto grabbed him and pulled him to safety.

"Thanks!" he muttered, breathlessly, as he bent over, resting his hands on his knees.

Relieved, she put her hand on his back. Thank God he was safe. Her heart still pounded from the exertion and the thought of losing him. "Are you all right?" She wanted to hold him.

He gazed into her eyes. Her eyebrows raised, she was hopeful he was fine. He nodded.

"My arms are a little weak," he straightened and stretched. He shook his arms out at his side.

"We'll take a break to let you recuperate, Adam," Berto took a sip of his water.

She offered Adam some of her supply. "What happened?"

He took the container and drank deeply and wiped his mouth on his sleeve. "A foothold gave way when I stepped on it. I lost my balance." He handed her the water, their fingers touching briefly. He caught her shoulder in his hand and squeezed gently. His touch sent a warm shiver through her. "I owe you one," he said, their gazes locked.

Her heart pounded. All she wanted to do was step into his arms and hold him. She was grateful he was alive.

"I'm glad you're safe," she managed to say. Lowering her gaze, she exhaled heavily, relief washing over her. She hadn't realized she'd held her breath. Adam thought he *owed* her? How could he think that way?

She'd taken him from the only home he had ever known and gotten him into this mess. Adam had rescued her from being raped by Z. How would she repay him for that except to return him safely to Earth?

"Here," Berto handed her and Adam some carabiners. "After that incident, we hook up together." He showed them how to tie their rope onto the object. He glanced at the darkening sky.

"Looks like a storm brewing. We should make it to shelter before it hits. There's a small alcove above on the left. There's room enough for the three of us to bed down." Berto said.

"You're right. We'll stop for the night soon." She hoped the storm was nothing like the one she'd experienced on Earth.

"We should be able to reach the top by late morning," Berto added.

Berto began his climb up the mountain. Using his anchor gun, he secured the metal ring into the rock. Each had to be loaded one at a time. She was relieved that they were all connected by ropes through their harnesses. Berto continued to use some handholds for climbing, as well as an occasional anchor. He shot another into the rock surface. Worry crept up her spine when she noticed he didn't thread the ropes in the anchors. They were high enough now someone would certainly die if he fell. And after almost losing Adam, she couldn't bear to experience it again. Berto reached the next ledge and she called out to him.

"Berto, we should run rope in the anchors."

He looked down at her. "Why?"

"In case we have an accident," she suggested.

"I think it's a good idea, too, Berto," Adam added, joining her on the ledge.

Berto shook his head. Reluctantly, he tied another rope to a carabiner and threaded it in the nearest anchor. He attached it to his harness. Adam helped her with her gear.

"Listen, Gen," Adam began, "I'm sorry if I made you mad earlier. I was just worried for your safety, especially after your experience with Z." His sad gaze made it difficult to stay angry with him. She'd almost lost him.

He held her by her arms now, and leaned close, kissing her forehead. "Can you forgive me?"

The warmth of that kiss seeped through her pores and flooded her body. She melted on the spot, he was so tender. She reached her arms around his waist. "Yes, I--"

"Hey! What's keeping you two?" Berto shouted from above.

She looked up. "I'm coming!" Disappointment took away her brief moment of happiness.

Adam helped her up to the anchor, and attached the excess rope to his harness. She continued her climb up and noticed the sinister clouds grew thicker and darker. Lightning bolts flared in the distance, and the air around them began to cool quickly.

Adam stood on the ledge and watched Gen's taut gluteus muscles push her weight up the mountain, when an image of someone falling flashed through his mind. His heart skipped a beat when he realized the person wore a blue flight suit. Oh, God. He swallowed hard, and followed Genesis, giving her plenty of room before coming up behind her.

The premonition meant one thing and he tried to block that thought from his mind. He'd noticed Berto wasn't threading his anchors as he went farther up the cliff.

While he waited for Genesis to continue, he took his extra rope and looped it through the anchor, giving his hand a rest from holding up his weight.

The wind picked up and a few loose stones fell beside him. He glanced up and saw another person dressed in a blue flight suit high above. Berto looked up, too.

"Traitor!" The man shouted. He fired a weapon. The laser hit some rocks over Berto's head, loosening them. He flattened himself against the mountain after seeing Genesis do the same but he was protected by the outcropping above him. Lightning flashed in the distance, as another shot was fired, closer this time.

Adrenalin rushed through him as the debris fell from the mountain. He pulled his anchor gun out of the leg holster and shot an anchor into the rock near the first metal ring. *Be prepared.* He remembered his Boy Scout motto as he slipped a loop of his rope through the second ring and secured it with a knot.

He heard Genesis scream and looked up. Berto was hit. He tumbled down the mountain below him but Berto's harness caught him, yanking Genesis off her perch. He swung hard, reaching his arms out and caught Genesis as she fell. Her quick thinking with the ropes had kept her from the same fate as Berto.

He pulled her close, burying his face in her hair. His heart thudded loudly, while he held her tight against him. The fear of losing her again paralyzed him. Her trembling arms tightened around his neck as he kissed her forehead. She clung to him, digging her fingers into his flesh. A sudden gust of wind blew them toward the rocks.

"Gen, I've got to check on Berto," he said, pulling away to look at her. Their gazes locked as she caught her lower lip between her teeth.

"I'm going to set you on the ledge," he loosened the carabiner attaching them together, after connecting himself to Berto. Slowly, he lowered her to the cliff below him. Then using one of the anchors for leverage, he pulled Berto up to her.

"I want you to heal him, Gen. Can you do that for me?" He was concerned for his friend but Genesis could help Berto more than he could since she had healing powers.

She nodded and knelt beside Berto in prayer.

Another shot went off above his head. He slipped his anchor gun out of its holster and reloaded it. He was too tangled in ropes to deal with his bow and arrows. He pulled the trigger and hoped it shot far enough. The anchor lodged itself in the man's chest. He stumbled backward and fell off the mountain, letting out a howl as he tumbled to his death. But something dropped as he bounced off the ledge where Gen and Berto were. He leaned back to see a small cloud of dust surround the man below and realized it was Ramen.

He loosened his own rope from the metal ring, and joined Genesis and Berto on the cliff. He knelt down and offered a prayer for Berto and for Genesis and watched her work on his friend. Helplessness crept in and he wasn't used to that.

Genesis felt along the back of Berto's head. "He has a large bruise here," she said. Closing her eyes, she prayed over him, cradling his skull in her hands. She gestured for him to hold Berto's head and moved to where he was burned on the shoulder from the laser weapon. She shut her eyes and spoke in soft, Micca Nulee, touching his wound. She continued for a long time while he looked on. He offered up prayers of his own but Berto never moved. When she stopped, she glanced up at him.

"Will he be all right?" he asked her, worry pulling at his gut.

"He is breathing now. The wound on his shoulder is healed."

"But?"

"His brain injury will take more time," she said.

"What do you want me to do, Gen?" he asked, concerned. He had to remember she was in charge.

She looked up at the darkening sky. "We must get him to safety." Thunder boomed in the distance, as the wind picked up on the mountainside.

"Stay with him, Gen. I'll go find that shelter and come back for you." He hated to leave her alone but time was running out.

She nodded and continued to pray as he left.

Taking Gen's anchor gun, he made his way up, planting the metal rings as he went. He found the shelter Berto had spoken of, not far from where Berto had been shot. He found a few trees and bushes at this elevation. He attached rope to the rings in a pulley fashion so he could bring Berto up easily. He set about finding a couple of large branches to use as a litter. He returned to Genesis but Berto was still unconscious.

Worried, he and Genesis hurriedly worked together making the carrier from their bedding and placed Berto on the makeshift support. He let Genesis go up first, following the path he'd made earlier. When she reached the shelter, she tossed the ropes he'd rigged back down to him. He attached them to the litter and pulled Berto up to Genesis a little at a time.

Anxiety washed over him as the storm drew closer while he moved Berto up the mountain. Too much wind, or moving too fast could cause Berto to tumble out of the litter. He waited for Gen's signal that she had Berto safely in the shelter. Finally, she tossed the rope back to him.

Thunder boomed a little closer now as the sky darkened and the cool wind gusted stronger. The air surrounding him was warm. This can't be good, he thought, as he climbed up to the shelter. He hated storms. His parents had died in an accident on a stormy night. A few drops hit him as he pulled himself onto the ledge then the sky opened up, sending torrents of rain and flashes of lightning all around the tiny alcove.

Genesis had Berto in the back of the alcove. Hmmm, he had forgotten how strong she was. He went to check on Berto. "How is he?" he asked, running a hand through his wet hair.

"Berto will be fine but he'll sleep for a long time."

"Are you sure? I mean, how can you tell?" Worry nagged him.

"He is healing as he sleeps. I can do nothing except pray and let him rest."

He had to do something. He cracked his knuckles one at a time. Berto was hurt and *he* had been the one with more experience in climbing. "I could find us some food," he suggested.

"We have some in our packs. It's storming, and I will not lose, I mean, let you go out there. You're soaked," she said, as she took the backpacks from him and lead him to the front of the shelter. "Besides, we have to get those wet clothes off you," she reached out to his shoulders. His pulse quickened at her touch.

He locked gazes with her and felt her fingers slide between the magnetic strips, releasing the fabric. Her hands remained on his bare shoulders, warming him instantly, while the top half of his flight suit fell to his hips. She let one hand drop to his chest, playing with the curly hairs and caressing his flesh. His heart beat faster and he swallowed. His skin burned from her touch. Her gaze went down his body and returned to his face. His groin reacted instantly and he pulled her close.

"I remember when I was wet and cold and you covered me in a blanket," she said, moving her other hand back to his shoulder. "But what warmed me the most," her hand circled his neck, "was when you," she pressed her body against his, gazing at his mouth, "kissed me." Her moist lips touched his in a soft, sweet caress before he crushed her to him. He devoured her, taking over the kiss, exploring her mouth hungrily. He tasted her sweetness and passion welled up inside him. She ran her hands through his hair, sending a fire throughout his body.

Desire for her overwhelmed him, burned him. He wanted her, every inch of her, but his friend lay injured a few feet away.

Her earthy, floral scent teased his senses as he deepened the kiss. He released her braid from its fastener and ran his fingers through her silky mane, combing it loose, while he kept her pressed against his swollen shaft.

She reached for his face, caressing his stubbled cheeks with her thumbs as she pulled him to her. She stiffened.

"What is it?" He gazed into wide eyes.

"Berto's awake," she whispered.

"Berto?" He moved toward his friend. "Hey, man, are you all right?" He studied Berto. His eyes were glassy, unseeing. Berto's mouth opened and closed, though he didn't speak. The gesture reminded him of a small baby awakening for food. He'd seen a co-worker's newborn do the same thing. He pulled out Berto's water container and lifted his head to give him a drink.

Genesis joined him, checking Berto's injuries. She prayed over Berto, while he leaned against the rock wall behind them, quietly watching her. She amazed him with her tenderness and skill.

Suddenly, a beeping sounded from the headset in Berto's pack. He dug through it until he found the device.

"Hello? Adam Davis here," he said.

"Where the hell have you been?" It was Lieutenant Howell.

"We, uhm, there's been an accident. Berto's hurt." He moved a little farther away to give Genesis more privacy in her healing prayers.

"How? When? Why didn't you contact me sooner?"

"It was too cumbersome to wear the headsets while climbing, so we left them in the backpacks. A couple of hours ago, Ramen shot at us and hit Berto. He fell, but we got Berto to safety. Genesis is healing him now."

"Where's Ramen?" Howell asked.

"You'll find his body at the drop off point."

"Let me talk to Genesis."

"I can't now, sir, she's in the middle of praying, and I don't want to disturb her," he whispered. "I'll have her contact you when she's finished."

"See that you do," Howell clicked off.

He leaned his head against the wall. Howell sounded pissed, but he wouldn't interrupt Genesis now, not while Berto's healing was at stake.

He returned to Genesis and continued watching her pray over Berto. She was in a trance, softly mumbling in her native language. Berto had just started trusting him, too. Why did this have to happen? Several long minutes later, Genesis sat still and stopped praying. She opened her eyes and turned to face him.

"Will he be all right?" he asked, worried.

She sat back on her heels. "We'll know by morning."

"Howell wants to talk to you." He handed her the headset as she sat next to him against the wall. He waited as Genesis returned Howell's call. Afterward, she gave him the device.

"Howell wants us to call about Berto's status in the morning." She gazed into his eyes. "We'll continue up the mountain. The other group captured the cook. All that's left is Dram."

Yes. He and Dram would fight. He should tell her about the premonition, but why worry her? He didn't know the outcome. Could he kill the man who claimed to be his father? If not for Dram, he never would have met Genesis.

He put the headset away and pulled out the rest of the bedding from the backpacks while Genesis started a small fire. When he finished fixing a pallet for the two of them, he sat down and took off his boots. He moved to sit beside her.

"What's for dinner?" he asked, looking through the backpacks, his hunger growing stronger by the minute.

"We have nutrition bars, fruit packs, and drinks, besides our water," she slipped her boots off.

He raised his eyebrows at her then looked at the wrapped bar. He took the object and tore the package open. Hesitating, he tasted the thick, chewy mass.

"Hmmm, not bad," he said, savoring the salty/sweet taste.

He finished the bar and a fruit pack before topping them off with H20.

Genesis shook her head. "It's better than space food at any rate."

"You got that right," he said, leaning back on his bedding.

Genesis put her container away and sat next to him on the pallet.

He put his arm around her shoulder and pulled her close. He had a stronger connection with her now. The warmth of the fire had knocked the chill from the storm. The lightning had lessened but the rain was steady.

"On **Atria**, when someone takes a mate, it is for life," Genesis said, breaking the silence.

He looked down at her as a twinge of panic flashed through him. "Mate? Is that like a wife?"

"What is wife?"

"Uh, you know, husband and wife, a couple?"

"A coupling? Yes, mates are a coupling," she said.

He caressed her arm as he squeezed her close. He could get used to someone like Gen as a... what? He had never entertained thoughts of marriage, although having a woman to love and settle down with had been in the back of his mind the past year.

Genesis wrapped her arms around his waist, turning toward him. He brushed her silky strands of hair away from her face and hooked his finger under her chin, brushing his lips against hers.

He pulled her backward, as he lay down beside her. His desire for her growing, he wrapped his arm around her and draped his thigh over her hip, cuddling with her. She wound her arm under his, caressing his back.

He fought the urge to take her with Berto so close. Along with the possibility he could awaken at any time.

Genesis felt comfortable in his arms. What had she done to him? He fought something much bigger than he was able to handle.

He brushed his lips against hers once more. "Good night," he whispered as he closed his eyes. Emotions flooded his senses. She meant a lot to him. Somehow he connected with her but he didn't understand how, it just seemed right.

Genesis had heard his mind speaking to her when he had kissed her. She felt his heart pounding. He wanted her but he fought his emotions. She struggled with hers as well. No man had affected her like this. His kiss caused so many sensations at once. The touch of his lips against hers began the first assault. Wave after wave of emotions followed as his tongue moved in her mouth, his hands on her body. The heavy aching between her legs made her want him.

Yet, if she gave herself to him willingly, she would commit to him as his mate. Did Earthens have the same meaning to their intimate actions? If he chose to go back to Earth, she couldn't take another. She had already given her heart to the Earth man. The thought she might lose him, saddened her.

As the storm outside intensified, Adam's arms tightened around her. She wanted to stay like this, safe in his presence. He had caressed her back as they lay together. Never had she seen such strength in a man as she witnessed in him today. She kissed his chest and fell asleep in his embrace.

Hours later, Adam bolted upright, awakened by the silence and a strange feeling that someone watched him. He looked down at Gen, her back to him. He covered her with the blanket. Then sitting up, his knees bent, he ran his hands through his hair, trying to recall the recent events. He snapped his attention to his left. Berto was on his side, facing him, a large grin on his face and his brown eyes wide open.

"Did I miss something?" Berto asked.

He jumped. "You scared the hell out of me, Berto! I was afraid you wouldn't make it. Welcome back," he walked over to Berto's pallet, squatted and reached out to him.

"What exactly happened?" Berto shook his hand and propped himself up on an elbow.

"Ramen shot you in your shoulder and you fell, banging your head on the way down. How are you feeling?" he asked in a whisper, while re-fastening his flight suit.

"Oh, I remember that part. I'm feeling pretty good, actually, just a little hungry. I want to know what happened between you two," he pointed at him and Genesis.

"Uh, not much with you here, thanks for asking." His face heated at the comment.

Berto smiled. "It looks more like something *did* happen if you ask me. You're changing colors again."

"Well, no one asked you." He turned to find Genesis awake.

Berto sat up. "Have we got anything to eat?" He looked around the area. "And where are we?"

He pulled packets of food out of his backpack.

"Here you go. Dig in," he tossed the packets to Berto, along with a container of water. He was glad his friend was back to normal. "We're in the shelter you told us about."

"How did you get me up here?" Berto scratched his head.

"Very clever invention Adam made," Genesis said, joining the conversation. "Are you better?"

"Yes, much better. Did you heal me?" Berto motioned to the gaping hole in his flight suit.

She nodded as she moved toward him. "You had a large bump on the back of your head yesterday, but it's gone now."

Berto reached his hand to the spot. "Thanks, Genesis."

"It took longer to heal the knot on your noggin," he teased, "because you're so hard-headed."

"And you aren't?" Berto snapped back.

Genesis interrupted their banter. "It's almost daylight. We need to get going." She handed him a nutrition bar.

He'd taken the bar and his water when he noticed Gen had none left.

"Here, have some of mine. I remember drinking a lot of your water yesterday."

Genesis drank from the offered container and filled Berto in on what Howell had said. He packed up the gear.

Afterward, Gen placed her call to Howell.

"Oh, I found this on the ledge when you fell yesterday. I thought maybe you dropped it." Genesis handed a small disk to Berto out of her pack.

"Oh. My. God."

CHAPTER ELEVEN

"What's the matter?" Genesis asked.

"I hope this is what I was looking for on Ramen's processor," Berto said, taking the disk from her. "He must have saved everything on it and cleared the unit."

"Gen," Adam placed a hand on her shoulder. "The disk could have the information to locate your father, mother, and the whole village," he said.

Ten long anos had passed since she had seen her friends and family, although her father, Malek, had only been captured three weeks earlier.

What would she say to her mother, Herda? She wasn't sure how she would react when they met again.

"As soon as we capture Dram, we'll start looking for Malek," Adam said. He gave her shoulder a little squeeze as he studied her face.

And after they found Malek, she would return Adam to Earth. Her heart sank at the thought she might never see him again. He had a life there, he had said so himself. *What could be worse than being abducted from your planet?* She turned away as her eyes filled with tears.

"We need to get moving," she choked out the words. She let Berto lead the way, but forced him to wear his harness and use the ropes. She couldn't afford to lose him again. The other team had made their way to the top last night. She had been hunting Dram much longer than *they* had, and *she* wanted to be the one to find him first.

Adam climbed up the mountain below her. She glanced down at him to make sure of his safety. He had saved both of them. She owed him more than her life. He glanced up and smiled. She looked away. Something about his smile warmed her. And he had kept her very warm last night. She almost wished Berto hadn't been there, so she could have experienced

Adam more fully.

Her body ached for him as well as her heart. She missed him already.

When she had climbed awhile, the sweat poured down her face and burned around her mouth. She tried to wipe away the moisture, but that made things worse. The skin under her chin and neck was raised like a rash. It became unbearable with the heat and perspiration mixing together, so she stopped. She couldn't remember reacting to anything before. What had happened?

She reached for her container. Empty. She called a break to get water from one of the others. She joined Berto on his ledge and waited for Adam to catch up.

Berto took a swig of his water and handed her the container. She poured some in her cupped hand and wiped her face.

"You were supposed to drink that," Berto said.

"My skin burns," she looked up at him.

He stared at her, his eyes wide, as Adam joined them on the ledge. Berto scratched his head.

"I've never seen anything like it before," Berto stepped away so Adam could see. She handed Berto his water container.

"What's the matter?" Adam asked. He took her chin in his fingers and angled her face to look at her. "Oh, Gen! I'm so sorry," he said, hugging her. His warmth radiated throughout her body as she wrapped her arms around his waist.

She was comforted in his embrace. Her heart raced when he kissed the top of her head.

"I got a little carried away last night." He pulled back slightly. "You have whisker burn from my beard." He rubbed his chin and gazed down at her. "I wish I had some lotion or vitamin E oil to put on you. Are you hurting?"

"My face burns." *Like fire*, but she had enjoyed the kisses which caused the burning.

He bent his head and gently kissed her mouth. "Can you forgive me?"

"Will this rash go away?" she asked, touching her chin and remembering how he'd forgiven her for almost killing him.

He nodded.

"Yes, I forgive you."

He hugged her once more but this time she felt a stirring in his flight suit, much like the one last night as they clung to each other.

"Ahhhemmm," Berto cleared his throat. "The headset is beeping. I believe it's for you," he handed it to her, his eyebrow raised.

Lieutenant Howell's voice came on. "The other group is heading your way, but they haven't encountered Dram."

"We should be at the top in a couple of hours," she said into the headset.

"Proceed with caution. Don't forget he is heavily armed and dangerous," Howell warned before clicking off.

As if he had to remind her! She drank from Adam's water container and offered a prayer of healing for herself. Then she continued up the mountain, behind Berto. They'd made it to the top much later than Berto anticipated with all the delays and stops.

Exhausted and tired, she glanced around the area. A few small trees and bushes were scattered along the trail.

"We'll need to find shelter for the night. Are there any caves or bluffs on this side, Berto?" she asked.

"Yes, up ahead. We can make it before dark."

"I'm going to hunt us up some food," Adam said, looking at both of them.

"There's nothing to eat around here," Berto replied.

"I've seen **eeya** and I plan on having one for dinner. You two find a place to camp, and I'll supply the meal."

"Yeah, right," Berto whispered to her. "We'll be eating nutrition bars, wait and see."

But she didn't doubt Adam. He had kept his word so far. Her mouth watered for the tasty meal.

Berto located the sheltered bluff. She set the packs down and searched for kindling to start a fire. But if she wanted to eat real food, she would need a lot of wood.

By the time she and Berto had gathered enough, stacked it and started the fire, Adam showed up with an **eeya** across his shoulders.

"How did you find one?" Berto asked.

"I've been hunting since I was eight. You've got to be able to read animal signs and know how to track them." He set the carcass down and pulled out his knife, ready to cut off the **eeya's** head.

"No, wait!" Genesis called out. They both stared at her.

"There's an easier way to skin the beast," she said.

"What do you know about skinning animals?" Adam asked, his eyebrows raised.

"My people eat this way on **Atria.** We use the hides for clothing. We waste nothing. Let me show you," she said as she knelt beside him. He handed her his Swiss Army knife.

She took the tool and cut the **eeya** from the neck to the center of his belly, while Adam helped hold the legs upright. Then, carefully, but swiftly, she cut the skin from the muscle, leaving the body intact. She cut off his head and hooves, leaving the carcass on the hide. She hadn't prepared a meal in several anos, but Herda's teachings all came back to her.

Adam sat back on his heels and ran his hand through his hair, watching Genesis work. He had never seen anyone like her before. She showed him how to rig a spit to put the animal on it for cooking. Amazed at her knowledge of the skinning of animals, he stared at her. Girls he knew never wanted to *talk* about hunting. He had learned over the years the subject was taboo with most women. Yet, she did all this as he and Berto watched. He helped her gut the animal, cleaning out the cavity. And not having a source of water nearby, she kept everything on the skin.

He and Berto supplied the manpower to raise the carcass so Genesis could insert the stick.

"You've got to love a woman who can handle a knife like that," he said.

Berto half smiled and shook his head, as the two of them hoisted the **eeya** on the forks of the spit. Berto took his place first at turning the carcass, while Genesis called Howell. He dug a hole and buried the guts.

"Wasteful," she said, when he returned.

"No offense, Gen, but guts don't appeal to me. How about you, Berto?"

"Uh, no."

He sat down beside Genesis, near the fire, while Berto continued to turn the spit.

"This reminds me of Boy Scouts," he began.

"What's that?" Genesis asked.

He glanced at both of them, remembering they were from other planets. "The Boy Scouts are organized groups of boys who learn about the outdoors, camping, and Indian lore taught by adult male leaders. It's a character-building type of experience."

Berto cocked his head. "*You* are truly a character, that's for sure."

"You, too, bud," he continued. "As I was saying, after my dad died, I went on campouts with our group leader from the Children's Home and my troop."

"Dad?" Genesis asked.

"My dad was my father, like Malek is to you. Dad is the name I called him. What do you call yours?" He glanced at her and Berto.

"I call him Malek."

"I thought Dram was your father," Berto said.

"Well, he may be my biological father, but Joshua Davis was more a dad to me than Dram will ever be. In fact, Dram doesn't even understand the meaning of the word. But you didn't answer my question, Berto. What do you call your father?"

"I don't have one."

He cocked his head and waited for Berto's response.

"I was seven when he left. I don't remember him much at all." Berto gazed at the fire.

He glanced over at Genesis, and caught her gaze, sadness in her eyes.

He began again. "This reminds me of when we cooked our food. We sat around the fire and told stories."

"What kind?" Genesis asked, turning toward him. Her eyes, wide and brows raised.

"Stories about ghosts or the crazy things we did at other campouts."

"Is that a spirit being?" Berto asked, glancing at him.

"Yes. Do either of you know any stories?" He looked at Berto then Genesis.

"The old ones told stories at night after we ate," Genesis looked between him and Berto.

"Tell us your favorite," Berto said.

"Mine is the story of the fight for a mate," she began. "Once a young man spent his early days lifting stones..."

Gen's soft, sweet voice was alluring as he listened. Of course, he thought of himself in the main role and Gen as the beautiful maiden princess.

"...the first fight would determine the best hunter, so each went off on their own to find baroo," Gen continued.

Intrigued with the story, he listened intently. He had hunted with his father until his death. Afterward, one of the scout leaders would take him, along with his own son every year, even though he lived at the Children's Home. The Boy Scouts was the one constant thing he'd had in his life growing up.

He sat forward to hear the ending, his elbows resting on his knees.

"On the third day, came another challenge. This time, a wrestling match in the village center," Genesis continued.

His mouth went dry at the word, wrestler. He had spent three seasons wrestling in high school.

"The winner would throw the defeated one into a pit to die. Life, love and glory hung on the outcome," Gen leaned forward, touching her heart with both hands.

She couldn't know he had wrestled before, but did she recognize the move he'd made against her when she tried to kill him? He swallowed hard.

"...Instead, the man chose the maiden for his mate in exchange for living peacefully among the villagers." Finishing her story, she sat dreamily gazing at the fire.

He thought about the sufficiency of his own strength. Could he overcome the premonition he had to face? As for the maiden, he glanced at Gen's profile--she would make a good wife. *Where did that come from?* He cleared his throat.

"What about you, Berto? Got any stories from your early years?" He asked.

"No." Berto stood up. "I didn't have a childhood." He stomped off down the trail leading them to this bluff.

He moved to take Berto's place turning the spit.

"He has a lot of pain inside from a past hurt," Genesis said.

"Is there a way to heal that kind of pain?" he asked.

"Yes, but I'm not the one who can do it."

"Who can?"

"Someone who can replace his bad memories with good ones," she said.

He remembered how the storm the night before had made him anxious when it had started. He always had nightmares about his parents' death during thunderstorms. But last night, he realized, he only had memories of Genesis and feelings he hadn't allowed himself to experience for anyone.

Dram sat in the shadows of the cliffs, watching. He understood Adam wanting to escape, but Berto? He ran a hand through his hair as he watched Berto from behind some boulders. He would settle the score. No one got away with blowing up his space cruiser without paying dearly for it.

"Traitor!" he called out to Berto, revealing himself.

Berto swung around at the sound of his voice. He had been standing there, kicking the dirt with one foot, while cursing, but he was alone.

Berto crossed his arms. "Yes and how many people have you turned against over the years, Dram?"

"I only exact vengeance on traitors." He raised the laser rifle and pointed it at Berto's chest."

"Yes, like you did with Derk because he quit working for you?"

"I killed him for different reasons."

"That's not what I heard."

"The truth is, Berto, Derk murdered the only woman I ever loved," he choked out the words as the pain rushed back into his heart. He hadn't spoken to anyone about it in years.

Berto's eyes widened.

"That's right. I made the mistake of taking him into my confidence and teaching him my business. I met Derk on the salvage ship that rescued me from Earth."

"Earth?"

"Yes. Anyway, Derk and I had an argument over money, mine. He tried to extort money from me, but I caught him." The thought of Derk brought up the overwhelming anger he had felt when he'd learned the truth. "Derk had returned to Earth, found Emma, and followed her and her mate one night during a thunderstorm, in one of my cruisers. He hit them from behind causing the fatal accident that left Adam an orphan. Derk tried to rub that in my face for not paying him off. But, instead, I got my vengeance." He tightened his grip on the weapon, his anger consuming him.

"Yeah, you cut his heart out," Berto gestured. "Why?"

"He cut my heart out the day he killed Emma," Dram struck his chest in her memory. The heartache and pain had returned. "He deserved no less."

"So, what are your plans for me?" Berto asked nervously.

"Well, I could kill you, but then, I know where your sister is." *Let's see how Berto likes the idea of me going after his loved one.*

"You leave Mara out of this, Dram," he shouted. "She has nothing to do with you and me. She's innocent." Berto clenched his fists. He had never seen Berto angry before. Berto had always obeyed without argument. *Something had changed.*

"I'll find some use for her, Berto, don't worry." Berto raised his arm as Dram pulled the trigger on his laser rifle, but it didn't fire. He took his eyes off Berto for a second to slap his weapon, but that's all Berto needed to tackle him to the ground.

He dropped the laser. He and Berto struggled in the dirt, with Berto getting in a few punches. He found the weapon and sprang to his feet. Berto lunged for him a second time but he managed to get off a shot on stun mode before Berto dropped in his tracks.

Well, he'll be out of the way for awhile anyway. His final battle would play out soon enough, and he'd be ready.

Genesis moved close to Adam and sat down.

"Berto has been gone a long time," she said.

"Yes, he has," he scratched his beard and glanced at Genesis. "How about taking over for me, Gen, while I go search for him?"

She put her hand on his back and warmth emanated throughout his body from her touch.

"Be careful, Adam," she said, gazing deeply into his eyes.

He leaned over and kissed her soft, warm lips. "I will." Rising, he hesitated at the worried look on her face. Cupping her chin in his hand, he gave her a half grin. "I'll be fine." He grabbed his bow and quiver of arrows and headed in Berto's direction.

He couldn't let Gen know what would happen. When he had gotten clear of the fire glow, darkness engulfed him. He had forgotten to grab a light stick. Fixing an arrow to his bow, he moved slowly, listening for sounds as his eyes adjusted to the dark.

"Berto?" he called out. No response. He prayed Berto hadn't fallen off the mountain. In the faint light from **Plexus'** second moon, he caught a glimpse of footprints, a lot of them, like there had been a scuffle.

"Berto?" he called out again. Still no response. Then it hit him. Genesis was alone and vulnerable.

"Genesis," he whispered. His heart pounded as he ran back to the camp. His heart skipped a beat when he found Dram holding her around the waist, his laser rifle pointed at her head.

"My plan would have worked, Adam, but you turned out to be

smarter than I thought."

"Yeah, I take after my mother." Anger rose up inside him. "Give it up Dram. There are I.S.P. agents all over this mountain." He raised his bow, the arrow still nocked.

"Oh, you mean the two I killed?"

Adrenaline flowed through him as he thought about his friend, his pulse raced.

"Where's Berto?"

"He's sleeping off the effects of being stunned. I would have killed him, too, but my laser jammed."

Maybe it was still jammed. He moved closer, taking careful aim. He didn't want to hit Genesis.

Dram fired a shot at his feet. "I know what you thought. The weapon is fine now," Dram pointed it back at Gen's head.

"You won't get away alive."

"One of us will, but which one?"

His premonition flashed through his mind once more. How had *he* learned about it? But Dram was right. He *didn't* know the outcome. He had only seen himself wrestling with Dram and Dram pointing the weapon at him.

"Let her go, Dram. This is between you and me."

"You could have taken over the business for me, Adam." Dram jerked Genesis away from the fire. The two of them were out in the open now.

He took a step closer. "Yeah, so I would take the fall when they captured me? No thanks." He aimed at Dram's exposed shoulder.

"Far enough." Dram shot another beam near his feet. Dram pulled Genesis in front of him.

Genesis glanced at him and spoke with her mind. He heard her voice as if she'd spoken out loud.

"Take Dram when I release myself."

In one swift movement, Genesis grabbed Dram's arm, sharply pulling it down, while bending forward. Dram flipped over her back, dropping his weapon when he landed on the ground.

Before Dram recovered, he dropped his bow and arrow and jumped him.

Dram rolled him, but he managed to flip Dram on his back. He struggled with him to get control of his arms. Dram was pretty strong for a man in his forties.

"I should have killed you both when I had the chance," Dram said.

"Why didn't you?" he asked as he pinned Dram to the ground.

"Because I thought my plan would work. If I had known you were this smart, I wouldn't have bothered to return for you." Dram managed to break loose, but he recovered and regained the advantage over him, taking him down once more.

Genesis quickly retrieved her headset and called Lieutenant Howell.

"Dram is here! He's fighting Adam. Dram said he killed two agents, and Berto's missing."

"Where are you?" Howell asked.

"I'm near a bluff on the side facing the compound. I can see the compound from here. I'll make a signal so you can find us," she dropped the headset and grabbed a blanket out of one of the packs. The confrontation between the two men could lead to the death of one of them. She wanted Adam to live, but it was out of her hands now.

She took the material and covered the meat and the fire then pulled it away quickly. She did this several times until smoke rose from her efforts. She continued until **The Guardian** came toward them. The spotlights on the Guardian's belly lit up the area. She tossed the blanket aside and grabbed her laser weapon.

The struggle between the two men had moved closer to the fire. Even with the spotlight, she couldn't tell them apart.

She watched as her stomach churned.

"Genesis!" A familiar voice cried out from behind her. She turned. Tremol ran toward her. She met him half way.

"What happened? I thought you were dead," she said.

"I went to relieve myself, and when I returned, I found the other two. I spoke to Howell on the headset and he told me what had happened. I saw your signal."

"Come with me," she said as she led him to where the two men struggled.

"Which one is Dram?" he whispered to her.

"I can't tell from this distance." She tensed her jaw.

Suddenly, one of them was on top of the other, strangling the one on the bottom. He struggled with the forearms of the man on top, unable to remove the man's hands from his throat. She bit her bottom lip watching, helpless to do anything.

Her heart pounded. The man on the ground drew his legs up to his chest, wedging his feet against the other man's torso. She nudged the knob on the laser into stun mode, as the man forced his legs out hard, shoving the top man across the ground.

She raised her weapon as the top man reached for the nearby rifle, the one she forgot to retrieve earlier. She fired at him the same instant he shot his weapon. Both men fell over. Genesis dropped her laser and ran to Adam, while Tremol checked on Dram. Her heart raced as she lifted his head. Please, God, let him be all right.

She cradled Adam's head in her lap. She checked him for a pulse. His heart beat rapidly against her fingertips. Thank God! She slid his hair out of his closed eyes and lowered her mouth to his. Brushing his warm, sweet lips, she gently cupped his whiskered chin in her hand. Before she pulled away, he reached behind her and lowered her into another kiss.

"I heard you, Gen."

She sat up and gazed at him, cocking her head. "Now?" She combed his hair with her fingers.

"No, when you flipped Dram."

"I've always been able to hear *you*," she said.

"Really?"

She nodded. "How long have you had *your* gift?"

"Only since I've known you. But you're the only one I can hear." He caressed her cheek with his fingers.

She leaned into his touch and glanced down when she noticed the gaping hole in his pants leg.

"You've been shot!" She moved to his other side and ripped open the material, revealing a large gash in his thigh. She placed her hand around the wound and began to pray, closing her eyes.

Gen's hands were warm and soothing, even though his leg hurt like hell. It hurt worse than the last time he had been shot, and in the same leg, too. He closed his eyes and tried to focus on her touch and prayers, and not the pain. He rested his hand across his forehead.

His premonitions were finally over. Now he could help her find Malek. Afterward, when he was back on Earth, life would be normal, quiet, peaceful, and lonely. Maybe then he would finally meet the right woman and settle down and raise a family.

His eyes opened wide. What was he thinking? He avoided those thoughts like the plague.

Genesis stopped praying and glanced at him. Had she heard him?

"Uh, Gen, how did you know who to shoot?" He propped himself up on his elbows to glance at her.

"I couldn't tell from a distance, but I seem to recall you tried the same move on me once, when *I* choked you," she smiled and moved a little closer.

"Yeah," he grinned back at the memory. He reached for her chin, letting his fingers gently stroke her face. "I seem to remember being at a bigger disadvantage with you, though."

She cocked her head.

"No hands, remember?"

She nodded and rolled her eyes.

"Genesis, what if *you* get hurt?"

She studied him, her brows furrowed.

"Can you heal yourself?"

"Other than the face burn, it's never happened to me before. But I received my healing shortly after I prayed that day."

"We're taking Dram to the base station," Tremol interrupted.

He glanced at Tremol, who stood near Dram's body.

"Is he dead?"

Genesis shook her head. "I used the laser on stun. I want him to suffer for his crimes, for all those he hurt in the past and to remember how he treated them."

"What happens now?" he asked, glancing at Genesis and Tremol.

"After he goes before the Council's governing board, he will serve out his life on **Plumaris**, which is a penal colony," Tremol explained.

"Is it like doing hard labor or something?" he asked.

"Exactly," Genesis said. She glanced up at the dark sky. He followed her gaze. **The Guardian** came in to land near the fire. He pulled both his knees up. His leg was normal again and the pain, completely gone.

"Help me find Berto, Gen," he said, standing.

She ran to the packs and retrieved a light stick, returning to him.

When he and Genesis got to the other side of the bluff, he heard a groaning noise not far from where he'd searched earlier.

"Berto, is that you?" he called out, as Genesis adjusted the light stick.

"There!" She pointed.

Berto was on his hands and knees, crawling toward him. He ran to Berto.

"Man, are you all right?" He helped Berto to his feet, too wobbly to stand on his own. He threw an arm around Berto's back and propped Berto's arm across his shoulder. Genesis was on Berto's other side. She let Berto rest his elbow on her shoulder.

"This would be much easier for me if you were a foot taller," Berto said to Genesis.

"Want me to drop you right here?" she asked.

"No thanks. I think I'll manage," he grunted.

"So, what happened?" he asked Berto.

"Dram surprised me. We struggled for the laser and he shot me," Berto explained.

"He killed two of the agents from the other team. His weapon jammed and that's why he stunned you," he said.

"He had planned to kill you, too," Genesis added.

"Yes, I know," Berto said.

"Need some help?" Tremol called out to them.

"Yes, Berto's complaining I'm too short," Genesis told him.

"Feeling the stun effects?" Tremol asked as he took Gen's place.

Berto nodded. "Adam," Berto began, "Derk killed your parents."

"What?" His breath caught in his throat.

"He hit them with his cruiser, causing their accident. That's why Dram killed Derk," Berto explained.

The police had never found out who'd done it. "Why did Derk kill my parents?" He asked.

"Extortion. He knew your mother meant everything to Dram."

He closed his eyes and inhaled deeply. The knowledge didn't erase the memory or the pain, but it brought closure to his parents' death.

Genesis went back to camp and retrieved the backpacks and gear. He and Tremol helped Berto into **The Guardian**. Dram, locked inside the cell, was unconscious, his hands and feet bound. Now *he* would know how it felt.

Genesis joined him, Berto, Tremol, and another agent at the galley table.

"Hey! Save some eeya for me," Genesis ordered as she dropped the backpacks.

Tremol and the other agent bit into the meat they had cooked earlier.

"I couldn't leave this food there. It looked too good to pass up," Tremol said.

"I'm glad you didn't." He ripped a piece of meat off and handed some to Genesis and Berto. He bit into the last piece himself. "Mmmm, this is good." The taste reminded him of lamb and venison mixed, but with added fat, and more tender.

Tremol took some eeya into the crew piloting **The Guardian**, as the other agent closed up the ramp. Within minutes, the ship hovered over the landing pad at Dram's former base.

The place was crawling with I.S.P. agents. More than he remembered seeing when he had first arrived.

Later, he met Lieutenant Howell and Genesis, while Berto retrieved information off the disk. Berto used Ramen's processing unit in the command room. Everything came back online, even the software.

It took awhile, but Berto was able to print out a list of the sales and trading points Dram had made with all the abducted people.

"There," Genesis pointed at the screen.

Berto's hand froze over the keypad. He leaned closer to view the dates.

"He was ambushed on **Tarsius** three weeks ago," she said.

Berto did a file search and found a ship departing with newly purchased slaves on the date in question.

"The ship went to **Ti**, a moon of **Tarsius**," Berto swung around in his seat.

"What is it, Berto?" Howell asked.

"Haven't you heard the stories about **Ti**?"

"**Ti** is a moon, rich in minerals."

"Yes and massive life forms. No one has been able to colonize the place either," Berto said.

"What do you mean?" Genesis asked.

"Two colonies were attacked while there. The last one was transmitting a message for help when their signal went dead."

CHAPTER TWELVE

" **W**hat kind of massive life forms?" Adam asked Berto. Gen's eyes widened as she glanced at him then Berto.

"Human?" She wrung her hands. He moved beside her.

"Hardly," Berto answered. "They were described as creatures before the transmissions broke up."

"How do you *know* this?" Lieutenant Howell glared at him.

"Because I was on a ship that picked up the broadcasts," Berto said.

"Well, did you offer them any assistance?" Howell asked.

"No. We were returning from **Chroma** with the girls."

"That's on the other side of the system." Howell's mouth dropped open. "How did you pick up those transmissions?"

"Dram's ships have always had good communications," Berto lowered his gaze. "You know, to avoid getting caught." His sorrowful glance moved back to Howell as he tensed his jaw. "I was a systems tech for Dram. I installed communications devices, worked on hyper drives, fusion engines, generators, or whatever needed fixing," Berto said.

Howell took the headset and called the I.S.P. headquarters.

He put his arm around Genesis. He wanted to comfort her as she stood nervously waiting for Howell's information.

"I want anything you can find out about **Ti** as well as any transmissions made from there right away," Howell clicked off. He glanced at him, Berto, and Genesis. "Bunk down for the evening, while I assemble a crew to assist you in finding Malek," Howell said.

"What about Dram and the cook?" he asked, wondering if he would ever see his biological father again. He pulled Genesis closer and her arm moved around his waist.

"They will be processed at headquarters and brought to the

governing board for sentencing then taken to **Plumaris,** where the two will serve out their punishments."

"Come with me," Danner said to him and Genesis. "I'll show you to your quarters."

"We've stayed here before, remember?" He followed Danner while giving Gen's hand a squeeze. He noticed how quiet she had gotten after Berto had informed them about the creatures.

"Yes, we've managed to locate the laundry facilities and removed all the linens from the beds. We've only got a few rooms prepared," Danner explained.

Berto remained behind, working on deciphering more of the codes Ramen had set up.

"You have your choice of these two," Danner pointed between his old room and the one beside it.

"I guess I'll take this one." He shrugged. "I'm used to it."

"The other is yours, Genesis," Danner said. "You'll find clean unicrins in the clothing cabinets."

Genesis pulled away from his grip and approached her door, her gaze lowered like she was deep in thought.

"Hey, what about meals, I'm still a little hungry," he said, rubbing his belly for emphasis. The **eeya** he had gotten wasn't enough to satisfy his hunger and morning was a long way off.

"Tremol found Dram's food supply on the mountain. He and Eakin went to retrieve it. The others are unloading the cargo transporter now."

"Great. I think I'll clean up."

His door hissed open. A hot shower would feel good right now. He noticed Genesis standing at her entrance, still deep in thought. "You okay, Gen?" He asked.

She nodded and went inside. Something bothered her. Maybe she needed to be alone with her thoughts.

He found the clean unicrin where Danner said it would be, and pulled the blue material out of the drawer. It was like the dirty one he had on. He sat on the bed and yanked off his boots and thought of Genesis. She must be worried about Malek, especially after what Berto had told them. Once they found Malek, though, he'd say goodbye to her. His gut tightened. He didn't know if he liked the idea of leaving. When she took him back to Earth, that's exactly what would happen. And, for the first time, he considered staying.

He had a job on Earth, building cabins. How could he make a living with Gen? She still had to find her mother and the women of her village. He would do the same if it were his mother.

He dropped his dirty flight suit on the floor, and turned the shower on. A knock on the outer door stopped him and he shut off the water.

He grabbed a towel and wrapped it around his hips as he hurried to the entrance. He pressed the button on the panel with one hand, while clutching the towel in the other.

"Gen!" He hadn't expected her. His pulse quickened. Still dressed in her white unicrin, she was barefoot, a surprised expression on her face.

"I, uh, wanted to give you something," she said, stepping into the room. The door hissed closed. She stood close as she slowly and deliberately let her gaze roam his body, a wicked smile growing on her face. The towel barely covered his thighs. His heart rate increased as well as his desire.

"I was just about to jump in the shower." He motioned with his thumb. She stepped even closer, so he cocked his head. Did she want to tell him something?

Her tongue flicked out across her lips, wetting them. He swallowed and heat rushed through his body. She always had that effect on him, and it was hard to ignore.

"I wanted to give you this," she said, reaching up to put one of her medallions around his neck. He lowered his head slightly, their faces close. Her warm breath brushed against his whiskered cheek. He inhaled her woodsy scent. Genesis held the object in her palm and glanced up at him through those thick, black lashes of hers.

"If you wrap your fingers around it, my medallion will light up. See?"

He watched the one she wore as it glowed. "Wow." She stirred up feelings in him again. Her blue-black hair was pulled back into a single braid. He wanted to take it loose and run his fingers through the silky strands like he had once before.

"The medallion lets me know if you're in danger."

"Is that why you wear it?" he asked, as he put his hand over the medallion in her palm, instantly feeling electricity emanate and shoot through his body.

"One belonged to my mother, Herda. The other one is mine.

Malek is too far away to detect anything, or alert me if he is in danger."

"Why are you giving this to me, Gen?" he asked, confused.

"In case we are separated, I will know your location. Or you'll know if I am in danger."

He didn't want to think about her being in trouble. She glanced up at him again through those long lashes. Her eyes were moist as she lightly pressed her hand on his chest, releasing the medallion at the same time. Her touch seared him, making him hard, as another wave of heat traveled throughout his body.

He dipped his head down and brushed his lips against hers. She reached her arms around his neck. He crushed her to his chest as he lifted her off the floor, his towel forgotten at his feet. She opened her mouth to allow him to explore her sweetness as his tongue mingled with hers. She, in turn, explored him, tasting and licking. At first it was sweet then demanding. He groaned as she wrapped her legs around his hips. His erection hardened more.

He wanted this woman, to savor her completely and to explore every inch of her body. He walked to the bed with her still attached to his hips, without breaking the kiss. He knelt down and lowered her to the coverlet.

If he gave in to his desires, he would experience the pain of loneliness once he returned to Earth. Was it worth the pain to start something with Gen he knew he couldn't finish? *Hell yes.* Her kiss intoxicated him.

She seemed to enjoy his touch as well. Finally breaking the kiss, he removed both medallions and her translator. He straddled her as he released the magnetic strips of her flight suit, peeling it off her body and tossing it on the floor. If she didn't want this, wouldn't she say so?

Genesis propped herself up on her elbows, allowing Adam to unbraid her hair. She gazed at him, swallowing her nervousness. He was hard, with tiny dark blond curls surrounding his swollen flesh. A trail of blond curls moved up to his belly in a thin line and stopped. The hairs sprinkled across his chest and forearms were lighter than below. She wanted to touch his arms and run her hands gently up and down, to feel the texture of his hairs. He smiled at her as he ran his fingers through her long tresses. God, she loved his smile. It melted her heart every time he glanced at her like that. His gentle touch soothed her and inflamed her senses. He massaged her head and she rose up to his chest, caressing and kissing him.

Gently, he lowered her to the bed and kissed her sweetly on the lips. He licked her skin and slowly trailed kisses to the flesh beneath her ear. The whiskers tickled and teased her tender skin. She shivered at his touch. He moved down to her throat and over to the other ear. She gasped and made strange noises she didn't recognize as her own.

She reached around him, caressing his back. His touch felt so good. She moved one hand up, massaging his head. He groaned against her ear.

"Does that hurt?" She stopped her fingers in his hair.

"No. Don't stop." He licked her throat and blew against her moist skin, gently brushing his whiskers over the sensitive area. The tingling was more intense, as the noises she made with her throat came out frequently. Did that really come from her?

She liked this and wanted more. The aching between her legs grew as he moved down to her breasts. She didn't think it could get any better but she was wrong.

He cupped one breast, and teased her nipple, pulling and twisting. He rolled his tongue over the other nipple, gently suckling her. Sensations ran down to her core. She'd never thought a man's touch could be so good, so right.

She cradled his head in her hands and ran her fingers through the fine, blond hair. He looked up at her with his pale, blue eyes and smiled. He switched breasts. *Oh, yes.* The aching in her core made her spread her legs for him. His swollen, warm flesh rested against her thigh. Waves of heat seared her.

All these new sensations were aroused by his mere touch. She wanted to please him the way he pleasured her now but she couldn't reach him.

He moved down her belly, kissing, licking, and blowing against her moist skin. He sent more sensations surging through her, making her dizzy. Her breath was ragged now and her body moved against her will, reacting to his hands and his lips. The closer he moved to her center, blowing across an area he had licked, the more difficulty she had breathing. She glanced up at his wicked smile from between her legs. What had he planned now?

"Oh!" She jumped as his tongue penetrated her. He tasted her and sent shock waves throughout her core. Each touch made her quiver, something she had never experienced before. Her heart raced, as she reached her hand to her head. Alien sounds escaped her. The pleasure he gave was unbearable. She wanted him inside her now.

The aching and throbbing need grew as he moved his kisses up her belly again. His fingers began tormenting her where his tongue left off.

He smiled now as he watched her. Her body quivered and burned. The intensity of pleasure was great.

"Adam!" she gasped. He stopped his fingers and moved toward her face, slowly kissing, licking and tasting her on the way. When he reached her lips, he placed a gentle, sweet kiss then a long, probing one. His knee wedged between her legs. Her thighs felt heavy now. She couldn't move them.

As he deepened the kiss, he entered her body in one fluid movement, causing a searing pain in her core. She gasped.

"Are you all right, Gen?" he asked, pulling back. His eyebrows rose as he gazed at her.

"Yes," she breathed, tears filled her eyes. The old ones had warned about this pain when she was a child, but she hadn't understood what it meant until now.

"This is your first time, isn't it?" he asked.

She nodded and chewed her bottom lip as the pain slowly subsided.

"Mine, too." He kissed her forehead and her temple, down to her mouth, while moving in a slow rhythm inside her.

"*I don't want to hurt you, Gen.*" She heard his thoughts.

She touched his whiskered cheek, letting her thumb brush against the hairs on his face. Her lids became heavy as he moved in a faster rhythm.

"*I want you, Adam,*" she told him in her mind.

"I need you, too, Gen, more than anything," he said aloud.

She wrapped her legs around his tight-muscled hips. He groaned as she squeezed, sending him deeper within her.

"Oh, oh, oh!" She moaned in her climax.

He moved faster and faster until he came, crying out her name in his release. "Gen!" His body stilled as his seed released inside her. He lowered himself and pressed his bare chest against her breasts. He embraced her and gave her a squeeze.

She wanted to stay like this, letting these new feelings wash over her. She held him tight.

Adam rolled on his back, drawing her on top. She sprawled across his body and drew circles on his flesh surrounding his nipples. She played with the blond hairs, while listening to the rhythm of his heartbeat. The sound lulled her to sleep.

She dreamed of him, the two of them, finding Malek. And in the dream Malek asked her about Adam. She told him Adam was the man who forgave her for almost killing him, the man who rescued her from Z, the man who saved her life on the mountain, and who fought Dram. The man she loved.

Her eyes opened. *Is this what love feels like?* She had to return him to Earth because he had a life there and she wasn't part of it. She blinked back the tears. She'd given him two gifts that no one had ever taken from her. Hers alone to give and she could never take them back, her heart and her body.

He'd claimed her when he'd called out her name in his release. But he didn't belong to her. A single teardrop fell, landing on his chest. A knot formed in her throat.

He mustn't see her like this. His chest muscles tightened as she reached for her medallion and translator.

"Gen, what's wrong?" He tried to sit up as she rolled off him.

"I must go," she choked out, while grabbing her unicrin off the floor. She draped the material around her torso and bolted for the door, hesitating briefly as she peered into the empty hall. She took off for her room.

Adam was up off the bed when he realized what she was doing.

He grabbed his towel and wrapped it around his hips as the door hissed open. No one was in the dimly lit hall so he ran to her room. Her door was locked, his heart pounded.

"Gen, let me in," he called out softly, but the entrance remained closed. He couldn't hear any sounds on the other side. What had he done? Why did she leave? When she didn't respond, he returned to his quarters.

Sitting on his bed, he raked his fingers through his hair. One minute they'd shared something special and the next, she'd bolted. He glanced down at his chest and saw the trail of a tear running down his body. *Oh, God. She was crying.* Did she regret this? He had wanted her and he'd thought she wanted him, too. Didn't she speak to his mind? Maybe she heard some things in his thoughts. He pounded his forehead with his fist. Think! What had he done to her?

When nothing came to mind, he stood up and walked to the cleansing compartment and finished his shower while trying to figure out why she'd cried.

He toweled off and dressed. It didn't matter anyway. After he and Genesis found Malek, he'd be back on Earth, building log cabins for Jeremy. And she would be the most perfect memory, burned in his heart. An ache that would never to go away. He slipped his boots on and tied them, as Dram's words came back to him. *'Maybe my life would have been different if she had come with me.' 'Then again, maybe I should have stayed on Earth.'*

'Why didn't you?' His own words echoed in his head.

'I didn't belong there.'

"And where do *I* belong?" he asked aloud. Part alien, part Earthen. He stood. "Where do I belong, Lord?" He raised his hands, pleading for an answer.

He headed for the kitchen. Maybe Berto was still around. He needed someone to talk to. The door hissed open.

Tremol and Danner put food into their version of a refrigerator.

"It took longer than they thought," Danner said. "Are you still hungry?"

"I could eat a bite," he replied.

Tremol put a miniature ham, about the size of a softball, into the rehydrator. Within minutes, Tremol pulled the cooked meat out of the unit.

"I didn't feel like fixing anything else since it's late," Tremol said.

"Well, I'm a little hungry, too," Danner replied.

"Got any bread?" he asked.

"Yes. We have a fresh loaf," Tremol handed one to him.

He searched the knife drawer and pulled out a sharp, serrated one, cutting off six slices of bread.

Berto walked in. "Got anything to eat around here?" he asked.

He cut two more pieces, then four, thick chunks of ham. He put them together in a sandwich, using a sauce the cook had used for salads. He couldn't find any mustard or mayonnaise.

"What in the worlds are you making?" Tremol asked.

He put each one on a separate plate and passed them out.

"On Earth, we call this a sandwich." He sat down and picked his up "It's a mini meal for when you're hungry, but not starving. It's really good with mustard and mayonnaise but you don't have that here." He took a bite while the others watched.

"Mmmm."

Berto reluctantly sat and ate his meal.

"Mmmm, not bad," he said, chewing. "Not bad at all."

Danner and Tremol each sat at the table. Danner poured four beverages.

"Hey, we ought to tell Howell that Adam volunteered to be our new cook," Danner said.

"No way, man. After we find Malek, I'm going home."

"Where's home?" Danner asked.

"Earth."

"Can you really do that?" Berto asked.

"What do you mean?" He cocked his head, while continuing to chew.

"How can you leave Genesis after all you two have been through?"

"We made a deal," he said, trying to convince himself.

"I've seen you two together, remember? There's something between you."

He set his sandwich down. Maybe Berto was right but he couldn't admit it, not even to himself.

—"Tell me you don't feel anything for her," Berto said.

He tried to swallow but the food wouldn't go past the lump in his throat. He stared at the sandwich. He could have gone back to Earth before the rescue from **Vestra Minor** but he had promised her he would help her find her father. Even Berto had tried to convince him to go but he couldn't. All he thought about was seeing her again, finding her unharmed and that was before they had been intimate.

He did care. He cared a lot. Too much, in fact. He'd done the one thing he had succeeded in *not* doing all these years, letting someone through the wall he had built around his heart. He didn't want to get hurt again by someone he loved. Did he love her? Is that why he couldn't get her out of his head? Did Berto see something he had not seen? He flushed his food down with his beverage.

Berto stared at him.

"Well, if you're going back to Earth, I plan on spending some time with her myself," Tremol announced.

His attention snapped to the man across from him. He cocked his head, his brows furrowed as he let this new information soak into his brain. Picturing Tremol kissing Genesis unnerved him. Tremol wasn't bad looking, either. His brown eyes and black hair, coupled with that uniform would make him attractive to women, he supposed. Probably thirty or close to it, Tremol had more experience with women than he had. Genesis had been his first, just as he had been hers.

"After all," Tremol said, "the women of Genesis' tribe normally take mates by eighteen. She is past her prime in that respect but she would make a good mate. She's headstrong with a lot of spunk. I like that about her."

"You're not her type," he stood and left the table, his sandwich half-eaten. He stormed out of the room, his hands fisted.

He hesitated outside Genesis' door but didn't knock. Maybe it was better this way, he thought, as he fingered the medallion. He headed to his room, when her door hissed opened and she ran to him.

"Gen," he called out, his heart beating harder at the sight of her.

"Are you hurt?" she asked.

"Uh, no, I..."

She glared at him and poked him in the chest. "This is not a fimjit...uh, plaything! Do not touch it unless you are in danger," she turned and walked back to her room, her hands clenched into fists at her sides.

He grabbed her arm and gently pulled her to him. Her medallion had been glowing and her blue flight suit was much too big on her. She was kind of cute in it, though. But her eyes were red from crying. His heart ached for her.

"Gen, why are you mad at me?" He lifted her chin with his index finger, running the pad of his thumb over her sweet lips.
He gazed into her dark brown eyes.

"I'm not mad."

"Why were you crying?"

She blinked a couple times before answering, her eyes still moist.

"After we find Malek, I will take you back to Earth. You can return to the life you had before we met. And I will have fulfilled my end of the bargain." She slowly pulled away from him and entered her room, the door hissed closed between them.

He stared at the cold metal entrance and mumbled, "What if I don't *want* the life I had before we met?"

CHAPTER THIRTEEN

The next morning, Genesis dressed early, her eyes puffy and her stomach in knots from the sleepless night. She headed to the galley to fix herself something to eat before the others got up. She didn't braid her hair. She rarely left it down but her energy for such things was gone. After eating, she went outside to be alone with her thoughts.

A large boulder sat beside the pond and she made her way to the spot. Climbing upon the giant rock, she dangled her feet near the water. The place had once been a prison to her but after yesterday, it held a special memory of the man she'd given her heart to. She wanted him but she wouldn't beg him to stay. They'd made a deal and she would keep her word. As next in line to chief of her tribe, she kept a vow when she made one.

Vaedra rose, illuminating the sky with beautiful shades of oranges, yellows, purples, and blues, as well as colors she couldn't name. The scene was remarkable. She had never been on a moon before, watching **Vaedra** come up over the horizon. She could see the planet, **Plexus**, in the distance. A long time ago, she had witnessed a **Vaedranrise** on **Atria.** She savored the moment.

Meta seemed smaller and much closer to **Plexus** than **Adara** was to **Atria.** Too bad Adam couldn't share this with her.

She glanced around the pond. The trees reminded her of White Mountain. The thought of her village and its women came to mind. Once found, would they be the same? Perhaps the men of **Atria** had gotten tired of waiting for their mates to return. Ten anos was a long time. Had Herda changed? Would she be able to recognize her own mother? She had been fourteen when Dram had captured Herda. She had changed a lot, no longer the scrawny child with shoulder length hair her mother had known.

The sound of a door hissing open startled her from her thoughts. Tremol walked around the corner of the building, carrying two mugs.

"I brought you something to drink, Genesis," he said, handing her one of the warm beverages.

"Thank you, Tremol. That's kind of you. How did you know I was out here?" She asked.

"I saw you through the viewing glass. A beautiful **Vaedranrise** like this should be shared, don't you think?" he asked.

"Yes, absolutely. We're lucky to be enjoying it," she said, wishing she shared it with Adam. She hadn't paid much attention to Tremol in the past, although she had known him for many anos.

"Howell has some items he wants us to take back to headquarters. He, Berto, and Eakin will remain here, waiting for the next cargo transport of supplies and trainees," he took a sip of his beverage.

"I'm glad they've found some use for this place," she said. Tremol was quite handsome with his black hair and brown eyes, but he didn't make her heart jump when she approached him, like her Earth man did.

"Yes. Berto will be a fine recruit, don't you think?"

She nodded and sipped her capu. "How did he get mixed up with Dram in the first place?"

"He'd have to tell you that story. He keeps to himself pretty much," Tremol said.

"Is everyone else awake now?" she asked. She only wanted to know about Adam.

"They're moving around."

She smiled as she sipped the warm capu and thought of how nice it would have been to wake up in Adam's arms this morning.

Tremol moved closer to her. "You didn't get much sleep last night, did you?" he asked.

"No," she hoped he wouldn't ask her any more questions. It was against her nature to lie but she didn't want him to know she had cried all night.

"I'd say sleep was difficult, thinking of reuniting with your father again after a long separation," he said.

She studied the concern on his face. It had been a little over three weeks and while she *did* miss Malek, she hadn't thought of him as much since Adam had entered her life.

She glanced down into the pond, holding her mug in one hand, and reflecting on her past actions. Since Adam had rescued her from Z, her thoughts had been filled with him. She gave little time to Malek or Herda. She should feel shame for that, but she didn't. Thinking about them had not helped in the past. Soon she would finally be able to find Malek. Together, she and Malek would find Herda and the village women. One good thing had come from knowing Adam and that was capturing Dram. Ten long agonizing anos of searching for him was over. She would have her family back. She finished her beverage and jumped down from the boulder.

"I need to prepare for the trip, Tremol. Thanks for the drink." She handed him the mug.

"Anytime, Genesis," he winked at her.

She froze momentarily. Had he done that before? She would have remembered if he had, wouldn't she? The only man to wink at her had been Adam. Her thoughts drifted back to the passion they had shared last night. Tremol remained outside after taking her cup. Before the communications door opened, she thought she had seen something move in the distance, behind some shrubbery.

She glanced back toward the boulder Tremol sat on. She found it strange that the pond reminded her of the place on Earth where she had met Adam. She walked through the eating hall and headed to her room. She had nothing to pack but her brushes, since all she owned was locked up on **The Guardian**. When her door opened, she heard the eating hall entrance open as well. To her left, Adam came toward her, drenched in sweat.

"What happened to you?" she asked, giving his fine body a slow gaze. Was he hurt?

"I went running this morning. I couldn't sleep last night." He reached for her arms and studied her face, sadness pained him. "Are you sure you're not mad at me?"

She gazed into his searching eyes, her breath caught in her throat. His mere touch awakened a desire for him as strong as the night before.

"I am not mad at you," she sighed.

"Didn't yesterday mean anything to you?" he asked, pulling her closer.

She swallowed. "Yes, it did." *More than he'd ever know.*

"Why did you run away and why are you ignoring me?"

"I'm not ignoring you," she lowered her gaze. She had to, or he would see the tears welling up in her eyes. She blinked them back. She wanted everything they'd shared the night before and more, like a future with the man she had almost killed, but he had to want it also.

"It sure as hell feels like it."

"I'm facing reality, Adam." She choked out the words.

"What do you mean?"

Her heart pounded, so she took a deep breath before she spoke. "Yesterday was beautiful. Wonderful. I gave you two things I've never given another man and I value them highly. But the reality is, you'll be returning to Earth soon, and I'll continue my search for Herda." She pulled away from him and hurried inside, leaving him standing in the hall.

Adam ran a hand through his sweat-soaked hair and sighed heavily. She had given up her virginity to him, something she valued highly. In return, he'd given her one night of pleasure to satisfy his lust.

"Reality bites," he said as he stormed off to the kitchen.

Eakin and Danner finished up a meal that Berto had prepared.

"What happened to you?" Eakin asked.

"I went for a run this morning," he said, tensing his jaw. The aroma of eggs cooking made him hungry.

"You ran without being told to?" Eakin asked.

He glanced at Eakin after his remark.

"I ran to exercise," he said. *And to think.* He had tried to figure out what he had done wrong to upset Genesis.

"You want some of these re-hydrated eggs?" Berto asked him.

"Uh, sure." He really wanted Genesis, the way she was yesterday—soft, warm, and naked in his arms. She had faced reality. He cherished the fantasy.

He took a bite of the eggs that Berto set before him on a plate. He remembered he had a job to do back on Earth. Jeremy counted on him to finish the cabin in Fox Meadow. Besides being his boss and best friend, Jeremy had promoted him to foreman. And when he didn't show up for work and Jeremy couldn't find him, would he have called the authorities? Would there have been a search for him? Would anyone miss him at all?

The image of Genesis and Tremol talking this morning as he came up over the ridge came to mind. He wished he had been able to share the awesome sunrise with her but Tremol had shown up. He'd moved in way too fast.

He choked down the eggs and thought of the sadness in Gen's eyes and the fact he was responsible for it.

"Hey, are you going to eat the food or play with it?" Berto asked.

He looked up at Berto. He hadn't really heard what Berto had said.

"Yeah, I'm finished." He pushed his plate toward Berto. Berto sat across the table, drawing his attention.

"You need to tell her how you feel," Berto said.

"I don't *know* how I feel," he stood up and stalked out of the room.

He continued outside and sat on some rocks by the pond. He thought of what his life would be like back on Earth, once he returned. People might think he was crazy if he mentioned any of this...until they saw Dram's ship.

He certainly couldn't tell them he was part alien. The scientists at NASA would study him like a bug under a microscope. *No thank you.* Or they wouldn't believe him at all and would lock him up in a loony bin. His life was forever changed. Could he work for Jeremy, building log cabins as if nothing had happened?

He tore a small branch off a nearby rhododendron plant and pulled off a leaf. Then he ripped the tender green piece into tiny shreds, thinking of how his life had been before the abduction.

He had gone to work every day, looking forward to the camaraderie of his crew. The physical part he enjoyed, taking large, hand-hewn timbers and creating a home that someone would live in, love in, and raise a family in.

But when he returned to his own cabin in the woods every

evening, it was always lonely. He threw the shredded leaves into the pond and pulled another from the stem. Slowly, he tore the new leaf as before. He had looked forward to the parties that Jeremy had on some weekends. Maybe because he had hoped to meet a woman he could love and who would love him back.

Berto came and stood by him at the pond. He looked up and threw the newly shredded leaves into the water.

"Remember the story Genesis told us by the fire?" Berto began.

"Yeah, what about it?" he asked glancing at Berto. How could he forget? All he thought about was him and Genesis while she recalled the story.

Berto squatted down beside the rocks. "Well, you remind me of the young man looking for a mate, and Tremol reminds me of the champion." Berto picked up the stem he had dropped.

"Hey, who said I was looking?" His brows furrowed. He *did* want someone in his life, but a mate sounded so...permanent.

Berto glanced down at the water. "Well, then, I guess there *is* no contest." He broke the stem in two.

"What are you talking about?"

"Tremol is planning to ask Genesis to be his mate since you're no longer interested in her." He snapped each half in two.

He stood, his hands tightened into fists. "Who says I'm not interested?"

Berto stood beside him, tossing the broken pieces in the water, glaring at him.

"You're talking about going back to Earth and she's planning on searching for her mother."

"So?"

"Well, if you're so interested in her, fight for her, damn it."

Adam's jaw tightened. A lump formed in his throat.

"You're giving up on her when you leave this place. If I had someone like her to love me, I wouldn't let her go."

"She doesn't... *love* me," he mumbled.

"Of course she does, you can tell by the way she looks at you,"

Berto insisted.

He stomped off toward the door to the compound. How could she love him? They barely knew each other.

"Adam," Berto called out.

He stopped in his tracks and turned to face Berto.

"Howell wants us to load **The Guardian**."

He rolled his eyes and waited for Berto to catch up.

The two of them walked to the ship and found Danner near a pile of boxes. He had a strange type of clipboard in his hands and tapped on it with a stylus.

"Hey, just in time to help me load this stuff," Danner pushed buttons on the black box. The ramp opened and he and Berto carried the boxes inside.

"I won't be going with you, Adam," Berto said, setting the box down in the center of the galley area.

"What do you mean?" he asked. He set his box beside the other.

"Howell wants me and Eakin to stay here. I'll be training with the new recruits when they arrive. I have to finish locating all the slaves Dram traded over the years," he said, walking down the ramp.

"You're not going to help us find Malek?" he asked, following behind Berto.

"No. Howell is bringing Ethan out here so we can locate the slaves from before I joined Dram's team." Berto bent down and lifted another box.

He stacked two smaller packages on top of each other and carried them, following Berto up the ramp.

"That means I won't see you again," he realized as he set his boxes down. His chest tightened.

"I guess not," Berto replied, setting his box beside the others.

"I'm going to miss you, Berto." He ran a hand through his hair. He hesitated, then offered a handshake to Berto. Berto took it enthusiastically.

"Yeah, same here," Berto said.

He pulled Berto into a hug. "You've been like a brother to me. I'll never forget you." How could he? He couldn't offer to write him. No way to send mail to another planet. Good-byes were so final. Most people expected to see friends again, but not in this case.

Genesis walked up to **The Guardian** with Howell and Tremol.

"Is everything ready to go?" Howell asked, looking at Danner, Berto and him.

"Yes, sir," Danner replied.

Howell looked at him. "Tremol's in charge of the mission, with Genesis as second in command. You and Danner are crew," he said. "Got any questions?"

He fisted his hands as he tightened his jaw. *Yeah, he had one question. Who the hell invited Tremol?* "No, sir," he said through clenched teeth.

"Good." Howell turned and left.

Berto faced him. "I never did thank you for saving my life, not to mention turning it around." Berto gave his shoulder a squeeze.

A strange sadness ran through him, like when he'd realized he would never see his parents again. He squeezed both Berto's shoulders. If he had to do it over, he wouldn't change a thing.

Berto continued down the ramp and stopped in front of Genesis. "I want to thank you, too, Genesis," he said.

Her hair was pulled back into the long braid she always wore. "What for?" she asked.

"For saving my life, for healing me, and for being kind to me." He hugged her, lifting her off the ground. He held her for several seconds. Her arms were around his neck as she held him tight. When he lowered her, she kissed his cheek. He saw Berto whisper something to Gen.

He turned and went up the ramp, swallowing the large lump in his throat. Would his heart ache this badly when he said good-bye to *her?* Could he walk away from her like he did to Berto?

He took a seat at the galley table with Danner, as he watched Tremol escort Genesis into the Nav-room. Tremol's hand rested on Gen's back as the door hissed open. His jaw tightened. He didn't like that scenario one bit. It was *his* idea to help Genesis find Malek. Tremol was in the way.

"Hopefully, Berto will be able to locate all the slaves from Ramen's disk," Danner said, bringing his thoughts back to the matter at hand.

"Yeah. How long had Dram been in the slave business anyway?" he asked.

"I'd say about twenty-five anos. Some of the people might not want to return home once we locate them."

"Why wouldn't they?"

"Sometimes, captives become sympathetic to their captors, even falling in love with them. Howell said the slaves can stay if they choose, but those responsible will be punished."

He thought about Danner's words and remembered his own to Genesis when he first met her, *'What could be worse than being abducted from your home?'* --*Falling in love with the woman who wanted him dead.*

Oh, God. *Do I love her?* The strength of his conviction to go home weakened the longer he remained here but was that so bad?

"Tell me, Danner, what is expected of a crew?" He had to ask, but he didn't have to like the answer.

"Anything the pilots want, from preparing a meal to cleaning the cleansing compartment."

He shook his head. This could be a long trip, with Tremol in charge.

"Tremol's not so bad. He doesn't care if you sit around and do nothing but you'd better be ready to jump when he calls you. Howell, on the other hand, will find busy work for you to do."

Sitting in the Nav-room, Genesis realized when she had flown with Tremol in the past, Malek had been there. She was younger, too. Being second in command meant she had to follow Tremol's orders, but he seemed preoccupied. She followed her own routine since they were on **The Guardian**. She had always done pre-flight for Malek.

"I've already completed the task," Tremol said, breaking the awkward silence.

"Sorry. Old habit." She shrugged. He must have gone through the checklist while she had her mind on Adam.

Tremol set the course for **Tarsius** and **The Guardian** lifted on its way.

She remembered Berto had been born on **Tarsius** but his words about **Ti** worried her. Was Malek alive? Could it be *his* transmission was cut short?

Berto had not discovered Herda's whereabouts before she departed but he assured her he would continue looking. Berto had started working for Dram long after the people of her village had been abducted.

Hard as she tried, she couldn't keep her mind off Adam.

She remembered his pale blue eyes gazing at her while they mated, and his soft, sensual kisses up and down her body. Her entire being warmed at the thought of him. She would rather be with Adam now, instead of here. She glanced at Tremol as he stared out the view port. She was uncomfortable in his presence. This would be a long trip.

After an hour of idle chit chat, she couldn't stand any more. She stood and stretched.

"I need a break." She yawned.

"Why don't you go lie down and take a nap. You can relieve Adam when you get back," Tremol said, his brows raised.

"Relieve Adam?" She had hoped to work with him.

"Yes. Have him come in."

Why not Danner?

"You really look tired, Genesis. Get some sleep. You'll feel better later."

Tremol meant to keep her and Adam apart. The door hissed open. Adam and Danner wrestled on the floor, much like he and Dram had done in their fight on **Meta**.

"What's going on here?" she demanded, her hands on her hips.

Both of them stopped.

"You catch on pretty quick, Danner," Adam said, shaking Danner's hand.

"Training," Danner replied, glancing at her.

"What manner of training is this?"

"Adam taught me some wrestling moves. Men wrestle on Earth. Seems quite effective for fending off an opponent, or defending oneself."

"Really? Why would you want to exert yourself? You are trained to use laser weapons," she asked, puzzled by Danner's exuberance.

Adam stepped close to her, gazing deeply into her eyes.

"Sometimes a weapon isn't available when your life is on the line," Adam said.

His pale blue gaze pierced her and she blinked. Her mouth went dry as she stared back. How could she forget her encounter with him in the cage here on **The Guardian**, or his exchange with Dram, when she almost lost him?

The memory of his heated look from the other night returned to her. Maybe wrestling wasn't such a bad idea, since Adam had a nice body to show for it. The thought of his perfect, naked flesh against hers, made her breasts tingle at the nearness of the man. She stepped back, her heart pounding.

Adam moved closer. Her skin heated, and she took another step backward, banging into the compartments behind her. She brought her hands up, touching his chest as he leaned his head down, next to her face. She inhaled deeply, closing her eyelids momentarily. *What was happening?* She felt his touch from the other night, all over again. She opened her eyes to find his hands on either side of her, penning her against the compartments.

"Would you like me to show you a few moves?" he whispered in her ear.

A sharp, warm shiver to her core awakened her senses at his words and with the warmth of his breath on her flesh. She became wet at the memory of the soft kisses delivered not long ago. A lump formed in her throat. *Yes!* Her mind screamed. She wanted him to move his body against her, kissing her like he had the other night. She opened her mouth to speak.

"I..." She remembered why she was out here in the first place. "Tremol wants you to relieve me," she managed to say, letting out her breath.

"That's *not* what you were thinking, Gen," he whispered in her ear. He pulled back to gaze at her and she dropped her hands to her sides. She'd forgotten he could hear her mind speaking to him.

"Why?" he asked. His brows furrowed as he stared at her lips, his arms straightened on the compartments, the muscles bulging beneath the material of his unicrin.

"Um, that's what he said." She swallowed. *I would rather fly with you, Earth man.* His scent, mixed with sweat, intoxicated her, like the other night. She wanted to wrap her arms around him and pull him close, to taste him once more. She caught her lower lip at the thought of his lips pressed against hers.

He lifted her chin. *You and I will pick up where we left off the other night, Gen,* his mind spoke. She sighed heavily after Adam left the room and moved away from the compartments.

Danner stood nearby, his arms crossed over his chest, a half smile on his face. She cocked her head at him.

"What?"

"Have you two got some kind of telepathy thing going on between you?" He motioned back and forth with his finger.

"Maybe," she said, lifting her chin and walking to the food compartments. She removed a water bottle and sat down at the table. Danner joined her as she pulled a long sip of the refreshing liquid.

"How long had you two been wrestling?" she asked.

"Oh, for about an hour," he began. "We started with exercises to strengthen the neck muscles. Afterward, we worked the arms and legs. I think it's a good workout for the training program, keeping us in shape, and giving us another option for fighting," Danner explained.

She gulped more of her water while he spoke. "Yes, looking at Adam, I can see his training was not wasted." She knew first hand how firm those muscles were. All of them, from head to toe, were in excellent shape. If she had the opportunity again, she would take her time exploring and tasting each and every one of them. She blinked hard. She had to stop thinking of him. No matter what he said. She had to concentrate on finding Malek.

"Tell me." She leaned forward at the table. "Have you heard the **Ti** stories Berto spoke about?"

"Okay, Tremol, what's going on?" Adam demanded when he entered the Nav-room. Tremol glanced at him as he sat down.

"Genesis needed a break. I thought you might want to co-pilot for awhile," he shrugged.

Tremol had ulterior motives, like keeping him and Genesis apart.

"Look, it was Howell's idea for me to lead this mission. You'll need help on **Ti** in the rescue efforts. When we get to **Tarsius** Station, we'll pick up another crew and cargo transport, brief them on our activities and head for **Ti**," Tremol said.

"So what's the plan?" he asked. He felt his idea no longer belonged to him.

"You tell me. Howell said you told Genesis you'd help her find Malek."

He studied Tremol, his anger toward the man abated somewhat. Why didn't Howell ask *him* about his plan before bringing in Tremol?

"When Captain Luc interrogated you, you told him the same thing to convince him you weren't Dram. Did you mean it?"

"Of course I did."

The monitor flashed a message while beeping.

"A transmission from Lieutenant Howell," Tremol said, pressing the com-link. "Go ahead, sir."

"I've gotten more information on **Ti**," Howell began. "The first colony discovered the massive life forms and began work on a camp, but were completely wiped out before finishing it. There were no survivors, only a few...bones."

He glanced at Tremol, then Howell's image on the monitor. This wasn't good.

"The second group completed the base and managed to put up force fields around the camp," Howell continued. "Their transmission stopped while they were en route to the compound."

He pressed the com link. "How long ago?"

"About a month," Howell said.

"Has anyone gone to check on them since?" he asked.

"No. It was a private venture put together by a mining group on **Tarsius**. They didn't want to spend any more money on the project. They cut their losses and got out," Howell explained.

He couldn't believe a company could be so cold hearted. He shook his head looking at Tremol. He hit the com-link. "How many people were lost?" He asked.

"About seventy total, unless some survived from the second colony," Howell said. "However, Berto said the trade made between Dram and another private mining group heading for **Ti,** took place after the last transmission received by the first group."

He swallowed. Too many people had died, in his opinion. "Was Malek part of the second group?" If he was part of the first group, Genesis would be devastated.

"Yes, as a last minute addition to the order."

"That must have been when Malek was ambushed on **Tarsius**," Tremol added.

"One good thing came of it, though," Howell said, interrupting his thoughts.

"Yeah?" He couldn't imagine anything good coming from the death of so many.

"We now have an exact location to start looking for Malck." Howell's image faded and was replaced with a display of the coordinates he mentioned. The screen read: GOOD LUCK!

He cracked his knuckles one at a time. He glanced at Tremol who pointed a finger at him.

"Unless she asks, don't mention this conversation to Genesis," Tremol said.

Genesis had a right to know if it involved her father. Besides, Malek's group, while not devastated, could still be in serious danger.

Tremol typed the coordinates into the memory of the processor. "Genesis would worry about Malek, and I don't want to upset her further," Tremol said.

He clenched his jaw. He didn't like the way that sounded, coming from Tremol. In fact, who made Tremol her protector anyway? He furrowed his brows as he pictured Tremol's arms around her in a protective manner.

"You know, Tremol, Gen's been worried about Malek since the beginning. Just because *you* don't want to tell her this information doesn't make her worry any less." Besides, Gen had more on her mind lately than Malek, the same as he did. Tremol might be right, though. No sense in adding to her worry, at least, not yet.

"Why don't you fix us both something to eat and tell Danner to take a nap, so he can replace me later," Tremol interrupted his thoughts.

He stood and looked down at Tremol. Yeah, Tremol wanted him and Genesis apart. He clenched his fists as he left the Nav-room. If Tremol tried anything with Genesis, he would answer for it. The door hissed open.

Danner was in the galley. "Where's Gen?"

"Gen? Oh, you mean Genesis. She went to her quarters to get some sleep," Danner said.

"Tremol wants you to take a nap, so you can relieve him later," he said. He pushed buttons on the dispensers. Danner waved and left the galley, while he selected several tubes of food paste. He glanced over his shoulder. Danner was gone. He set the tubes down on the table and headed for Gen's compartment.

Her door hissed open. She was on the bottom bunk, her back facing him. He sat on the edge of the bed next to her.

"Gen, are you asleep?" he whispered as he leaned closer. She turned toward him but her eyes remained closed.

She looked so sweet and vulnerable like that. He put his hands on either side of her and dipped his head, brushing his lips against hers. Her arms reached around his neck, pulling him close. Her mouth opened to receive him. He scooped her in his arms, kissing her hungrily. She returned the kiss with the same passion that welled up inside him. His heart pounded as his groin tightened.

He rolled on his back, pulling her on top. His arms had ached to hold her. She fit comfortably against him. He slowly pulled away to gaze at her.

Her eyes opened wide in surprise and she stiffened as she glanced at him. "What happened?"

"From the feel of it, Gen, you kissed me," he said half smiling.

She blinked a few times, her arms on either side of him, while he held her tight. He wasn't about to let her run off again.

"I kissed you good night then you kissed me back. I thought you were asleep," he explained.

"It was a dream," she sputtered, still propped up and blinking at him.

"Yeah, well that was a hell of a dream, Gen. Mind if I join you?" He rolled her onto her back with him on top. A smile escaped her lips.

"We belong together, Gen," he spoke against her mouth. She captured his bottom lip in her teeth and gently pulled. When she let go, he kissed her below her ear on her throat. Her breath caught as she arched her back. He groaned. Her soft skin tasted so good. He wanted more of her, but Tremol expected him to return.

"I've got to go, Gen," he reluctantly pulled away.

"I want you to stay," she grabbed the neck of his flight suit and brought him down to face her. He kissed her nose and her forehead.

"Believe me, Gen, I'd really like to, but Tremol is expecting me back."

She pouted. He dipped his head down and kissed her again, his groin tightened more. He slowly backed away.

"Sweet dreams, Gen." His voice, thick as he stood. His loins ached as he left her sleeping compartment. *Damn it, Tremol, why did you have to come along anyway?*

He gathered the containers of food from the galley table and headed for the Nav-room. He dropped into his seat and handed some tubes to Tremol.

Tremol stared at the objects he gave him, then at him.

"You were gone so long, I thought you'd actually prepared a meal," Tremol remarked.

"Yeah, right," he said, sucking down the protein matter.

He caught Tremol studying him out of the corner of his eye, but he didn't turn to look at him. He wouldn't give Tremol the satisfaction of an explanation.

He and Tremol sat for hours with little conversation between them. He had tried to keep his mind off Genesis, but she drifted in and out of his thoughts like a sweet breeze.

Finally, Danner strode into the room to relieve Tremol. Tremol filled him in on what was going on when Genesis came in through the door. He stood to let her have his seat, and spoke to her with his mind. *Did you sleep well, Genesis?*

She half-smiled. *A little better than last night, thank you,'* she spoke back.

"If you get tired, Gen, come and get me, okay?" He winked at her. She nodded and he left the Nav-room.

Sleep didn't come easily for him. He tossed and turned thinking of his life on Earth and trying to imagine it with Genesis.

In the midst of his dreams flashed the face of a dinosaur, running toward him, shaking the ground with every step, as he tried to make out what kind it was. As the creature got closer, he realized it was a T-Rex with front legs much larger than Earth's scientists claimed they had been. The hulking creature didn't stop. It charged at him, its mouth wide. T-Rex was so close, and the dream so vivid, that T's stinking breath, coupled with his loud roar knocked him off his bunk.

CHAPTER FOURTEEN

Genesis glanced at Tremol after docking **The Guardian** at **Tarsius** Station. When she stood to leave, he reached for her hand.

"Genesis, I want to ask you something," he said, rubbing his thumb across her knuckles.

She looked down at his warm, long fingers, then up to his dark, brown eyes. His actions puzzled her.

"We've known each other for several anos now and, well, you've grown into a beautiful young woman."

Her heart pounded. This led somewhere she didn't want to go. "Thank you for noticing," she managed to say while gently pulling her hand free.

He captured her wrist and brought her fingers to his lips.

"I admire everything about you, Genesis. Would you...consider being my mate?" His warm eyes pleaded.

Her heart skipped a beat. She had longed to hear those words, but not from him. Tremol was attractive, but she had given herself to Adam. Her mouth fell open but nothing came out.

He moved from his seat and pulled her up, standing very close. His hand still clasped hers. "Think about it, Genesis," he said, lifting her chin with his forefinger. "I know you have a lot on your mind right now. You can give me an answer after we find Malek."

She closed her mouth and swallowed hard then nodded. What could she do? He was tall, well built, and sure of himself and his abilities, but Tremol wasn't the man she wanted. After Adam returned to Earth, she couldn't love another, not the way she had come to love him. Besides, Tremol wouldn't want her if he knew she was no longer innocent.

Tremol moved his hands to her arms gazing deeply into her eyes. "Promise me you'll think about us," he said, his brows raised.

The door hissed open, and she jumped at the sound.

"Am I interrupting anything?" Adam asked, glaring at Tremol. He glanced worriedly at her, his mind spoke, penetrating her thoughts. *'Did he hurt you?'*

'No,' she spoke back. She couldn't explain more now. It would have to wait until they were alone.

"No, we've just finished here," Tremol said, putting his arm around her to escort her out. "We'll be meeting in the interrogation room with Captain Luc," he added. "You *do* remember the location, don't you?" Tremol raised an eyebrow at Adam.

"Yes," Adam tensed his jaw. His hands fisted at his sides.

She swallowed as she watched their interaction. Were they testing each other? *Is this what males did when both wanted the same woman?*

Adam glanced at her. *'Can I talk to you, Gen?'*

"You go ahead, Tremol. I'll join you in the interrogation room," she glanced at him then at Adam. Tremol's gaze saddened, but she had to explain to Adam before he jumped to conclusions.

Tremol hesitated in the doorway, a worried look on his face as he left. She tried to smile but her heart was in her throat.

Adam faced her with an unreadable expression.

"Tremol asked me to be his mate," she said. No use trying to prolong this.

Adam's mouth dropped open. "And what did you say?"

She swallowed. "Nothing. He's giving me time to think about it, at least until after we find Malek."

Adam reached for her arms, pulling her toward him but she put her fingers against his lips. She had to be strong. Leaving him would be hard enough but continuing to hope for more tore her apart. Tremol would never match the feelings she had for this man but Tremol was considerate and willing to take her as a mate although she was older than most men preferred.

"I think we should go," she whispered, looking away from those pale blue eyes.

Adam leaned his forehead against her brow and took a deep

breath, slowly letting it out. He nodded and turned to leave. A wave of betrayal washed over her as she followed him through the doorway and down to the interrogation room.

She would miss his firm body, as well as the beard he grew. It had become softer than when he had first kissed her. Each time he nuzzled her neck it sent shivers of pleasure through her. The memories of the few moments they had shared together had to sustain her.

Genesis sat beside Tremol, so Adam sat on her left. Danner sat on Tremol's right. He fought back the sadness welling up inside him. He tensed his jaw and tried not to think of her. She was free to choose a mate. He couldn't interfere anymore.

Captain Luc sat at the head of the table and addressed the group. Six other I.S.P. agents sat with them, two he recognized from the mission on **Vestra Minor**.

"Everyone will be armed with laser rifles," he began. "Their fire range is much farther than the laser pistols."

He ran a hand through his hair, his heart rate kicked up a notch as he sat forward, resting his hands on his thighs. He had to warn them. "You're going to need something a lot bigger than laser rifles," he said, pulling everyone's attention to himself. He glanced at Genesis as she studied his face.

"How do you know this?" Captain Luc asked.

He sat back and crossed his arms over his chest. He looked at Captain Luc, avoiding Gen's gaze, especially since she sat next to Tremol. He tensed his jaw.

"You're going to need Ion Cannons and turbo lasers along with laser rifles," he began. He felt Gen's stare, but he avoided it.

"The firing range on those weapons is too far," Tremol said.

He continued looking at Captain Luc because if he glanced at Tremol, he would see Gen.

"Sir, if you don't use long range weapons, by the time the dinosaurs are close, the laser rifles may not be strong enough to take them out. We'll end up as dinosaur appetizers."

The other agents looked at each other and talked loudly among themselves. He felt a tug on his flight suit. He looked down at Gen's hand on his sleeve and up at her face. Her brows were raised.

"Again, how do you come by this information?" Captain Luc asked before Gen could speak.

"I had a premonition, sir."

Captain Luc knew about the other premonitions since he'd grilled him on them before he ever released him from this room the last time he was here. Genesis still had her hand on his arm but he wouldn't look at her. He couldn't.

"You expect us to believe that?" Tremol asked, leaning forward.

He quickly glanced at Tremol and back at the Captain.

"Every premonition I have ever had has come true. You can believe what you want." He tensed his jaw but kept his eyes on Luc. His heart ached for a glance at Gen but he had to be strong. He had to let her go.

"We need a plan," she patted his arm then removed her hand.

A sense of loss hit him when she withdrew her touch.

"I *have* a plan, Genesis." He stole a glance at her. *Be strong, Adam, be strong*.

She blinked.

"Do you care to share it with us?" the Captain said, dryly.

"Yes, sir." He cleared his throat and turned his attention to Captain Luc. "We use scanners like we did on **Vestra Minor** to locate any people. We take out the bad guys and load up all the slaves and bring them home."

"What about those dinosaurs?" Tremol asked.

He leaned forward. "That's where you come in, Tremol. You blow the dinosaurs to pieces using the Ion Cannons from **The Guardian**, or the cargo transport in the air." He glanced at the other I.S.P. agents. "You'll have the scanners and will be able to see them coming. We can get these people out with air protection, while we cover the ground."

"How many cannons can we get?" Genesis asked.

"You have the one on board **The Guardian**, and two turbo lasers. We can probably get you one more canon and two more turbos for the cargo transport," Captain Luc said.

"That's it?" he asked.

"They're expensive. We can't spare any more right now. The crew of the cargo transport," Luc gestured to the others in the room, "will remain in a hover position as air support, over the site with one Ion Cannon and the two turbo lasers. When you've released the slaves, they land and take them on board, while **The Guardian** serves as back-up. You all return here. Any questions?" The Captain asked.

No one raised a hand so Luc stood and left the room.

As he got up to leave, Tremol ushered Genesis out the door. Danner caught up with him.

"Adam, Captain Luc wants us to unload the boxes we brought here from **Meta**. Then load the ship with supplies," Danner said.

"I take it we're crewing again," he asked.

"You got it," Danner raised his thumb in acknowledgement.

Using a hover-trol, he and Danner finished loading food, weapons, and supplies in record time. Afterward, the two of them walked back to the docking station. He ran a hand through his hair and scratched at his beard. Somehow, he had to get a turbo or Ion Cannon on the ground. It should be *him* looking for Malek since he'd conceived the idea, but then, Tremol called the shots.

"How are you at shooting a turbo laser or Ion Cannon?" he asked Danner.

"Pretty good, why?"

"If I need you to take out some dinosaurs, do you think you could do it from on board **The Guardian?**"

"You mean I can't go with you?" Danner asked.

"If *I* was in charge, I'd have you on the ground as my back-up." He would take one of the turbo lasers and leave one of each on **The Guardian**, with two shooters and one pilot. The cargo transport needed four men-two pilots and two shooters.

"The transporter crew is ready to go," Tremol announced as he approached them. "Is everything loaded on **The Guardian?**"

"Yes, sir," replied Danner.

He crossed his arms over his chest. "We'll need two shooters, Tremol. Can the transporter spare two of their men?" he asked.

Tremol's brows were furrowed as he studied him. "What's your plan?" he asked.

"Three on the ground to search for the others-one carrying a turbo laser, while the other two use laser rifles. That leaves two shooters on each ship, with one pilot on **The Guardian** and two on the transporter. Each ship has an Ion Cannon. **The Guardian** would have one turbo laser. The transport would have two. One pilot could help shoot on the transport if he had to."

Tremol crossed one arm in front of his waist and propped the other on it while tapping his chin with his fingers. "It might work," he said.

It *would* work. But who would search for Malek?

"All right, let's go. We'll use your plan for now," Tremol said. "Danner, get two men from the transporter and bring them here." Tremol turned and headed for **The Guardian**.

Genesis walked up and he glanced away. He had to keep his thoughts on the rescue and not her.

Tremol opened the hatch and entered the ship with Genesis behind him. Danner returned with Spencer and Tamlin following. The four of them climbed aboard **The Guardian**, and sat in the galley area.

"This trip won't be as far as the one from **Meta**," Danner said.

"I hope not. I don't like the idea of the two of them alone for long periods of time," he said without thinking. He ran a hand through his hair then propped his head up, while leaning his elbows on the table.

Danner cocked his head. "I thought you were returning to Earth."

"I am."

"Well, if you go back, then Tremol will ask her to be his mate," Danner said.

"He already did." He leaned back in his seat, his arms folded across his chest.

"Did she accept?" Spencer asked, leaning forward.

"Not yet."

"Tell us about these dinosaurs, Adam. What do they look like?" Tamlin asked.

"You mean you don't know?"

The three of them shook their heads.

"Didn't any of you study history?" he asked.

"Yes, but what does history have to do with dinosaurs?" Tamlin asked.

"On Earth, pre-historic creatures lived before humans existed. Some of them were the size of a football field," he tried to explain.

"What's a football field?" Spencer asked.

He scratched his beard. "Hmmm, let's say longer than four cargo transports put end to end."

"Wow," Danner said.

"Yes, and some were taller than the I.S.P. headquarters," he added.

"How can we kill something that big with laser rifles?" Spencer asked.

"My point exactly." He pointed his index finger at Spencer. "That's why you're using the turbo lasers or Ion Cannon."

"If the dinosaurs are that tall, we won't be able to hover near the ground to pick up the slaves," Tamlin said, looking at him.

"Yeah," Spencer added, glancing at Tamlin. "Those dinosaurs could step on us and we'd be dead."

"That's why we have back-up," he gestured, his arms outstretched. "When **The Guardian** lands, three of us jump out and search for the slaves, while the transporter takes out any large dinosaurs in the area using the turbo lasers or cannons. We take out the smaller creatures with the laser rifles," he explained. "**The Guardian** pulls up and waits for our signal."

Danner shook his head. "I don't want to end up like the others."

"We won't. You've got to pay attention, watch for anything that moves, but don't shoot until you're sure it's not human," he said. He realized Genesis didn't know what dinosaurs were either.

"I've got to warn them," he stood.

"Warn who?" Danner asked.

"The pilots. If they hover too low, we could hit one. He left the galley and headed for the Nav-room.

The door hissed open, revealing Tremol with his arm around Genesis, their backs toward him.

"Hey, what's going on here?" he demanded, his hands balled into fists at his sides.

The two of them turned. Genesis had been crying.

"Gen, what's wrong?" He went to her, but Tremol put his arm out to stop him.

"Everything's under control. Go back to your seat," Tremol ordered.

"It doesn't look that way to me." He stepped closer.

Tremol moved between him and Genesis. "You'd better leave." Tremol crossed his arms over his chest and stared him down.

He stopped inches from Tremol's face, his jaw tensed and his hands still in fists. He didn't like being ordered around by others, but he had to remember he wasn't in charge any more.

'Gen, are you all right?' He spoke with his mind.

'Yes,' she said back to him.

He glared at Tremol, then left. When he reached the door, he faced Tremol again. "You might tell the transport crew not to hover below sixty feet...uh, I mean 1800 centikiks until we pick up the slaves."

"And why not?" Tremol asked. His arms were still crossed over his chest.

"Because some of the dinosaurs are larger than that," he said, then left.

Genesis was so upset with Tremol for holding back information about the last colony, she hadn't spoke to him since they'd departed the station.

The Guardian entered **Ti's** atmosphere behind the transporter. Tremol had told the other crew not to hover below 1800 centikiks, but he didn't follow the advice himself.

She adjusted a lever to stay on Howell's coordinates when something came toward **The Guardian** in the sky. As it got closer, it resembled a bird of some sort. When it neared the ship, she realized the object was larger than **The Guardian**.

"Pull up!" she shouted at Tremol, grabbing the controls.

She banked sharply to avoid the hideous creature. Nothing like any bird she had ever seen, yet it flew. The monster was too large to fly.

"Did you see that?" Sergeant Teague, the leader of the transporter called out over the headset.

"Yes, we did," Tremol answered, glancing at her.

"I've never seen a bird like that before," Teague responded.

"That wasn't a bird," she said, remembering Adam's explanation about dinosaurs.

"Get those scanners on, Sergeant Teague, and let us know what you find," Tremol said.

Tremol turned to her. "We're getting close to the last known transmission, Genesis. Hopefully, we'll find Malek here with the survivors."

"We've found a large energy source seventeen kiks to our left, possibly a force field of some sort," Sergeant Teague said.

Tremol yawed in the direction of the scanner findings.

Within seconds, she spotted the lighted fenced-in area. It was dusk and the sky darkened quickly.

"Pull up," she glared at Tremol.

"Why?"

"We're below 1800 centikiks. We could be spotted if we were much lower."

"I'm not so sure Adam knows what he's talking about. He isn't from this system. How could he have a premonition of our planets without living here as we do?" Tremol said.

"Well, I believe him. At least *he* hasn't lied to me," she said.

Tremol's jaw tensed at her words. She regretted saying them the instant the words left her mouth, but it was true. Adam would have mentioned the colonies' problems, but Tremol had lied about the seriousness of the situation. He'd said he didn't want to worry her.

Tremol pulled up and **The Guardian** responded instantly.

"Why would they have a gate so large and so high?" she asked, barely hearing the hissing sound of the door.

"To keep the slaves from escaping, I imagine," Tremol said, looking at her.

Hardly," Adam interjected as he walked up behind her. Danner followed Adam, along with Spencer and Tamlin. "It's to keep the dinosaurs out, Genesis."

She swallowed at the thought those creatures could be so large.

He knelt between her and Tremol's seats. "We've got to get inside the compound, Genesis." Adam's fingers clasped the medallion around his neck. She reached over and pulled his arm.

"Don't play with the communicator, it's not a toy," she admonished him. Why couldn't he remember? She watched him release the disk.

"Sorry, Genesis, I wasn't thinking," he glanced at her.

Did she imagine it, or was he being more formal with her name? She had gotten used to him calling her Gen, while no one else used the name. Now he used her full name, as if they had not been intimate. It hurt.

She glanced down at his hand against his thigh and noticed the medallion still blinked, as well as her own.

"He's here!" she shouted. Her hands fisted on the arm rests, her heart pounding. *Please let him be all right,* she prayed.

Adam touched her arm, and she rested her free hand on his, gazing in his eyes.

"Who's here?" Spencer asked in a whispered tone.

"Malek, her father. You remember him? He's the bounty hunter who went after Dram so many anos ago," Danner explained.

Spencer nodded in recognition.

"And Adam here, helped capture Dram," Danner added.

"We're coming, Malek," Genesis spoke aloud while clutching the medallion.

"Can he hear you?" Adam asked.

"Yes. Malek designed the medallions himself as communicators, but also as locators, in case one of us got lost."

"Large masses of life forms coming this way," Sergeant Teague said across the headset.

"How many do you see?" Tremol asked, pressing the com-link so all could hear.

"It's a herd."

The sky was black now as they got within range of the compound.

Adam turned to Tremol. "Tell them not to shoot until we have to but only use the turbo lasers," he said.

Tremol glanced at Adam, but before he relayed the message, Danner shouted.

"Look, over there!" Danner pointed to a dwelling on the far side of the compound. Shots rang out from an Ion Cannon at that very spot.

Tremol pulled up hard, throwing Danner, Spencer, and Tamlin to the floor. Adam lost his balance too, but was already down.

"Let's go!" Spencer shouted at Tamlin as the two headed out of the Nav-room. Adam jumped up and after them.

"Where did they go?" she asked Danner.

"To the engine room to get the weapons."

Adam followed quickly behind the other two down the metal steps to the engine room, his hands sliding along the rail as he went. His adrenalin pumped through his body.

"I'll take one of the turbo lasers. You two can fight over the cannon," he said.

Tamlin sat at the Ion Cannon, and Spencer took the other turbo.

"Remember, save the cannon for the large dinosaurs, Tamlin," he said as the two men put on the headsets. "The cannon would be too big a blast for the building. That perimeter fence is there to protect the people inside from the creatures."

He pulled the turbo laser out of its nest and carried it up the steps. Heavy enough for a man to carry, there was no way Genesis could lift the thing. Whether Tremol liked it or not, he would find Malek. He slipped the shoulder strap across his chest, with the laser resting against his back.

When he got to the Nav-room, the transport hovered to the right.

"Did you tell them what I said?" he asked Tremol. As he finished speaking, a blast left the transport, hitting the building where the other shot originated, blowing it to bits. The lights around the perimeter flickered and went out.

"Thanks, Tremol. Our safety net is now gone," he said, raising his hands in the air. He tensed his jaw and crossed his arms over his chest.

"What are you talking about? They took them out with one shot. We won't have trouble from the abductors any more. You can go in and get the slaves." Tremol turned in his seat to look at him.

"The abductors weren't the problem, Tremol."

"We took out the guard shack!" someone yelled from the transport. There was shouting in the background. He reached over and hit the com-link.

"Yeah, the cannon you used blew out the only protection we had against the dinosaurs," he said. He turned and glared at Tremol.

"Take us down, Tremol," he said, taking a headset from Genesis and putting it on. She put another one on herself.

He pressed the headset. "You men on the transport will have to keep the large dinosaurs back with the cannon. We're going down and hunt for the slaves." He clicked the headset again to speak to Tamlin and Spencer.

"You two watch our backs while we search."

"Sure thing, Adam," Tamlin said.

"Now wait a minute," Tremol turned in his seat. "Genesis, you're not going down there. Danner can go, but you're staying here."

"I tried that before, Tremol, remember?" He raised an eyebrow. Genesis stood and stepped beside him.

"As first in command, *you* need to stay with the ship and call the shots." Genesis pointed at Tremol. "I'm the second and will head the search party for my father." She gently nudged him and the two of them left the Nav-room.

Danner stood out in the open area near the cell with four laser rifles and a pack on his back. He handed two to Genesis, and made a thumbs up sign when she took them.

"Do you know how to use the turbo?" she asked him.

He pulled the laser up onto his right shoulder, feeling for the trigger on top and propped the front up with his left hand. She moved close to his side.

"Kneel down," she said.

He knelt down and she inspected the top of the weapon.

"This lever is only at half power. Push it forward for full," she nudged the lever. He stood up, and Genesis bent and walked under the barrel of the turbo laser to where she faced him. Her rifles, slung over her left shoulder. She grabbed him at the back of his neck. His heart beat kicked up a notch as he cocked his head and gazed at her, puzzled. She pulled his lips to hers and kissed him hard on the mouth.

"I love you, Adam Davis," she whispered, then turned away.

He swallowed at her words. "Bring your scanner, Genesis," he said, his voice thick.

Danner handed her the box he pulled out of the compartments. She then checked the laser rifles.

Within moments, the ramp lowered, but they were several feet off the ground.

"Jump," she shouted as she took the first leap. She landed on her feet, her rifle ready with the spare over her shoulder.

Danner jumped next and did the same thing. But when *he* followed, he landed hard. The weight of the turbo laser knocked him on his back and the laser itself. A sharp pain seized him momentarily.

"Damn, that hurt," he said, trying to stand. Danner helped him to his feet. The extra weight made it difficult to right himself.

The Guardian pulled up and shone a spotlight onto the three of them. A building stood behind them.

"Let's check this out," Genesis said as she pointed her rifle at the door. She shot at the latch, popping it open. He faced away from the dwelling and watched the jungle, while Danner had his back.

"Nothing here," she called out.

He tapped his headset. "Shine the light ahead of us," he said. The spotlight moved forward. What he thought were palm trees were actually ferns, taller than the building behind them.

The Ion Cannon went off in the distance, along with the turbo lasers from the cargo transporter.

"Boy, did you see the size of that creature?" a voice spoke into the headset.

"Look at this!" another one said. "There must be twenty to thirty of those damn things feeding off the carcass of the big creature. They didn't even wait to let the body cool off."

Danner glanced at him and he nodded. No telling what's out there, but they had to find those people fast.

He moved forward through the ferns, while Danner and Genesis brought up the rear. He listened for sounds, but it was eerily quiet. In the past, he'd looked for animal signs whenever he hunted. Out here, *he'd become* the prey.

Suddenly, a strange clucking sound came from his left. He swallowed hard and turned toward it. Was it a warning to the other creatures? Now they were surrounded by the clucking noise. He held his breath. "Make a circle," he whispered into the headset. The noise stopped.

Their small black eyes glistened in the light from the spotlight. The creatures were about his height and similar to something he'd seen in history books. Bird-like in appearance, minus the feathers, they had large clawed feet, tiny arms and longish beaks. When the clucking started up again, a bird-like creature stood about six feet away. The beak, full of sharp looking teeth, snapped open and closed.

"Shoot them," he whispered harshly as his heart pounded. "Go left in a circular pattern."

Danner handed him a rifle as he slid the turbo down his back. He fired shots at the bird as he turned left. The lasers marked a circular pattern, killing most of them. Those that weren't killed screeched horribly and ran through the jungle. He managed to hit a couple on top of the building behind them. The creatures had been hunting in a pack. Not good at all.

The Ion Cannon went off again but this time from both **The Guardian** and the transporter. Too close for comfort.

"Malek, where are you?" Genesis called out.

He glanced down at the medallion and noticed it glowed.

"Straight ahead, Adam, in your direction," she said.

He moved a little quicker through the ferns, the turbo laser on his shoulder. **The Guardian** provided some light but Tamlin and Spencer needed it more to search for the larger threat. The cargo transporter, at a higher altitude, lit up more area. Why didn't Tremol do the same?

Genesis pulled out her scanner as they moved through the thick foliage.

He heard scurrying noises moving around him. He didn't like the sound. The creatures were either big or there were a lot of them. Night feeders were dangerous because they knew how to adapt to the darkness, and had vision for that purpose. His heart beat so loud, he had difficulty distinguishing which noises he should be wary of.

He felt a tug on his flight suit and froze. He swung around hard. Genesis and Danner ducked to keep from being hit by the barrel of the turbo.

"Watch that thing, man, you almost hit us," Danner whispered loudly.

"I felt a tug on my clothes."

"It was me," Genesis said. "There's a cave ahead holding twenty or more people inside." She glanced at the scanner then his face. Slowly, her gaze moved above his head, widening with fright as her mouth dropped open.

He swung around again and managed to get off a shot at what looked like a giant lizard, with a tongue whipping out toward him. The turbo was at half power and only stunned the creature. The lizard shook his head, blinked a few times then moved off in another direction. The spotlight left them in darkness.

"What's wrong with this thing? It should have blasted that creature to pieces," he said.

"Let me see," Genesis reached up with her hand to touch the slider mechanism.

He bent down so she could inspect it, while Danner took a

defensive posture.

"The lever must have gotten stuck when you fell on your back." She hit it hard with her hand. "Ouch!"

"What happened?"

"It's jammed." She took the butt of her laser rifle and whacked the lever into position. "That ought to do it." She offered her hand to help him up.

"Thanks, Gen. Come on." He motioned, as he moved toward a clearing between them and the cave. He took off running, Genesis and Danner followed.

"Anyone in here?" he called out.

"Yes," a voice responded.

"We've come to rescue you," he shouted. "We don't have much time."

Men poured out of the opening as Danner guarded the perimeter to the left and Genesis to the right. He took the mouth of the cave as well as the top.

One of the men had a rifle. "Who are you?" the man asked.

"We're with the I.S.P. Drop your weapon," he pointed the turbo laser at the man.

The man followed orders, and moved toward the others.

"Is that everyone? And is everyone all right?" he asked, retrieving the rifle.

"Yes, all but this one," a man answered. His face seemed familiar, but it was too dark to make out any features. The man had his arm around another who held up an injured leg.

"Malek?" Genesis turned.

"Genesis, is that you?" the man called out.

She ran to him, lowering her weapon. The two of them embraced and he lifted her off the ground.

"Here," she said, handing Malek her other rifle. The ground shook ever so slightly.

He listened and realized it was deathly silent. The rustling had stopped, and so had the small night noises of bugs.

He tapped his headset. "We're ready for pickup. Keep alert for large creatures."

"We've got your location, Adam. We'll be there in a few. We had a large life form on the scanner, but it vanished."

He glanced at Genesis then searched for the spotlight from **The Guardian**. Where was **The Guardian?** It had hovered low all this time. Had Tremol decided to heed his advice now?

The ground shook again but a little stronger this time. The men from the cave huddled against the outside wall. Danner and Genesis had their backs to him to guard in a circle. Malek and another man had the two extra rifles.

The turbo lasers went off in the distance. He located the smoke from their hit. Afterward, the transporter came at them in the clearing. The ramp lowered, but the cargo ship remained in hover position. The two shooters stood at the opening.

"Everyone get on the ship, now!" he shouted. His heart beat faster. All of them were vulnerable. He felt the presence of the T-Rex but he couldn't see him. Malek helped the injured man up the ramp when the ground shook again. A large creature came at them from the far left.

"Pull up!" he shouted. He had a good shot at this distance, but the ship was in the way. It lifted slowly, the last three men dangling from the end of the ramp. The two shooters got the men inside as it pulled straight up.

He squeezed the trigger. A bolt of white light erupted from his weapon, hitting the creature's snarling muzzle. The dinosaur flinched, but kept coming. "Damn! What's wrong now?" He banged the turbo laser with his fist, sending a stronger jolt to the animal, and the hideous thing fell over.

The ground shook, harder this time. Genesis, Danner, and Malek formed a circle with him, their backs toward each other, watching, listening, and waiting.

"I can't see anything out here, but I can feel its presence," Danner whispered loudly.

His adrenalin kicked in, as he waited for the inevitable. *God help us.*

The ground shook again, bam, bam, bam, bam. It ran toward them from his left. He turned and fired but the turbo didn't phase the T-Rex. He kept coming. He banged the weapon with his fist once more, and the weapon kicked back, sending him to the ground. He scrambled to his feet, his heart racing. The creature was momentarily stunned. Panic engulfed him.

Danner and Genesis stood paralyzed beside him.

God, T-Rex was huge, making the other large creatures seem like toys in comparison. His heart hammered so loudly he didn't hear Genesis yell. She hit his shoulder and he jumped.

"Kneel down!" she shouted in his ear as T roared. He smelled the stench of T's breath blowing across his face.

He knelt and kept his hand pressed on the trigger, jolts of electricity flew at T. T-Rex roared again and moved in for the kill, while Genesis slammed the butt of her laser rifle against the lever of the turbo. One blast at full power blew T-Rex into big chunks of flying carcass. One large chunk hit Genesis, knocking her to the ground.

"Gen, are you all right?" he called out to her as he set the laser down his back. Malek was beside her, helping her up. Blood covered her white flight suit. She hugged Malek tightly.

"Adam, are you there?" Sergeant Teague's voice came over the headset.

"Yes, we're here and we're ready for pick up," he said, pressing the headset.

Small creatures scurried out of the jungle to feed on the chunks of the dead T-Rex. He pulled the turbo laser back on his shoulder. His arms ached to hold Genesis and comfort her.

"We've got to get away from here before larger creatures show up." He ushered Danner, Genesis and Malek in the opposite direction.

"We can offer you air support, but the transporter can't hold any more people," Sergeant Teague said.

He glanced at Genesis. "What's that supposed to mean?"

Her brows furrowed as she cocked her head to glance at him.

"**The Guardian** was supposed to pick you up, but we haven't been able to reach them," Sergeant Teague replied.

Gen's eyes widened.

"**Guardian,** come in," she said, tapping her headset. "**Guardian,** this is Genesis, do you hear me?"

His jaw tensed and his gut tightened. "Damn it, Tremol, where the hell are you?"

CHAPTER FIFTEEN

Genesis pressed the voice override key on the scanner as she stood with her back toward Adam, Danner and Malek. The three of them watched their surroundings for signs of creatures, while the cargo transporter supplied the light she needed to work.

"**Guardian,** awaken," she said into the scanner.

"Responding," a feminine voice replied.

"Who was that?" Adam asked, looking over his shoulder.

"**The Guardian**. The ship is now in voice mode," she explained. "Tell me your condition."

"Scanning. The sensors tell me we are not on level ground. We are partially submerged in liquid."

"What condition is the crew in?" she asked.

Silence, then..."No one is responding, but my sensors tell me three life forms are on board. All are functioning at a diminished capacity."

She turned to glance at Malek. "They may be hurt."

"Have her sensors pick up our location," Malek said.

Adam touched his headset. "Sergeant Teague, can you see **The Guardian**?"

The spotlight circled the area.

"It's impossible to see below the foliage," Teague began, "but we're picking up massive life forms all around you. They're much larger than the last one you shot, but don't appear to be moving."

She backed into Adam, her heart rate kicked up. *Larger*? Panic seized her. She didn't want another creature, especially bigger or meaner than the last, to show up. Would she ever forget the horrible face that came within a few feet of eating her and Adam?

"It could be they've bedded down for the night," Adam said to Teague.

"Flesh eaters?" she asked him.

"The largest dinosaurs ate plants, Gen, during the day. But the carnivores, well, I'm not sure about their feeding habits. I didn't pay much attention in school," he said, glancing over his shoulder.

She looked at Adam, in the dim light of the transporter. She was amazed at his knowledge. He knew more about these creatures than anyone else did. She hoped he was right, but it didn't make her fears go away. She pressed the com-link button on the scanner.

"**Guardian**, take a reading from my signal, and let me know your location." She held down the planetary locator system button.

Silence surrounded them for a few moments except for the feeding frenzy going on several metikiks away.

"You are point six kiks to the north," **The Guardian** said. She studied the compass on the scanner.

"That way," she pointed, moving out in front of the small group.

"All right," Adam whispered. "We stick together and keep quiet. We don't want to wake anything."

Her laser weapon was slung over her shoulder as she held the scanner in both hands. The thick foliage proved difficult to move through, so she made sure she could touch Adam if something jumped out at her. Behind him, Danner and Malek followed.

Quietly, she pushed the large leaves aside as she passed. She couldn't shake the feeling someone watched her.

Adam tried to be careful with the turbo, but a few times he swung around sharply and almost hit her in the head. The transporter offered dim lighting from above.

Suddenly, the scanner blinked. She stopped in her tracks, with Adam bumping into her. He reached over her shoulder pulling aside the taller foliage. He held a finger on his lips and pulled her to him. He whispered in her ear, and his heated breath sent shivers of sensations throughout her body. It was hard to concentrate on what he said. She inhaled his scent as he spoke.

"Genesis, have them dock with **The Guardian** and pull it to **Tarsius** Station. We'll get on the transporter and go through the docking rings to check on the others."

"They won't be able to connect as long as **The Guardian** is not level," she whispered, wrapping her hand around his neck to reach his ear. His fingers remained on her back, pulling her close. She savored every moment of his touch, knowing it would end all too soon.

"**The Guardian** doesn't seem heavy. Couldn't several men lift one end to make it level?" he whispered.

"Maybe," she said. She tapped her headset and relayed the information to Teague. As she finished her conversation with the Sergeant, something jumped up from her left and knocked her to the ground. The weight of the creature penned her down. Sharp claws dug into her back and forced her face into the mud. But just as quickly, she smelled the burning dinosaur flesh as one of the men shot it with the laser rifle.

Adam helped her to her feet, after Danner and Malek pushed the carcass off her back. Adam took his sleeve and carefully wiped her face, clearing the mud from her mouth and eyes.

"Gen, he must have smelled the blood on your clothes," he whispered as he gently cleaned around her nose. She blinked a few times. He had called her Gen, like before. She tried to smile, but tasted mud in her mouth. She spat out the dirt.

"Oh, Gen," he laughed as he drew her into his arms. She reached around his waist. This is where she belonged, where she wanted to stay.

"Uh, hem," Malek cleared his throat and glared at the two of them. "Her name is Genesis, and she appears to be injured," Malek said.

Adam pulled away and inspected her face. "Where are you hurt," he asked.

"My back," she said, pointing to where the creature clawed her. Adam moved behind her. "Genesis, you're bleeding in several spots." He removed her rifle so she could heal herself. She placed the back of her hands on her back and began praying. Moving her hands up and down her flesh, she touched the injuries as much as she could. The skin tightened under her hands as she prayed. Concentrating on her injuries, she pictured them closing up and healing. When the pain diminished, she stopped praying.

Malek didn't know about her relationship with Adam. She would have to explain her behavior later, since women were not allowed to act familiar with a man unless they were mated. But it would have to wait. Now they needed to move a ship.

The cargo transporter hovered over **The Guardian** while the ramp lowered. Four men quietly climbed out, stunned to see a creature three times the size of the one Adam had blown apart, lying with its tail near the ship. **The Guardian** was half-submerged in a small pond beside the beast.

She and Malek stood guard while Danner and Adam stepped in the water and helped the four men lift the end of **The Guardian** out of the shallow pool. One of the men slipped and fell on the creature. She held her breath and aimed her rifle. The huge animal lifted its head to watch the men. Then the beast raised its tail, moving **The Guardian** out of the water. Relief ran through her. How did the creature know what they needed?

The men on board the transport worked feverishly to connect the two ships. Finally, the docking was completed.

"Everyone load up," Sergeant Teague's voice came over the headset.

The beast moved its tail out of the way. Her mouth fell open as Adam patted the creature.

"It's okay, girl. We mean you no harm."

The creature grunted softly in response. Was Adam communicating with it?

She followed Adam up the ramp with Malek behind her. She continued watching the creature as she climbed aboard the transporter. The plant eating animals on **Atria** came to mind. They were always more docile than any flesh eaters she had ever seen. It was a shame they were the ones eaten, especially when they could be so helpful. "Thank you," she whispered to the creature. She felt Malek's hand on her shoulder as the ramp closed up behind them.

The cargo transporter pulled straight up about half a kik and hovered. With a full load of people, it couldn't pull **The Guardian** all the way to **Tarsius** Station. Any repairs would have to be made now so the ships could be flown individually.

Please let the men be all right, she prayed. She and Malek headed to the Nav-room and her heart thudded when she found Tremol unconscious. She checked Tremol for injuries and found a large bruise on his head. Malek inspected the Nav-U-Com and followed with a systems check.

"Everything seems to be fine, here," Malek said.

Adam burst into the room. "Is Tremol okay, Gen?" he asked.

"He has a head injury. I was about to pray for his healing," she said.

"Will you be all right if I take Malek with me?"

She nodded. His request was odd, though.

"We need your help in the engine room," Adam said.

Malek nodded and followed Adam.

Adam ran a hand through his hair. It was going to be difficult to get Tamlin and Spencer up the narrow steps that led to the weapons cache. Malek was built bigger and looked much stronger than Danner.

"Why do you call my daughter, Gen when her name is Genesis?" he asked as they reached the opening.

He swallowed. "Uh, it's a nickname, sir. Back on Earth we use them when people have long first names," he explained. *Or for terms of endearment,* but Malek wouldn't like that explanation.

Malek studied his face. Was he telepathic as well?

"I prefer you call her Genesis." He tensed his jaw.

"Uh, yes sir," he said. What *could* he say? He took the steps two at a time, Malek right behind him. He saw where Genesis got her looks. Malek's high cheekbones and elegant features had been transferred to her. His dark coloring was the same as Gen's, but his blue-black hair was much shorter, coming to the middle of his shoulder blades. He wore a dirty white, worn-out flight suit. Malek had broad, muscular shoulders and narrow hips, with powerful thighs, where Genesis was slender and toned all over. Maybe she'd inherited her body type from her mother.

"Are they still unconscious, Danner?" he asked when he reached the weapons area.

"Yes, and I can't seem to budge either one of them."

He knelt down beside Tamlin and checked his body for broken bones, while Malek and Danner watched. He moved to Spencer and did the same. Both were unconscious, but breathing, he would leave the healing to Genesis.

"Can you carry a man over your shoulder?" he asked Malek.

"Maybe," Malek replied. "I've never tried but I am strong," he said, hitting his chest in a salute.

He squatted down and lifted Tamlin off the floor. He reached under his arms and pulled up. "Get in front of him and I'll drape him over your shoulder," he said.

Malek cocked his head, a puzzled expression on his face.

"Here, I'll show you. Danner, come and hold Tamlin," he said. Danner picked up Tamlin under the arms while he stood facing Tamlin. He bent his legs so he could prop Tamlin over one shoulder. Then stood, shifting Tamlin's weight. He grunted from the strain and headed for the stairs.

Tamlin was the heavier of the two. Hopefully, Malek could manage Spencer, because he didn't know if he had enough strength left to carry another man. The turbo laser had weighed a little less than Tamlin. He held the rail and pulled himself up the stairs, supporting Tamlin with one hand. He made it to one of the sleeping compartments, and lowered Tamlin onto the bottom bunk.

He tried to straighten his back and stretch when Malek came toward him with Spencer over his shoulder.

"In here," he moved to the compartment next door. It was much easier to set them down on the bottom bunks in separate rooms.

"Thanks, Malek," he said, running a hand through his hair.

"All systems good in the engine room," Danner reported coming up the steps.

He helped Danner close the lower compartment hatch.

"I'll do another check for air leaks and other damage if you two want to find something for us to eat," Malek said.

"Sure," Danner replied.

Later, he took some tubes of food and water in to Genesis and

Malek.

"Everything all right in here?" he asked as he entered the Nav-room. He didn't want to interrupt their reunion, but he wanted to bring them something to eat. No telling how long ago Malek had eaten. *He* was hungry, and food paste was better than nothing.

"Yes," Genesis responded. "Tremol will be fine. He needs to sleep for awhile."

He handed some tubes to Malek, stepping across Tremol's unconscious body. With Malek here, he didn't have to worry about Tremol. Surely he wouldn't try anything while Gen's father looked over his shoulder.

"You and Danner can begin the undocking, and we'll be under way when you're finished," Malek said.

"Yes, sir," he turned to leave. It felt strange taking orders from Malek, but much easier than from Tremol.

"I'll check on the other two, Malek," Genesis said.

She followed him out the door.

While Genesis tended to Tamlin, he and Danner worked on closing off the cargo transporter. By the time he finished locking the inside hatch of **The Guardian**, Genesis had healed Spencer as well.

"They will both sleep for awhile," she said. "I have a lot to explain to Malek," she lowered her eyes, "before we return you to Earth." She turned and left him.

Earth. The word stuck in his throat and caused his heart to drop. He had longed to go home. That's all he had thought about in the beginning, and now it would happen. He'd kept his word to her and now she would fulfill her promise to him. He couldn't ask for more.

He joined Danner in the galley. Suddenly, he was no longer hungry. He sipped his water and stared at the tubes of food. Danner squeezed every bit of his vegetable matter into his mouth and swallowed.

"Yum," he said.

"How can you eat that crap?" He shook his head.

"Hey, it's all we've got. I thought you were hungry, too. I heard your stomach growling an hour ago," Danner said.

"I've lost my appetite," he mumbled.

Inside the Nav-room, Genesis told Malek everything that had happened since they had been separated, except the intimate details of her relationship with Adam.

"He's Dram's son?" Malek raised his voice as he glared at her.

She rolled her eyes. "He's nothing like Dram," she tried to explain. "Didn't you notice the way he acted around you?"

"It's a good thing we're taking him back to Earth. The less I see him, the better I like it," Malek said.

Her heart was saddened at his words. "He looks nothing like Dram with his beard," she mumbled.

"You mean the monstrous growth on his face?"

She nodded, anxiety flooded her senses. He actually looked sexy with his facial hair. Not to mention what he did to her senses when he rubbed his beard across her skin. The thought sent shivers to her core.

He cocked his head and stared at her. "You find him... appealing?"

"Yes, I do," she lowered her eyes.

"He is not of our race," Malek said.

"Neither is Tremol, and he asked me to be his mate," she argued.

"You have been promised to another," Malek said.

"I know." She stood. Malek glanced up at her. "The son of Nikyuk is not my idea of a mate. He is not worthy of me. Besides, what if the men of our village chose mates from another tribe? Ten anos is a long time for anyone to wait." She fisted her hands on her hips.

"You will be his mate if he has not chosen another," Malek said, sternly.

"And did Malachi choose Herda for your mate?" she asked, knowing the story behind Herda and Malek's union.

Malek tensed his jaw and glared at her. Malek had fallen in love with the Chief of another tribe. Herda had been twenty when her father had died in a hunting accident and she became Chief. Herda had sent for help for her people to re-plant and farm the land after a blight had wiped out their forests and crops. Malek, son of Malachi, the chief, had been dispatched to teach them all he knew about crops.

She crossed her arms over her chest. She knew what she wanted in a mate, but did Malek?

"And what will happen if I choose not to take a mate?" If she couldn't have Adam, then she would have no one.

"There would be no one to take your place as chief after you die. Our blood line would die with you."

"And what happened to Herda's tribe when she left them for you?"

"Her sister, Yanna, became chief."

"I want to choose my own mate."

"And live in exile for the rest of your life?"

"It's time that edict was challenged," she said.

Adam was chatting with Danner at the galley table when Spencer woke first and joined them. Spencer scratched his head. "Got anything to eat around here?" he asked.

"Take this," he offered his tubes of food. "Knock yourself out."

"I already did," Spencer said, rubbing the back of his neck.

He cocked his head. "What do you mean?"

"Tremol kept hovering low to the ground, even after Tamlin told him to pull up. The beast raised its head, so I jumped from my seat. We must have hit the creature, because after that, I don't remember anything."

After docking at **Tarsius** Station, Spencer, Tamlin and Tremol reported to Captain Luc. Genesis, Malek and Danner filled out reports, and *he* went to speak to the one person he had never planned to see again.

"Hello, Dram," he said, looking through the bars of Dram's cell. He sat on the only piece of furniture in the small, confined space.

Dram stood and walked toward him. "Why are *you* here?"

"I wanted to say good-bye and, well, even though you caused some problems in my life, I can't say it was all bad." In fact, he would never have met Genesis if it hadn't been for Dram.

Dram crossed his arms over his chest and studied him. He shook his head.

"You amaze me," Dram said, finally.

"Really?"

"You remind me of Emma somehow. If things had turned out differently, we might have gotten along as father and son."

He let Dram's words sink in. He couldn't imagine anyone taking Joshua Davis' place, but for Dram to run an illegal operation for twenty-five years without getting caught, the guy must have done something right.

He clutched the bars as he stared into Dram's eyes. It was uncanny seeing himself as an older man. "Gen and I found Malek," he began, "so I'll be leaving for Earth."

"You've got it all planned out, don't you," Dram said.

He cocked his head and studied Dram's face. "Gen and I made a deal."

"You think by going back to Earth everything will be as it was. You'll meet some woman, fall in love, and settle down, right?"

Surprised by Dram's remark, he sputtered, "Ye...yes."

Dram moved close to the bars and reached through them, smacking him hard on the side of his head.

"What was *that* for?" He pulled back, rubbing his temple.

"I needed someone to do that to me when I was your age," Dram said.

Why had Dram hit him? He cocked his head, his brows furrowed.

"Love can't be planned, son. It just happens. When you least expect it, love grabs you by the heart and holds on," Dram made a fist with his hand.

"What are you *talking* about?" he asked.

"If you don't grab it back," Dram stared at his fist, "love will slip through your fingers and be lost forever." He slowly opened his palm, looking at his empty hand, and into his eyes. Dram moved back to the small cot and sat down.

He crossed his arms over his chest. Maybe Dram was crazy. He'd lost his mind since he had been locked up.

"Think about it, son," Dram glanced at him. "Will you grab it back and hold on or let it go? Don't make the same mistake I did." Dram leaned his elbows on his thighs, clasping his hands together and stared at the wall.

He didn't know how to respond to that. Had Dram just given him some fatherly advice? He shook his head and left.

He found the I.S.P.'s version of a lounge, where pilots and crewmen hung out. Spencer and Tamlin played something similar to pool, except there were four different colored sets of balls. Each person had to knock their own colored balls into matching colored pockets then go for the larger black ball. The round table made it more difficult to get the balls into specific holes.

Danner walked up.

"Hey, why don't you two join us?" Tamlin said.

He shrugged, and before long, the four of them bet drinks for the winner.

"You've been pretty quiet tonight, Adam. What's up?" Danner asked.

"I've had a lot on my mind," he said, hoping the conversation wouldn't go any further. He tried not to think of Genesis, but that was like holding back a river with his arms.

"You're leaving for Earth soon, aren't you?" Danner asked.

"Yes." He leaned over the table, aimed the stickit and took his shot. He couldn't get excited about going home for some reason.

"I heard Malek tell Tremol they would search for Herda once they dropped you off," Danner added.

Adam raised his head and straightened after watching the ball miss the hole. "Damn!" He took a gulp of ale. Not bad for a dark beer and it dulled the ache in his chest.

"Have you thought about joining the I.S.P.?" Tamlin asked.

He wiped his mouth with the back of his hand, watching Spencer lean over the table to take his shot.

"No, I haven't. Why would I?"

"Well, the pay is good," Tamlin said.

"Not to mention you get to travel," Spencer added, straightening after missing his target.

"Oh, but the best part is the fringe benefits," Danner said, gesturing with his hand. He leaned over the table and studied his shot.

"And what are those?" he asked, glancing at each man.

Spencer moved close and spoke to him in a low voice while Danner took aim.

"For every mission you complete, you get four days off and bonus pay. And you can hop a ship and travel for free while you're off."

"Yes, and women love the unicrins," Danner said, standing.

The ball Danner hit dropped into its pocket, earning him another shot.

He shook his head. "I've seen more impressive unicrins on our armed forces back on Earth."

Danner pulled at his sleeve. "What's wrong with ours?"

"Lack of color, for one thing." He shrugged, and scratched his beard. "If I didn't know better," he began, looking at each of them, "I'd think you guys were trying to recruit me."

"We get a bonus if we bring in new people," Spencer added.

"Oh?" He raised an eyebrow.

Suddenly, the three men turned away from him, and he followed their gazes.

Genesis had walked into the room and headed toward them.

"Gen!" he said. His heart rate increased at the sight of her.

She stopped in front of him and glanced up. Her eyes were red and puffy. "We leave in thirty minutes at docking station ten," she tensed her jaw and left.

He watched her leave, his heart pounded as sadness overwhelmed him. A lump formed in his throat as he thought about the hurt in her eyes, and the fact he was responsible for it. He leaned both hands on the table after placing his stickit across it. His gut tightened.

"You're actually letting her go?" Tamlin asked.

He shook his head, while staring at the table. "No," he choked out the word. "Tremol asked her to be his mate." Nausea set in at the thought of her and Tremol together.

"Yeah, but she turned him down," Spencer added.

His attention snapped to Spencer and he straightened.

"What did you say?" He tensed his jaw.

"Tremol told me she'd decided not to take a mate at all." He shrugged.

His heart thudded then resumed pounding. A flicker of hope crossed his mind. "I've got to go," he said, his throat tightened at the thought of leaving her.

He shook hands with each of the men and they wished him luck. He took one last glance at them before he turned away. Danner gave him a thumbs-up and he returned the gesture.

He hurried down the corridors to get to docking station ten. He wanted to talk to Gen, to hold her one more time, but it would only make matters worse. She would search for Herda after she dropped him off. She must be anxious to reunite with her mother after all this time. He would be.

The tightness in his throat grew at the thought of the long trip back to Earth with plenty of time to think. He didn't look forward to it.

Once on board, he found his gear in one of the compartments and made himself comfortable at the galley table, waiting for her.

Malek came out of the Nav-room.

"Good, you're here," Malek said, walking toward him. "I wanted to talk to you before we left." Malek joined him at the table. He wore a clean flight suit now, and looked much better after cleaning up. The man's long, blue-black hair fell below his shoulders. Too bad Genesis didn't wear hers that way.

"Genesis told me what happened. I apologize for her error in your abduction. I hope there are no bad feelings."

He swallowed hard. If Malek only knew the intimacy he and Genesis shared, he would be apologizing to Malek.

"No, sir," he said.

"She spoke highly of you. I thank you for saving her life. On **Atria**, when someone saves a life, we pledge a life-debt."

"What's that?"

"We pledge to stay with that person until we repay the debt," Malek explained. "But you will return to Earth and Genesis won't be able to repay you," Malek glanced down at his clasped hands.

"Sir," he leaned forward, "she *has* repaid the debt, more than once." He studied Malek's reaction.

"How?"

"She saved my life on the mountain, when I almost fell off, she healed me several times when I was injured, and on **Ti**, you remember what she did to save us all from becoming a T-Rex snack." Then he realized something he hadn't admitted to himself. He admired her. "She's the bravest woman I know." His eyes watered at the thought of losing her.

"It makes me proud to hear you say such things. She will be chief one day, and that is a desirable quality for a leader."

"Yes, sir."

"We'll leave now," Malek said, standing.

"What about Gen...esis?" He almost forgot Malek's warning. He hadn't seen her get on board. "Is she here?"

"Yes. She's in the Nav-room, preparing for take off," Malek cocked his head and furrowed his brows.

"Can I see her?"

Malek let out a breath. "She prefers to talk to you later," he said.

His stomach knotted. He must have hurt her deeply. How could he undo this and make things right? "Yes, sir," he choked out, his throat tightened on the words.

Malek returned to the Nav-room, after closing the ramp to **The Guardian**. He left him alone with his thoughts.

Inside the Nav-room, Genesis glanced over her shoulder at the sound of the hissing door. Her breath caught in her throat. It was Malek. She exhaled. What did she hope for? She had made a deal with the Earth man and she would keep her word.

"Let's go," Malek returned to his seat.

She punched in the information on the keypad and manually lifted **The Guardian** from the docking station. When they were clear, she spoke commands to the ship.

"**Guardian**, return us to Earth."

"Responding," **The Guardian** said.

She went over details in her mind, every little thing she could pull from her memory about Adam. She wanted to savor all of them, but she couldn't bring herself to see him. She'd cried for hours thinking about letting him go. To speak to him would weaken her. She refused to let it happen. Time passed. He would be a fond memory...eventually.

"Why don't you get us something to eat," Malek suggested.

She glanced at him. "I can't," she said.

"Of course you can," his brows furrowed.

"I refuse to see the Earth man," she said.

Malek cocked his head. "But you spoke so highly of him. Why won't you? He asked to speak to you," Malek said.

"He did?" Hope rose up in her chest.

"Yes, but as you requested, I told him you'd speak to him later."

Her stomach tightened at the thought of seeing him at all.

What could she say? Bye, have a nice life?

Malek touched her arm. "Genesis? You have been acting strange lately. I agreed to let you choose your own mate. Isn't that what you wanted?"

She nodded. But the mate she desired didn't want her. How could she tell Malek? The daughter of the chief would have no children. There would be no descendants. Who would take her place when *she* died? Malek was an only child, just like she was.

"Did you give him the tulin?" she managed to ask, staring out the view port.

"No, that is your obligation since you and the Earth man captured Dram."

"You and I share the reward, Malek, but the Earth man deserved some as well. He saved me from death at the hands of Dram."

"You need to thank him when you give him his portion," Malek said.

She lowered her head, slowly nodding. How could she face him without breaking down?

"He told me you were the bravest woman he knew," Malek said. "If you are so brave, show it."

She stared at Malek. Adam had said those things? She leaned back in her seat and glanced up then closed her eyes momentarily, and prayed for strength. She would get this over with now, before they reached half way to Earth. Slowly, she stood and walked to the doorway, where she found the sacks. She grunted as she picked up the heavy bag holding 100,000 pieces of tulin. Dram had a high price on his head, but the coins were meaningless to her. All she wanted was to be reunited with Herda and maybe one day, start a family of her own.

She blinked. After losing her family, the thought of having her own was fresh on her mind. The door hissed open.

Adam sat at the galley table with his head on his folded arms. He raised up slightly at her approach then straightened.

"Gen?" He stood.

She carried the heavy sack to him and set it down.

"This is yours," she said, looking at the tulin to avoid eye contact.

He stood in front of her with his arms around her, pulling her close but she refused to look up. Her palms were on his chest. His heart beat hard against her fingers. *Be strong*, she told herself.

"Gen, I'm sorry I hurt you," he said.

She reached up and touched his lips with her fingers. The sadness in his pale, blue eyes pierced her soul, making her throat tighten.

"Thank you for saving my life," she choked out. She pulled away and ran back to the Nav-room.

For three days, he tossed and turned in Malek's sleeping compartment, but sleep escaped him. The words Dram had said to him played over in his mind, along with the things Tamlin, Spencer and Danner had told him before he'd left. He remembered conversations he and Genesis had shared and the intimacy they'd experienced. He couldn't get them out of his head.

His stomach growled, but food wouldn't go past the constant lump in his throat. He was miserable. He'd never felt this way before. What was wrong with him anyway?

Genesis wouldn't talk to him, and Malek didn't talk either.

"We are here, Earth man," Genesis finally announced, standing in the doorway of the sleeping compartment.

He blinked a few times and realized she meant Earth. He jumped out of the bed and was on his feet. He ran a hand through his tangled hair, glancing at her. Her eyes were red and she looked tired. He probably looked like hell.

She left the compartment and he went to the galley to retrieve his bow and arrows, his bundle of clothes, and the sack of tulin Gen had given him. He was hollow inside and dazed. He hadn't slept much in the time they had been traveling.

He walked to the ramp, while Genesis stood at the entrance and waited, her arms crossed over her chest. He stared at her. He wanted to say something, but he was numb. What could he say to someone like her after what they had been through?

"Gen, I will never forget you," he choked out and walked down the ramp. He stepped into the old cornfield, and tromped toward the cabin.

The Guardian pulled up and was gone in a matter of minutes. He saw his home in the distance, a place that once held a young family full of love.

When he approached the spot where he'd first met Genesis beside the pond, it hit him. He'd just made the same mistake Dram had made with his mother. He'd left the only woman he had ever loved.

A lump formed in his throat and heaviness filled his heart. He realized he would never see her again, or touch and hold her. His heart had been ripped in two as he fell to his knees. He closed his eyes.

'God, what have I done?' his mind screamed. He dropped his possessions and grabbed his chest, the pain was unbearable. His fingers hit something familiar. The leather strap of the medallion.

He opened his eyes and tightly clutched the metal object in his palm. *'Gen, I love you! I always have.'* Without her he was hollow and empty, like his cabin. His home wasn't the same anymore. He glanced at his surroundings. He realized he didn't have to be on Earth to love someone or to be happy. He had let Genesis slip through his fingers, like Dram had warned him not to do. He held his head in his hands and cried out.

"Genesis, come back!"

Genesis sat at the controls of **The Guardian**, clutching her chest. The pain was intense and she doubled over.

"What is it, child?" Malek asked her.

"It hurts, Malek," she managed to say. She heard someone scream, *'God, what have I done?'*

"What afflicts you?"

"My heart," she sat back slightly and listened. *Adam?* It sounded like him. She tilted her head.

"Genesis!" Malek glared at her, his brows furrowed. "When a healer takes a mate they feel the mate's pain when their mate is hurt or injured. Tell me you *didn't* mate with Adam," he demanded, his jaw tensed.

"I cannot," she doubled over. Was Adam in pain? She hadn't known this. It didn't matter now. She loved him whether he loved her or not.

Malek slammed his fist against the armrest when she heard Adam speak to her once more. *'Gen, I love you. I always have.'*

"What is *this*?" Malek reached for her medallion which glowed. "Herda?"

"No, Adam. He loves me!" She grabbed the controls and yawed sharply to the left.

"What are you doing?" Malek demanded as he fell back into his seat.

"He loves me!" she shouted. *'I'm coming, Adam,'* she spoke to his mind.

Adam still clutched the medallion as a tear ran down his cheek. He should have told her when he had the chance. He couldn't imagine his life without her.

"Adam?" a male voice called out.

He opened his eyes.

"Jeremy?" Jeremy came toward him from the cabin.

He stood up.

"Where the hell have you been? I've searched everywhere for you. It's like you dropped off the face of the Earth," his boss said, grabbing him by the shoulders. Jeremy studied his clothes.

"I was abducted by aliens," he managed to say.

Jeremy chuckled. "Seriously, Adam, where have you been?" Jeremy glanced up at the sky behind him, his mouth dropped open. He turned and saw **The Guardian** setting down in the cornfield. His heart lightened.

"Here, take this gold and pay off my Jeep and my cabin. The papers are in the box on my table," he said, handing the bag of tulin to Jeremy.

Jeremy took the bag and studied Adam once more. "I don't understand."

"A space ship crashed in the woods over there," he pointed. "Tell the authorities."

Jeremy stared past Adam to the cornfield.

He swung around. Genesis ran toward him.

"Gen!" He ran to meet her. At the edge of the pond he scooped her up and kissed her passionately. Her arms encircled his neck.

"I love you, Gen, I didn't realize it 'till now," he managed to say, pulling away slightly. His heart pounded with happiness.

"I love you, too, Adam." She smiled at him.

"My heart belongs to you, Gen and my home is wherever you are, as long as we're together." He kissed her sweetly on the lips then set her down. Her arms moved to his waist.

"Uh hem," Jeremy cleared his throat.

He walked toward Jeremy, holding Genesis' hand.

"Jeremy, this is Genesis, the woman who abducted me," he gestured to her. He put his arm around her back and pulled her close.

"I love her."

Genesis reached toward Jeremy to shake his hand. Jeremy's mouth hung open.

"I'm going back with her to help her find her mother." He gazed at her and then glanced at Jeremy.

He picked up his bow and quiver of arrows. "I'll return after we locate Herda." He turned and ran with Genesis toward the cornfield...to a new home and life with the woman he loved.